VENDETTA STONE

For Michael,

VENDETTA STONE

A Novel By

Tom Wood

Thanks for everything!

Tom Wood

Walnut Hills Press
2013

Copyright © 2013 by Tom Wood

All rights reserved.

ISBN: 1490331522

ISBN-13: 978-1490331522

Library of Congress Control Number:

Walnut Hills Press, Nashville, Tennessee

www.tomwoodauthor.com

AUTHOR'S NOTE

Angela Stone was *Pure Palomino*. The name of her 1993 debut album, which boasted two Top 100 songs in the title cut and "Sweetie's Pie," also described her look—flowing, taffy-colored tresses surrounding a creamy-golden oval face capped by an upturned nose, full lips, and striking eyes. One critic labeled Angela as her generation's Farrah Fawcett.

Born and raised in Houston, Texas, Angela went to New York City with her mother in 1990 to begin a successful modeling career. They moved to Nashville in 1992 to launch a solo singing career after becoming disenchanted with the modeling scene. Angela fell in love with the Music City vibe and decided to stay when her father got sick and Mama went home to Houston to nurse him back to health. A few years later, she met Jackson.

But this isn't Angela's story, not really. Today marks the second anniversary of the 2010 murder of Angela Stone, to whom this book is dedicated.

I never met Angela, though as a veteran reporter at Nashville's daily newspaper, *TenneScene Today*, I've come to know her through conversations with family, friends, and people whose lives she touched. I'm certain you'll become acquainted with her, too, in these pages. Instead of focusing on her murder, I'm concentrating on her husband, Jackson Stone, and his wholly unexpected reaction to her premature death and his quest to hunt down the killer.

I'm writing this book because I'm a reporter who got a little too close to this story and Jackson, who was trying to do something right, even if it was wrong.

For the record, I reconstructed some scenes from first-hand accounts, journals, countless interviews, police reports of certain incidents that occurred to which there were no living witnesses, and other public records. In those passages, dialogue was remembered from my hearing it, deduced from a written source, or presented verbatim from an interview. But evidence suggests this is how events took place, and every speculation is fact-based.

—**Gerry Hilliard,** *August 3, 2012*

FRIDAY, AUGUST 13, 2010
1

Jackson Stone lumbered to the front of the media briefing room at the East Nashville precinct. He forced his legs forward, his arms swung funny, and his face was pasty white. I sat transfixed on the front row, one of a dozen reporters, photographers, and cameramen summoned to the police station that hot, humid afternoon.

Zombies don't call press conferences.

But Jackson Stone did. At least, that's what this felt like. He slumped behind the lectern, shoulders curled, sport coat rumpled, and his glassy-eyed stare went above the crowd. He fit the image of the undead—not really dead, not really alive—a man in mourning. His wife had been murdered.

What happened next sucked my breath away.

"I don't want justice," Jackson said in what began as a hushed tone, but grew in resolute strength with each word, his cheeks flushing to their normal ruddy color. His palms came together, then his fingers balled into fists. A tear rolled down his cheek. He let out a long, whooshing breath of air, a sigh of deep despair.

Angela Stone had disappeared from their Lockeland Springs home in East Nashville ten days earlier, and after a massive city-wide search, police found her bloody and broken body three days ago. Because of her notoriety as an established model and country music singer, the case drew intense coverage from my newspaper, *TenneScene Today*, as well as other media. As other reporters scribbled notes and cameras rolled, and my mini-cassette tape recorder captured the details, I focused all my attention on Jackson Stone. He wasn't done.

He brushed his tear away in a brusque, cold manner, then his hand covered and slid down his face, an unconscious move that struck me as perhaps the unmasking of his true personality.

"I want revenge." It was a guttural sound.

This uncoordinated, mindless mass of man changed before my eyes into a hardened, embittered force, hungry for human flesh.

That man just bit a dog.

One of the oldest adages in the news business: When a dog bites a man, it rarely makes the paper, but if a man bites a dog, that *is* news. Big news. This was once-in-a-career news.

This forty-five-year-old advertising executive just called out his wife's killer in a very public challenge.

Had he lost his mind? Or his humanity?

2

Jackson had been staying in the guest bedroom of the West Meade ranch home of his brother Patrick since police discovered Angela's body. This morning, he was awakened by the radio alarm in Patrick's room across the hall. The heaviness of his loss kept him in bed, and he listened to the stirrings of Patrick and Sheila. Their shower rattled the old bathroom pipes, and he heard their kids, Brianna, three, and Jonas, five, run down the hall.

Their lives were normal. His wasn't.

Jackson closed his eyes and looked back on the past ten days that had changed his life.

On the morning of August third, a six a.m. US Airways flight awaited Jackson for a day-long, emergency business meeting in Charlotte, North Carolina. As he dressed, Jackson watched Angela sleep. She was the same blonde bombshell he'd met after returning from the first Gulf War in 1992.

The previous night, they'd dined at one of their favorite upscale East Nashville restaurants, an intimate atmosphere where she escaped the spotlight that went with being one of Nashville's recognizable citizens. Residents and Music City celebs coexisted in public settings. You might spot Nicole Kidman and Keith Urban shopping in Green Hills or Vince Gill at one of the many local golf courses or at a Belmont University basketball game. And rarely were they heckled or harassed for an autograph.

Angela didn't go out of her way to avoid publicity like others who might have covered up in a scarf and sunglasses. It wouldn't have worked. She would've still stood out.

Their last conversation played over and over in Jackson's mind. When he returned from Charlotte later that evening, apologizing with a dozen red roses topped his to-do list.

The Stones enjoyed a rock-solid marriage, according to friends and family. Not perfect people, but perfect for each other. Jackson's strengths made up for Angela's weaknesses and vice versa. Their temperaments ran hot and cold. Whereas his emotions hit a hot boil, her anger resembled a slow burn that turned ice-cool.

Such a scenario had played out that final night at Margot Café & Bar, a one-time filling station in East Nashville converted in the mid-1990s into a cozy-casual, brick restaurant that exuded plenty of Old World charm.

Jackson had gotten tied up at work, so they missed their reservation and waited for the first available table. Over appetizers, Angela wanted to discuss something important with him.

"Okay, I'm all ears . . . hey, look who's coming in—Stephen and Connie. Hey, y'all."

Forgetting all about Angela's news, the gregarious Jackson invited the couple to join them for a few minutes. Those few minutes turned into about ninety as the couple ordered a bottle of champagne, and Jackson returned the favor after the pan-seared scallops arrived. Two more bottles of champagne came and went.

Angela limited her intake to one glass, Jackson recalled, as she turned down all refill offers. Pushing ten o'clock, the impromptu party ended, and Jackson stood while they bid the couple farewell. Angela still wanted to talk to Jackson and asked him to sit back down.

"Aw, hon, if it's that big a deal, let's talk about it tomorrow night. It's late, and I've got a six o'clock flight out. I'm due back on the six-thirty, so I ought to be home by seven, seven-thirty. I'll bring you back to your favorite restaurant. Just you and me this time, I—"

Jackson's smirk died, and the words froze in his throat in mid-sentence.

"Uh, sure," he continued. "I'd like another glass of bubbly anyway. Want one?"

He sat, and she stood.

"No way," she said. "I've wanted to talk all night, and now it's too late? You know what, Jack, you're right . . . as usual. Twenty-four hours . . . twenty-five days . . . twenty-six weeks. I'll let you know when I'm ready to discuss it again. Just take me home."

On that warm August night, a distinct chill blanketed the car all the way home.

Jackson propped himself up on one elbow on the soft mattress and turned on the bedside lamp. From the way Angela had acted at dinner, he assumed she'd planned to announce her intentions to quit drinking and to also ask him to cut back. They never got to that conversation, though, and it haunted him. Guilt weighed down on him. Don't beat yourself up, he told himself. You'd change that now, but it still wouldn't change what happened to her.

Maybe because of the sudden burst of light from the lamp, but in his mind's eye flashed an image of Angela's battered body in her own bed, a dark, hulking figure standing over her. Jackson blinked and shook his head to shut out the horrifying vision.

He picked up the engraved, silver heirloom watch she gave him for their tenth wedding anniversary, turned it over, and reread the inscription. "Love Always, Angela." His chest tightened in a flood of emotions. The luminescent clock glowed five-fifty-two as the television came on in the den, and he heard the kids fussing over what to watch. Sheila settled the argument by turning on the DVD classic "Three Little Pigs." He heard Brianna singing, "Who's afwaid of the big bad wolf, big bad wolf."

Jackson headed to the bathroom and caught a glimpse of himself. The mirror didn't lie. The salt-and-pepper stubble on his face matched the color of his hair, and the overgrown

mustache needed trimming. He had large bags under his
eyes. He brushed his teeth, splashed cool water on his face,
and combed his sparse, oily hair by running his hand through
it several times until it settled on his head. He dressed in the
same Dockers and navy knit shirt he'd worn the last three
days and ambled down the long hall to the sun-splashed
open kitchen.

Patrick, Sheila, and the kids watched him pour a cup of
coffee. Jonas, dressed in his favorite Buzz Lightyear
pajamas, froze with a spoonful of cereal in his hand. Daddy
explained why Uncle Jack always seemed upset since Aunt
Angela went to heaven.

"Uh, g'morning," Patrick said, wearing a University of
Tennessee orange shirt, maroon pajama bottoms, and beat-up
house shoes. "Guess we woke you. Sorry 'bout that."

"Saw-wee," Brianna echoed.

Despite the lack of sleep, despite all the horrors of the
last week, the innocent concern on the little girl's face
touched Jackson. Instead of his usual grunt and grab of the
morning paper, he squatted in front of his niece and put on
his smiley face. Sheila and Patrick shared a look of relief,
For a moment, at least, good old Unca Jack was back.

"You didn't wake me, honey, but thanks," he said,
smoothing the little girl's auburn hair. "Got a hug for me?"

Brianna's arms wrapped around his neck, and as
Jackson squeezed back, she planted a kiss on his cheek and
squealed. "Ooh, your beard tickles." She didn't see the tear
roll down his face, but Sheila and Patrick did and began to
worry anew. Good old Unca Jack was gone.

Jackson stood, picked up the front and local sections of
the newspaper, and headed for the den. He settled on the
green-suede sofa, then flipped through the newsprint looking
for the latest article on his wife's murder. On Page 2B of
TenneScene Today, he found what he sought, and he read the
words I'd written the previous afternoon.

I fumed that my story about the police all but clearing
Jackson as a suspect failed to make the local news section's
front page. Even worse, it got cut in half to about ten inches

6

of copy. True, it stood above the fold, but I thought it deserved better play.

I sat in my breakfast nook perusing the paper. "This woman's big fan base and her name recognition make coverage of every aspect of her murder worthy of front-page display," I said to my wife, tapping a finger against the newsprint. Steam was rising off the mug of coffee beside me. Jill nodded, but never looked up from spreading her toast with strawberry jam.

I thought I had a pretty good nose for news judgment. I'm Gerry Hilliard, 1979 graduate of the Henry W. Grady College of Journalism and Mass Communications at the University of Georgia, former reporter in Athens. I passed up a chance to go to the *AJC* (that's *Atlanta Journal-Constitution*), and latched on at *TenneScene Today* where I've been for a long stint. I rarely questioned how or where a story was played, but this one did not belong on 2B.

The murder made national headlines, though most newspapers carried it as a celebrity column brief. The tabloids, on the other hand, were already rife with speculation into circumstances of Angela's death. "MODEL CITIZEN'S DEATH POSES QUESTIONS" read the inch-tall, bold headline in *Country Weekly*. I argued my point later in the day, but city editor Carrie Sullivan stood firm. She countered that a mundane story on the husband *not* being a suspect, offering almost no new developments on the case itself, didn't deserve better treatment. In hindsight she made the right call, but reporters were always challenged by editors, and vice versa. It was a constant battle.

Writing for a newspaper is unlike any other profession. It's often called "instant history." The rise of the Internet and other social media has brought many changes on how information is distributed, but not how news is gathered. Reporters must still develop sources, ferret out facts, double- and triple-check, then check them again before they put it all together in a cohesive, readable manner in a very short time frame. As a great editor once said, "Get all the facts, get them fast and get it out first. But first, get it right. We get one chance to get it right, so get going."

Once printed, it's out there forever . . . or at least until it's used to line the birdcage. You can run a correction the next day, but the original error is in black and white. Even if the story is error-free, nit-picking journalists always find something that needs a re-write, or they wonder why an editor changed a word or phrase, or they gripe over how the copy desk trimmed the story.

Jackson felt no relief at being "all but" cleared. He understood that the police almost always looked first at the husband as a prime suspect, but he was angry because it took so long for them to reach the obvious conclusion, that they were wasting time looking at him while Angela's true killer eluded them. He also disliked reading about it first in the paper instead of hearing it officially from the cops or his attorney, Stan Allenby. Stan had called on Thursday morning to say the medical examiner released Angela's body and that the family could make funeral arrangements. He also mentioned the likelihood that the police department's preliminary findings would be released in the next twenty-hour hours, hopefully clearing Jackson as a suspect.

A cheery Sheila Stone, still dressed in her favorite plaid nightgown, came into the den and asked Jackson if he wanted breakfast. Patrick sat down in the easy chair across from his older brother, who had one leg propped up on a knee as he held the paper about six inches from his face. When Jackson didn't answer, absorbed in the paper and his thoughts, Patrick leaned across and flicked the paper with his forefinger to get Jackson's attention. It worked.

"What?" Jackson snapped, dropping the paper into his lap. "Don't *do* that again."

"Sheila asked if you'd like something to eat. Say yes. You need your strength."

Jackson uncrossed his legs, giving her a forced smile.

"No, thank you, Sheila. But I will take a little more coffee," he said, raising the mug.

The crow's-feet wrinkles around Jackson's eyes were prominent. Concerned for his health, she gave him a peck on the cheek and took the oversized cup, then headed back to the kitchen, calling over her shoulder, "I'll fix something."

"You didn't sleep again, did you?" Patrick asked.

"A little. Maybe. I don't know."

Patrick's cheeks puffed up then deflated as he exhaled. His impatience festered after a reluctant Jackson agreed to spend a few nights with them. Jackson at first had resisted Sheila's pleas as he felt an overwhelming need to be near his home telephone, just in case. When Angela's body turned up late Tuesday afternoon, Patrick led the grief-stricken Jackson to his car as television cameras rolled. Word spread among friends and neighbors, and quite a few were waiting for them at Patrick's house.

Patrick had finally had enough, and he now unloaded on the older brother who had wasted countless hours on recriminations and waves of self-pity bolstered by the overuse of alcohol. The rumpled, downtrodden guy sitting across from him wasn't the strong-willed war-hero brother he'd grown up admiring. Patrick pushed his horn-rimmed glasses up on the bridge of his nose and leaned in closer.

"Look, I know you're hurting, but don't let one tragedy lead to another. Angela's gone, but you're still here. You can make her death count for something."

Jackson noted the concerned look and the worry in Patrick's voice and recognized the truth of the situation. Rubbing his temples as he closed his eyes, he half-whispered, "You're right, by God, you're right."

Patrick sighed with relief. His message got through to Jack. But not in the way he intended. Jackson took the reproach in a different manner, knowing he must begin training to somehow hunt down Angela's killer himself.

Patrick's harsh words had been echoed by an unrecognizable Jackson Stone, one shaped by horrific war experiences. Those harrowing combat-zone moments had made Jackson into a man of swift, deadly action when the need arose. With the help of Angela, Jackson thought he'd buried that dark side of his personality. But it would soon come roaring back with a vengeance.

9

atrick could see the pain on his brother's face, but he saw other emotions pushing to the forefront—anger, ,olve . . . and something else. It was like Jackson was .norphing into someone else. His eyes showed he was turning the tables. Instead of remaining a victim, along with his victimized wife, he was becoming . . . a savage hunter.

It was dusk when Jackson's US Airways flight from Charlotte landed in Nashville. He speed-dialed their house number as he got into his royal blue Honda Accord. No answer. He had already tried calling three times since disembarking. By the time he was a mile away from the house, it was dark, and he was ticked. Still no answer.

He called Angela's cell phone number, thinking she might be next door, and was briefly fooled when her voicemail answered. Her voice bubbled, and so did his in hopes she'd gotten over her mad spell from the night before.

"Hi hon. I'm just off the plane, and I'll be home in a few minutes if traffic's not too bad. Can't wait to take my favorite gal to her favorite restaurant. See ya."

He had a foreshadowing that something might be wrong when the setting sun was blotted out by a huge dark cloud. He turned on the car radio, preset to one of the news channels. "And for tonight," the announcer said, "there is a thirty percent chance of rain, extending into—"

Home. Jackson pressed the garage door opener and turned into the driveway. The outside security lights were off. Angela always turned them on for him. Her champagne-colored Subaru was not there. Jackson stopped in the driveway and got out. The first thought to cross his mind was that Angela was still so incensed that she'd gone to dinner without him. It was his turn to throw a tantrum if that turned out to be the case. Maybe she'd left a note.

Jackson reached into his pocket for his keys. They snagged on a thread, and he gave a yank. He pressed on the keychain's LED flashlight, and the garage lit up pale blue. Reaching for the lock on the side door to the kitchen, he realized the door was slightly ajar and gave it a push.

"Angela? You home?"

He flipped on lights as every nerve tingled. Nothing seemed amiss in the kitchen. All the off-white chairs were pushed neatly against the tiled table, and the fresh flower arrangement in the center exuded a strong, sweet scent. A lower cabinet drawer stuck out half an inch. Meticulous Angela always wanted everything in place and orderly. Jackson always kidded her about being a neatnik, so he immediately sensed something wasn't right. Below the drawer . . . was that a small dirt spot? He leaned over and peered closer. That darkening spot, not quite dried, was red. Blood red.

"Angela?" Jackson's body tensed, then he screamed. "Angela!"

His frantic and fruitless search began, and he shouted again for his wife as he raced into the den, hoping to find a note . . . something, anything. Nothing seemed out of place. His chest tightened as he hit the stairs, slapping light switches before throwing open the bedroom door.

"Annnnngel-uuurp."

The physical illness came at first sight of the streaked, blood-stained bed sheets. Jackson dropped to his knees, wailing like the proverbial banshee.

"Oh my God. Oh. My. God! OHMIGO-O-O-O-O-D!"

He struggled to his feet, checked the bathroom—where was she?—looked in the closet—was an intruder still in the house?—grabbed up his cell phone and called 9-1-1.

The cops' arrival led to the discovery of the Stones' Wolfhound out back, its neck broken. Investigators pored over the house and issued an all-points bulletin. Neighbors, curious about the flashing blue lights on their quiet street, came to see what was wrong, and community watch volunteers began a search. Patrick and Sheila arrived and tried to keep Jackson calm. But at one point Jackson ran to the closet and came back with his hunting rifle. Patrick grabbed hold of the gun, forcing the barrel toward the floor. "Jack, you can't do that! Let the police handle this. They'll find her. Don't go off half-cocked and assume the worst." Jackson let go of the gun, slumped to the couch, and cried.

11

3

One of the most often-repeated clichés about revenge is that the taste is sweet. As Sheila walked in with plates for the brothers, revenge smelled like eggs. Scrambled, with smoked cheddar cheese, and a dash of Worcestershire sauce.

After a couple of bites, Jackson set the plate on the ottoman, leaned back, and closed his eyes, and Sheila headed back to the kitchen to clean up. Patrick scraped the eggs off Jackson's plate onto his own. The sudden blare of the "Halls of Montezuma" telephone ringtone made both men jump. Sheila answered at "to the shores of," and handed the phone to Jack. Patrick left to get dressed and give Jackson privacy.

"Good morning, Jack. Did you see the newspaper?" attorney Stan Allenby asked.

"Yeah. When did the cops decide I'm no killer?"

"It's not over yet. The police want to interview you one more time this afternoon, then they'll release an official statement. Can you be at the East Precinct between three-thirty and four? We should be done by five."

"That'll work. I need to take care of a few things beforehand." Jackson hung up, went to the kitchen, and topped off his coffee. It was nine a.m., and Sheila and the kids were leaving for a shopping expedition to get them suitable attire for Aunt Angela's funeral.

Once Jackson figured a course of action, he mapped out the best way to mobilize. Once a "lean, mean fighting machine," he now had a routine workout of little more than raising a coffee mug or a beer bottle to his mouth.

12

But for the most important ad campaign this award-winning advertising executive would ever undertake, he hoped and prayed that one certain individual would receive his message loud and clear.

Jackson folded the paper where my article appeared and drew a bold circle around the small agate print at the end of the story, the part that read, "Got a news tip for us? Please contact ghilliard@TenneSceneToday.com." He handed the paper to Patrick, who came into the room buttoning his cuffs.

"Look, I've got some errands to run, and then I'm going to meet Stan Allenby over at the East Precinct," Jackson said. "Call this Hilliard guy, all the TV and radio stations, The Associated Press, and anybody else you can think of, and tell them I'm ready to make a statement about Angela's murder. Tell them to be at the police station at five. I'd like you to be there, too."

Patrick looked up from the circled number and studied his brother. Jackson appeared calm and rational for the first time since the whole ordeal began.

"Are you sure this is the best time to talk to the media? Why not wait until after the funeral?"

Jackson shook his head adamantly. "No, it must be today. Stan expects the cops to say I am no longer being considered a suspect. I'll make a statement that needs maximum exposure."

Jackson strode to the entry closet with Patrick hot on his heels. Digging out the tan sport coat and slipping it on over his navy short sleeve, Jackson bolted out the door.

"At least clean up a little. You need a shave," Patrick shouted while his brother backed his Accord out of the long driveway.

Patrick called right at noon, just as I turned off my computer and started to head out for lunch somewhere on West End. A little annoyed, I picked up on the second ring.

"Newsroom. This is Gerry Hilliard."

"Mister Hilliard? My name is Patrick Stone, Jack's brother."

ʎy tone changed from business-like to sympathy. "Of
se. I've tried calling Jackson a couple of times. How's
doing?"

"It's been tough on him . . . tough on all of us, but Jack
most of all. Anyway, Jack asked me to call all the media and
let them know he's willing to talk to all of them. He'll be
over at the East Nashville Precinct this afternoon about
five."

I said I'd be there, thanked Patrick for calling, and
looked for my city editor, Carrie Sullivan. She emerged from
the mid-day news meeting and headed for the stairs,
probably on her way to the lunchroom two flights down,
with managing editor Ken McGuire and a couple of other
departmental editors. Catching her between floors, I told her
about Patrick's call. The fact that he called a press
conference instead of doing one-on-one interviews meant it
wouldn't see great play in the Saturday paper unless I
cornered him alone and got something fresh after the news
conference.

"Go ahead and put out a photo order, and I'll try to clear
it with Brad," Carrie said. Brad Moore was our photo editor.
"They've got at least two other assignments, so it might get
canceled. I'll tell Ken now, and we'll go over it at the three
o'clock news meeting. Stop in before you leave."

I went back to my desk and keyed the information the
photographers needed into the assignment template, then
called Brad to give him a heads-up.

"Yeah, I'll see who's least busy," he said. "We've got
two high school football jamboree assignments, but
somebody can catch it if it's quick. We need something for
the B-section front."

I thanked Brad and headed to lunch myself. The menu
selections downstairs were grilled salmon and vegetables
and a slice of bread or Salisbury steak with green peas,
buttery mashed potatoes, and a roll. I went with the latter and
added a Diet Coke out of the fountain machine. Carrie and
the other editors finished, but she lingered while I dug in.

"Your cop sources got any leads now that Stone looks
to be in the clear?"

I shook my head and swallowed a mouthful of my scrambled peas-and-potatoes mixture before answering. "I don't think so. It's pretty puzzling. I heard this morning that Stone's being grilled about four, and his brother confirmed it, so it makes sense that he'd talk to us after that meeting. I'll swing by the station house right after I finish here and see what else I can learn."

"Keep me posted," Carrie said, picking up her messy, half-eaten tray of food. She headed back upstairs, and I sat there wondering what Jackson Stone could possibly say that differed from the grief expressed by hundreds of other family members of crime victims. I had no clue.

4

En route to the East Nashville police station, Jackson stopped to bid a final, private farewell to Angela at Eddie Paul's Pub. Just about every afternoon for at least a decade, Jackson had stopped off at his favorite hangout, now part of a local chain of family-oriented restaurant/bars. On weekends, Angela joined him, and they'd spend a few hours in front of one of the big-screens. Often they ate. At other times, it was a launching pad for dinner elsewhere or maybe a movie or a ballgame.

He waved to a couple of old cronies as he took a familiar stool at the oak-paneled, sports-themed bar and ordered a LandShark. Louie, the gray-haired, overweight bartender, recognized when a guy ached and needed to be left alone. Louie pushed the beer toward him and resumed clean-up duties.

Jackson drained half the bottle in a gulp and reflected on how his life had changed over the years, from his tough, fit Marine days to a middle-aged ad exec who might—just might—be dealing with a drinking problem. Jackson felt that the years of entertaining clients had finally caught up with him and admitted to an excessive, addictive lifestyle. But it didn't mean he'd forgotten all his military training. He almost made it into the Scout Sniper unit. The elite USMC school washed him out because of a severe back injury, not his accuracy. That dream died and now another loss.

Angela. My God, why did this happen?

Jackson had first met Angela at a 1995 Halloween fundraiser at Eddie Paul's Pub for one of Vice-President Al Gore's go-green global initiatives. The fundraiser itself wasn't held at the intimate sports bar, but the post-party was, and Angela Crosby was the featured entertainment. Jackson's firm, Martin and Robbins, handled all promotional aspects for the event, and Jackson, assigned to stage the after-party reception, chose Eddie Paul's because of its proximity to Shelby Park, where the formal fundraising announcement took place.

Jackson had booked Angela as a favor to his boss, Marty Martin, who knew her political leanings and musical talents. Just like Angela, her audition tape had proved a knockout for Jackson, who didn't hesitate hiring her. It ranked as the smartest decision he ever made, both personally and professionally. He'd watched her move easily back and forth across the stage, playing to the distinguished guest of honor. Angela paid equally close attention to Jackson, first noticing the lean, muscular, six-foot-two former leatherneck talking with his boss. His lazy, easy-going grin put a smile on her face, and she was drawn to the magnetizing eyes that sparkled when he looked her way.

After the show, Marty made the formal introduction. "And this is—"

"Jack Stone," she said real cool-like in her soft Texas drawl, extending a demure hand and thrusting her hip playfully. "I caught you watching my . . . aaact. Howdja like?"

Jackson sure did, but he wasn't letting on just yet. His voice took a more serious tone.

"You were wonderful, Miss Crosby. One thing bothered me, however."

The smile vanished. "And what might that be?"

"Those tight-fitting jeans you're wearing. I was going to ask how you breathe. But I think I know the answer because you've taken my breath away."

A corny line, but she laughed at the set-up. He'd won her.

They were inseparable after that and married a year later on Halloween at Eddie Paul's. All the guests wore outrageous costumes.

During their first year of marriage, Jackson and Angela had adjusted to different lifestyles, him working days and her nights. Jackson went to most of her local club appearances and missed her something terrible when she hit the road.

Angela had confronted Jackson head-on about the darker side of his personality. It scared her. Much of their heart-to-heart conversation focused on his military background, a time he rarely discussed. Angela could touch his physical scars, but not the mental ones.

"What happened to you in Kuwait musta been horrid, but everything I know and trust and feel tells me it happened to you for a reason. Everything happens for a reason. Never forget that," Angela had told him. "Someday, Jack, you'll be able to draw on those experiences, and they'll get you through whatever test you face in this life. And if you don't get through it, there'll be a reason for that, too. And I'll weep over you, pray for you, and then get on with livin'. Same rules if it's the other way around."

Jackson, sitting at the bar with tears in his beer, half-laughed, half-sobbed to himself, thinking about Angela and how good she was to him and for him. Am I going crazy? "I'm losing it," he mumbled. He wiped his eyes dry. Marines don't cry. Nobody could help him now.

"Hey, Jack, you okay?" Louie asked as he wiped the counter.

"No. No, I'm not," Jackson said. "Nothing's ever going to be okay again."

"Look, I know I'm just your bartender. But I'm your friend, too. You've been coming here a lot of years now, and some guys don't like to talk much about their problems. But you've got more friends than you know. So if you want to talk about this—now or later—you know where to find me. And if there's anything you need—anything—all you gotta do is ask. What happened to Angela is unforgivable. If I could get my hands . . ." His voice trailed off.

Louie's gesture touched Jackson. He experienced an emotional overload during the last week—shock, horror, grief, and a lot of anger—so much so that he thought nothing remained. But this crusty bartender reached out, and more importantly, reached him. Considering his plan, he just might need a friend—someone who wouldn't turn on him or turn him in. Jackson smiled and spoke an octave lower out of the right side of his mouth in his best Humphrey Bogart imitation.

"Thanks, Louie. Is this the beginning of a beautiful friendship?"

Louie grinned back, causing his sagging wrinkles to change direction. Glad to see the sudden switch in Jackson's demeanor, he fired back.

"Watch it, pal. This ain't no Casablanca."

"And I'm no Bogey, right?" said Jackson. "Well, I appreciate the gesture, and I'm going to take you up on that someday soon, if you want. But I've said enough. I've gotta get going right now."

"Whattya mean?" Louie said, surprised-like. "We ain't even talked. Grab a table, and I'll be right over."

Louie started to take off his apron, but Jackson held up a hand to stop him.

"Catch the six o'clock news, and you'll see what I mean. I'll come by in a few days and we'll see if you still want to talk."

Jackson drained the rest of his beer and raised the bottle in a final silent toast to Angela, as a puzzled, but curious Louie watched him exit. Jackson looked around the old bar, unsure if he would ever return.

Stepping from the dark interior into the bright sunshine made Jackson half close his eyes while he fished the Ray-Ban aviator sunglasses out of his jacket pocket. In the car, he pulled the visor half-down, backed out, and made his way through the stop-and-go afternoon traffic on Gallatin Pike, the city's major route north out of downtown that wasn't an interstate. Like all of East Nashville today, businesses along that road reflected a cross-section of the community on the comeback. An influx of new retail and chain grocery stores and restaurants stood alongside the numerous Hispanic and other ethnic eateries and time-worn, outdated 1960s shopping centers and strip malls.

Jackson took a left on East Trinity Lane and soon pulled into the parking lot of the Metro Police Department's still-new East Precinct. The facility opened on July 24, 2007, and the state-of-the-art precinct delivered on everything the aging station house lacked, except character. Three years later it still exuded a sterile, wet-paint, look-but-don't-touch feel. At just over twenty thousand square feet, this precinct was six times larger than the one it replaced. One hundred and thirty officers—sergeants and detectives, including supervisory officers, and then another twenty or so support personnel worked at the facility. The design included a two-thousand-square-foot community meeting room, where outreach programs, seminars, and media briefings were held.

The precinct's nerve center communications department, AKA "the bubble," a reinforced glass enclosure, helped coordinate officers and served as a lifeline for the public, where someone coming in off the streets first reported a crime.

Jackson arrived at the station house about three p.m. and sat in his car waiting for Stan Allenby to arrive. The blazing sun made it too hot to stay out long, so he went inside and stood in the reception area. The officer in "the bubble" asked if he could help, and Jackson explained his presence.

"Someone will be right with you," the officer said. "Would you like a cup of coffee or soft drink?"

"Got anything made by Budweiser?" The amiable smirk wasn't returned.

Allenby was late, so Jackson called the lawyer's office.

"Mr. Allenby got stuck in court proceedings, but called and said to tell you if you called that he would be leaving soon for East Nashville," the secretary said.

That delay gave Jackson time to shake off the effects of the couple of beers downed at Eddie Paul's and scout around outside. The sudden change from the climate-controlled police lobby to the burst of August heat made Jackson break into an immediate sweat. Removing his sport coat, he walked the station's perimeter to get his bearings, taking note of the precinct's unobstructed views in all directions. A chain link fence topped by a coil barbed wire surrounded the parking lot full of cruisers and personal vehicles.

Jackson anticipated his plan would cause a major public reaction, and he wanted to make a quick getaway without answering a bunch of questions from either the media or the cops. He walked up and down Trinity Lane several times, then down a couple of side streets in each direction. Then he went back to the station and moved his car a couple of blocks away, parking behind the white-bricked Nashville Public Health facility. His car looked out of place in the run-down residential area that showed its age. Several kids were out playing in yards, paying no attention to Jackson. Walking back to the precinct, he checked to see if his car could be seen from the street. Nope. Good. He wiped his brow several times, threw his sport coat over his left shoulder, and huffed a little as he walked up the hill.

"Man, I am so out of shape," Jackson mumbled as he went back into the lobby and used his smartphone to call his brother. He barked out two questions.

"Yeah, I called all the media, and everybody said they'd be there by four-thirty," Patrick said. "What else?"

"You planning to come? I might need a fast ride outta here."

"What's wrong with your car?"

"I'll explain after I meet with the cops," Jackson said and clicked off.

Twenty minutes later, Allenby wheeled his white Cadillac into the parking lot. Detective James Williams, the lead investigator since Angela disappeared, greeted them. So far, Williams failed to impress Jackson. His cool demeanor didn't fit Jackson's stereotypical mental image of a hard-boiled detective. He expected Shaft, and instead got the shaft. A thirty-five-year-old black man, Williams stood about five-foot-eleven and weighed right at two hundred pounds. A pencil-thin mustache seemed too small for his moon face, but his dark, intense eyes revealed a keen intelligence. A sharp dresser, Williams spoke with an easy-going drawl that exuded the same laid-back confidence of a sax player down at one of the jazz clubs in the Printer's Alley entertainment district.

Williams, a member of the Nashville force for thirteen years, proved good at his job. A thorough check into Jackson and Angela's backgrounds revealed no hint of dirt or scandal, no financial or marital problems, no cheating by either spouse.

Williams had checked the airlines and Jackson's business connections in Charlotte to verify every statement Jackson made in those first few days of the investigation. There were no discrepancies, no hints that Jackson had hired a hit-man in order to collect an insurance payoff. Angela's modeling career had allowed her to amass a sizable bank account, but her will specified that unless it involved a personal injury settlement, seventy-five percent of her estate would go to various local charities, designating most, but allowing Jackson to select two charities. Word for word, codicil for codicil, their wills matched. The couple agreed the surviving spouse could take care of him/herself and wanted their earnings to be put to work after they were gone.

But instincts told Williams he missed something. He'd seen some good actors and always saw through it. Jackson might be telling the truth, the whole truth, and nothing but the truth, but doubtful. He might be the bereaved, grieving husband, yet still hiding something. But what?

"So, Mister Stone, everything seems to be in order, and I guess we're done," Williams said. "We'll be in touch, but rest assured we're doing everything we can to find your wife's killer." The detective paused as Jackson returned a firm handshake. A grimace replaced the smile.

"So, one last time. Is there anything else you can tell us, something that can shed some light on what happened to your wife?"

Anxious to meet the press, Jackson let his anger spike and introduced the cops to a very different Jackson Stone.

"What happened to my wife is that whoever did this is still out there," he said, "and you guys are clueless. You've spent a week wasting time looking at me instead of tracking the butcher who killed her."

Williams' eyes widened at the verbal assault as Allenby pressed hard on Jackson's shoulder and told him to get hold of himself. Precinct Commander Mark Reynolds emerged from an adjoining room to defuse the situation, adding, "I'm sure you understand we look at everyone and everything in every case that comes our way. Detective Williams thoroughly checked out other leads and details. We'll share them with you at the appropriate time, but today we're going to let the world know, while we are still looking at anyone and everyone, you are no longer being considered as the primary suspect."

The lawyer answered before Jackson popped off again, but Jackson's stare said plenty.

"That's fine. We look forward to regular updates on how the case is proceeding and hope your hunt comes to a swift, satisfying conclusion. Please forgive Jackson's outburst."

Reynolds' plan to just release a statement changed when he was informed that the media awaited in the briefing room. The commander felt the public nature of the case warranted an assurance that his department undertook a pro-active approach in the search. Allenby didn't know Jackson had alerted the media.

"Are you sure you want to talk about this? Now might not be the best time," Allenby advised.

"No, I need to get this done today," Jackson said, and turned to the precinct commander.

"Sir, I'll make a brief statement after you finish, but I don't want to take questions afterward. Can you get me out of here without running a media gantlet?"

"There's an exit right off the community assembly room that goes out into our parking lot. It's not accessible by the public, and the fence can only be opened by a cruiser making contact with the sensor panel. But we can override if you pull your car inside," Reynolds said.

Jackson didn't apologize for his earlier outburst, but thanked the officers and looked at his watch. At five till five, they headed into the lobby. Jackson peered in and saw the media gathered around the front lectern, his brother sitting in the back. He motioned for Patrick to step outside as Allenby went inside.

"Look, I need to borrow your car," Jackson half-whispered. "I can't explain right now, but mine's parked behind the public health center just down the street. That's where your car will be in about fifteen minutes. Pull your car around the building and inside the fence and park by that door. Leave the keys in the ignition."

Reynolds talked to a patrol officer, who went around out front and let the civilian car enter the restricted area.

Patrick nodded and followed the cop outside. Jackson went into the briefing room and sat next to Allenby up front.

5

Jackson studied the reporters and camera crews as Reynolds discussed various aspects of the investigation and then offered to take a few questions. Several hands raised, and Reynolds fielded them deftly, answering in the vaguest of terms. Jackson's intense concentration broke when Reynolds called his name.

I remember thinking how bad he looked. I glanced around for our late-as-usual photographer, Casey Leiber, and spotted her. She blew hair out of her face and squatted just below camera range of the television lighting so she didn't use her flash. Out of the corner of my eye, I saw Jackson's brother Patrick re-enter the room, take a seat in the back, and nod. I looked forward and a somber Jackson Stone nodded back.

As Jackson stepped to the lectern, he seemed to lapse into a fog as if deciding whether he wanted to go through with his plan to talk. The collective media grew silent, tension filling the room. Those hushed seconds seemed to last forever.

"Jack?"

Allenby's barking voice cut through the fog, and Jackson recognized his surroundings and the difficult path he'd chosen. He cleared his throat and mumbled a "scuze me" and wiped a tear from the corner of his left eye. Steeling himself, he understood his dangerous plan would change his life forever. He couldn't imagine how many other lives it would alter—and in some instances end.

After he said his first two shocking lines: "I don't want justice . . . I want revenge," a resolute Jackson stood there for several long seconds, watching the various reactions of the media—eyes popping wide open with astonishment, words forming but only mimed, the note-taking freezing in mid-scribble, some audible gasps. We were all caught off guard at this unexpected development.

For veteran newsmen and women, press conferences like this were supposed to be routine. For the electronic media, it meant interviewing the police spokesman, getting the grieving family member on tape for a thirty-second sound bite, followed by sympathetic words from the anchor back at the station, then moving on to the next big story. For print media like myself, I wanted hard facts from the cops to wrap around some colorful comments that might warrant better play for my story.

"Colorful" described my face as I flushed with excitement, realizing the impact of the story that had fallen into my lap. In all my years on the police beat, I'd never heard a victim's relative issue such an outrageous declaration. And he wasn't done.

Click-click-click-click-click. The cameras of the print media whirred non-stop as Jackson shook with rage, then took a deep breath. He looked down at his hands. When they no longer trembled, Jackson clinched them and continued. He stared at the cameras, his outward calm making his words more chilling.

"Whoever did this to my wife, he better hope the police find him before I do. I will spend the rest of my life hunting down this scumbag if that's what it takes."

Jackson then aimed his right index finger at the cameras as he spoke with an air of assuredness, glaring from camera to camera for maximum effect. Cameras zoomed in for close-ups of the unshaven, haggard face. Rumpled as he looked, his mind remained clear and his eyes blazed. This guy meant business.

I stole a quick glance at others seated up front. Commander Reynolds and Jackson's attorney, Allenby, appeared stunned. Allenby, in particular, looked ready to jump out of his chair and wrestle the mike out of Jackson's hands. But with every wrenching second of this "meltdown" being recorded, neither man moved. I didn't dare turn to the back of the room to gauge Patrick's reaction.

"And when I find you, you won't die quick. That's no threat, that's a promise," Jackson continued, speaking slow and sure with occasional pauses for emphasis. "I promise you I will start by breaking both of your legs. While they're healing, I promise I will torture you for the rest of your miserable life in ways I've just begun to imagine. When I think you've finally suffered enough—and that's going to be awhile, I promise—I'll gut you like a deer and take my time doing it. Then I'll feed your carcass to the dogs. You're real good at hurting helpless women. Let's see how *you* cry, how *you* bleed.

"Look over your shoulder every day, because I'm coming. It may not be tomorrow or next week or next year, but I'll find you. And if the cops find you first, I'll still find a way to get to you." He paused. "I will end you."

Then it was over. Just like that. Jackson turned to his left and darted to the exit door, gave it a shove, and stepped outside. He jumped in Patrick's white Ford station wagon and sped away.

6

What had pushed Jackson to this point?

Not the first question racing through my mind at his shocking press conference, but it required answering first.

I would eventually discover that it was not a snap decision, but one Jackson had reached over several hours through a series of recollections followed by a connect-the-dot chain of events.

The plan came out of his most memorable hunting trip with his father in 1975.

"That's what makes this a sport, Jacky," Larry Stone explained that crisp, late October day as they walked the woods of northwest Davidson County near the Cumberland River. "It's just you and me, relying on our senses and our tracking skills to find that big boy. Then you watch and wait for the shot—count on getting just one—and when that moment comes, you're going to use all your well-honed abilities to make that shot count. You don't want the animal to suffer. You want a clean kill."

The ten-year-old nodded. Deer hunting differed from other sports he played, but pitting newfound skills in a test of man versus beast challenged Jacky. A glance down a path off to his right quickened his pulse.

"Dad, look over here. Fresh tracks."

"We're close, kiddo, keep your eyes and ears open."

Crack! The morning's silence shattered at what first sounded like a firecracker exploding, then another.

Cr-a-a-a-a-ack! A furious whistling followed that echo, and the youngster looked up. A flock of small birds flew overhead.

"Stay alert, Jacky." They double-timed it over the outcropping toward the shots and stepped into the clearing where two twenty-something hunters stood over a ten-point buck. The heavyset redhead drew his knife, preparing to gut the deer.

"Howdy, fellas, looks like you just beat us to him. We've spent all morning tracking that big boy for a few—"

The salt block on the ground melted Larry's smile, and Jacky recalled the lecture about luring deer into the open. His shivers came not from the October winds blowing in off the nearby river, but in the startling transformation in front of him. His six-foot dad seemed like a giant as he stared down the two young hunters who were of equal size, just not equal heart.

"You two are gutless," Larry said. He then leaned back and talked over his shoulder to explain to his son, though his eyes never left the men. "Deer love salt, real hunters hate it. Little punks like these give real hunters a bad name. Baiting a field may be legal, but it ain't sportin' . . . it's just killin'."

The uncertain younger hunter on the left glanced at his friend as Larry Stone took three methodical steps to his right so that the sun blinded the youths. A savage grin came across Larry's face as he glared.

"And anybody can kill, can't they, fellas?"

The hunter still gripping the knife took a slight step forward as he started to say something, but Larry cut him off, elevating his rifle enough to let them know he meant business. Eye contact broke as the hunter looked down to realize the barrel pointed at his belt buckle. Maybe an inch or two lower.

"Way I see it, you've got two bad choices, kid," Larry said. "Use that blade or try for your rifle." He paused and sneered. "I'm feeling generous, and I'm giving you a third, one-time-only offer. Get out of here. *Scram!*"

It produced the same effect on one as if he'd shouted "boo!" Jacky stifled a laugh as the younger of the two hunters fled for the surrounding brush.

Then Jacky stiffened, realizing the knife-wielder stood his ground. Unlocking eyes with Larry, the scruffy hunter leaned to his right and spat a stream of tobacco juice on the ground. He dropped the knife point-first, and it stuck.

"You're pretty tough with that rifle, old man. You're not taking our deer."

Larry's sneer turned into a threatening grin.

"Jacky." The boy didn't move, and his father spoke again, harsher. "Jacky!"

"Yes sir?"

"Take this," he said, handing over his rifle.

"Yes sir."

Larry Stone then began removing his hunting jacket, speaking calmly yet chillingly to his son. "Jacky, take this and go stand over by the trees. This won't take long."

"Yes sir." Jacky's adrenaline surged as he grasped the camouflage jacket and stepped back while his father stepped forward. That decided the young hunter. He didn't want the deer—or his knife—and cut into the woods in the same direction as his friend.

"I'm calling the cops. You're crazy, mister," the fleeing hunter shouted as he scrambled out of sight.

"That's right," Larry Stone yelled back. "Run! And don't come back!"

Larry turned and winked to Jacky, then picked up the knife. "C'mon, son, let's get to work. We've got maybe an hour. The food bank is going to love us."

Thirty-five years later, Jackson still remembered how easy those two guys had lured their prey with a baited field. What bait might lure Angela's killer into the open? What bait would be impossible for the murderer to ignore? The answer came in a burst of clarity, he'd mapped out his plans based on it, and he had just voiced it to all of Nashville.

Himself.

He'd put the target squarely on his back.

7

Almost before any of us journalists reacted, Patrick Stone's car sped around the back of the building, went through the opened gate, turned left, and emerged on the far side of the precinct beside the adjoining railroad tracks. Jackson took a right, drove under the train trestles, and disappeared. The car switch baffled the media. When we learned of the ruse much later, it struck me as pretty clever. Jackson whipped the station wagon behind the by-then closed Public Health Building, stuck the ignition keys under the front seat, got into his Honda, and pulled away. The getaway plan worked perfect as we all watched for the wrong vehicle.

Channel 11's Dan Clarkston, with his cameraman hot on his heels, headed for the front door, knowing the route of the police lot's only exit. I watched a couple of the other TV people go out the same side exit as Jackson, then reverse course and head for the front door. The precinct commander, Reynolds, tried to gain control of the confusion, but gave up and retreated to his office, recognizing a disaster when he saw one. Disgusted, the lawyer Allenby berated Patrick Stone. I jotted down all this to spice up what I now considered a Page 1A story. First, I needed to find my photographer.

Clarkston's bolt out the front door made him the lone reporter to see Jackson's vehicle and the direction it took. A recreational runner, Clarkston still couldn't get to the street quick enough to see what other maneuvers Jackson made after dropping out of sight.

But he spotted a couple of teenagers walking along the road in the same direction and hoped they remembered seeing a white wagon. Clarkston caught up to them just before the train underpass. So focused on the young couple, he failed to notice the royal blue Honda Accord that drove in the opposite direction past the police station and turned left on Ellington Parkway to head toward the city. Flabbergasted, Patrick Stone recognized his brother's car, but he wasn't tattling.

"Did you kids notice the station wagon that just drove up that way," Dan Clarkston asked the teens, "or which way it turned?"

The vacant-eyed girl didn't respond at first, and then recognized Clarkston, the most popular electronic journalist in the mid-major market. In his late thirties, Dan's lean, angular face fit his runner's body. Known around the media for an inflated ego, occasional outbursts of temper, and bouts of vanity, Clarkston wore a light gray summer suit, with a striped red tie to play off the teal shirt.

"Hey, you're that guy on TV that my parents still watch," the girl said.

"Yeah. So did you see a car like that?"

"Nah," the slacker boyfriend said, flicking his cigarette. "What'd the guy do, rob a bank? Police station's right back there if yawanna report it."

Clarkston grinned.

"Tune in at ten to find out."

"Stuff it, old man."

The teens went on their way as Clarkston turned back to Greg Pittard, the cameraman he was teamed with. He moved around Pittard so the background shot included the police station.

"Ready to roll?"

Clarkston gathered himself, smoothing down a few stray gray hairs.

"On three . . . two . . . one."

Clarkston spoke with an air of authority while also trying to show a degree of compassion. He'd practiced this "signature style" thousands of times and nailed it again.

"You've just heard the shocking first public statement from an angry Jackson Stone, whose wife Angela was brutally murdered ten days ago in East Nashville. A senseless crime like so many others, it sent shockwaves through this community and put pressure on police across the city to find the murderer who committed such a heinous act. But Jackson Stone just upped the ante and gave Metro police a new mandate—find a killer before he does. How will police react to this unprecedented—and most public— challenge? Is Jackson Stone the kind of man who can carry out such an act of vengeance? We'll try to answer some of those questions on our ten o'clock report."

"And cut," Pittard said. "If we hurry, we can make the six o'clock newscast."

"You drop it off, then get back over here for some police reaction. And then we're going to try to find this nut-job for an exclusive."

Spotting my photographer, Casey Leiber, I waved her over and speed-dialed city editor Carrie Sullivan.

"Newsroom. This is Carrie."

"Got a big one, boss. Can you take some dictation and get this posted ASAP?"

"Go," she said, opening a new Word document on her note-covered, coffee-stained computer.

This called for old-school journalism, not at all the normal procedure these days. But Carrie, twenty years younger than me and just five years out of journalism school, lived for moments like this. In the Internet era, print remained a passion for the fast-tracking daughter and granddaughter of two of Nashville's finest newsmen of the previous generation.

I'd known Carrie all of her life, dating back to when I began working for her dad as a young reporter. Harry Sullivan took me under his wing, seeing a fire in me, I guess, that matched his own. We broke some great stories and I spent many a weekend at my boss's house playing cards and watching ballgames like a surrogate son since Carrie was an only child. After Harry retired, I tried my hand at editing when the time came, but soon returned to reporting.

So Carrie trusted me enough that when I called in with "a major breaking news story," she believed me.

"Hang on," I said, then lowered the phone.

"What'd you get?" I asked Casey. "Something good, I hope."

"I like this one." She thrust the digital camera at me.

"Me, too. Okay, get something to the paper as quick as you can and then we're going hunting."

I paused to collect my thoughts while Casey went inside to transmit her photos.

"I'm back, Carrie, with a wild one here. Seems our Mister Stone has gone off the deep end. Casey's about to send some art from his press conference. Get this up as quick as you can, and I'll start writing as soon as I get a police statement."

"I'm ready," Carrie said, having already typed in my byline.

"Open paragraph. Grieving husband Jackson Stone swore revenge Friday against the man who brutally murdered his wife Angela ten days ago. Period. New paragraph."

A sucking gasp. "Oh, wow. Okay, go."

"In making his first public statement since this crime sent shockwaves through an outraged community comma Stone's vow for vengeance at the East Nashville precinct appeared to shock police officials comma his lawyer and family members. Period. New paragraph. Quote. I don't want justice comma I want revenge comma close quote said Stone comma who then described in detail how he would kill the perpetrator if he found him before the police could. Period. New paragraph. Stone then abruptly left without taking questions. Period. Close."

It had been years since I last dictated a story, and it felt good. And I deemed the effort well worth it if we posted our story online before the TV guys hit the air at six p.m. I glanced at my digital sports watch. Five-forty.

"Great job, Gerry. Try to find a friend, family member, or someone who can reach him, get some police reaction, not just the official line but the guys on the street, if possible. Then we'll update online and come back with the print version. I need everything by eight o'clock."

I sprinted toward the parking lot and Patrick Stone.

8

Back at the office, Carrie Sullivan's brain cranked into overdrive as she looked over my dictation one last time before sending it to the online editor to post. In the next-to-last sentence, she inserted the word "graphic" between "in" and "detail" to give it more oomph, then wrote the headline that she wanted used by the online people. After a couple of tries, she settled on "Stone-cold killer? Husband says he'll hunt down wife's killer" and then deleted it. She'd used "killer" twice and dismissed "Stone-cold killer" as too trite for a news flash of this magnitude. She rewrote it to say "Husband Jackson Stone vows to avenge wife's death" then deleted it, and wrote "Angela Stone's husband vows vengeance," saved it, and forwarded it to online to post.

Sullivan punched in Online Editor Alan Moore's number while also emailing copies to Managing Editor Ken McGuire and Executive Editor Judy Flint.

"Suze, take over that school funding story. I've got my hands full," Sullivan yelled over her shoulder.

"Online. This is Alan," Carrie heard in her earpiece and turned to the computer screen, looking at her version of my story.

"It's Carrie. Take down the Titans practice as your top story and put up what I just sent you. I forgot to add a tagline 'Check back at TenneSceneToday.com for details' at the end of the story. Also give it a 'news alert' keyword. There's art coming, and I should be able to file an update within an hour or so. But get this up pronto. We want to beat the six o'clock newscasts with this one."

"Sure, but replace the topper? You know how many hits Titans stories get."

"That's an editorial decision, not online's. And unless I'm way off base, this story will get more hits than anything in a long time. Gotta go," she said as her other line buzzed.

"Newsroom. This is Carrie."

"Start tearing up the front page. Heard back from Hilliard?" Ken McGuire said, his baritone voice causing her to lower the headset volume.

"Not yet. I talked to him about ten minutes ago, and he's getting some reaction and then going looking for Stone. Where, I don't know."

"What else?"

"Stone's brother called and told Gerry to be at the East Precinct at five p.m. Casey's shooting and supposed to get something here ASAP. We'll re-post and add a photo, and then I'm meeting with the page designers."

"I'll be down in five minutes. Judy's at a seminar, but I'll text her. I'll inform the publisher, too, for this one. Tell Hilliard he's got as much space as he needs."

"The six o'clock news is about to start. Let's see how they handle it."

On the other side of town, Channel 11 news videographer Greg Pittard weaved in and out of rush-hour traffic to get to the station located just off Interstate 65 South and Harding Place. Clarkston called, and gave the news editor the gist of the footage.

"So where is Pittard? We go on the air in fifteen minutes, and we sure don't want to wait until ten o'clock for video," said a frustrated Sam White, the fiftyish, pot-bellied director of the six o'clock newscast. He tried to keep up with producer Ellie Bligh, a former weekend anchor often referred to as "Captain Bligh" for her take-no-prisoners news judgment and a snappish attitude toward her staff.

Bligh glanced out a window as they walked toward the set. "That's him now. Is the intro ready?"

"Everything's good. We're just waiting on the tape," White said. "I'll go over it with Julia."

Pittard rolled halfway out the door before the news van's brakes screeched.

"About time," Bligh snapped as Pittard went straight to his editing bay. He hooked in to the machine and started punching buttons as the raw footage fed into the playback unit. Editors huddled with news writers around the screen, then scurried to edit what he'd shot. The producer and director came over to offer input.

"Five minutes," Pittard heard Bligh say as he concentrated on his final cuts.

Getting a newscast on the air is in many ways like putting out a newspaper, except they produce five to six "editions" a day. The Internet has given us a chance to compete with their immediacy, without the chaos and equipment failures that sometimes accompany a live broadcast. Their jobs must be handled with precision both in front of the camera and in the control room, ready to deal with any glitches. In a frantic setting, most everybody stays cool. But not Ellie. For this story, she bounced from one task to the next, understanding all the ramifications after they hit the air.

Ratings had slipped for the six o'clock newscast in the past quarter, falling two percentage points farther behind Channel 7, even though Bligh's team consistently performed well and remained locked in a dead heat for ten o'clock viewers. She expected this story to put them back on top in the ratings, translating into more advertising revenue, and assuring her of a contract renewal for at least another two years. But she realized all the things that might go wrong if she didn't crack the whip, explaining her frenetic leadership style.

Coming out of commercial, the six o'clock theme cued the teleprompter's start. The red light on camera one flashed.

"Good evening and here's what's happening," said Karen O'Day, the feisty, red-headed counterpart to graying, homespun co-anchor Cameron Knight. They worked well off each other and talked about syndicating their weekly gab-fest, "O'Day and Knight." Bligh and other station officials saw the potential. "Our top story is an anguished husband's emotional and angry reaction to his wife's violent murder."

In the control room, White's directions were precise. "Camera two, cut to Knight, get ready to cut to video one," White said. Camera two's red light flashed. Knight spoke in grim tones.

"It's been almost two weeks since Angela Stone disappeared from her East Nashville home and seventy-two hours since searchers found her body across town in the Warner Park area. Less than an hour ago, husband Jackson Stone finally talked about her mysterious death. And it was a reaction no one expected. Our Dan Clarkston filed this report."

Cut to video one. Jackson Stone's disheveled image and rage-filled message beamed across the Midstate. Cut to video two. Clarkston, professional but clearly sympathetic.

"You've just heard the shocking first public statement from an angry Jackson Stone, whose wife Angela . . . ."

9

Jackson Stone moved swiftly after his disappearing act from the precinct. Nearly six p.m., as he pulled off Ellington Parkway, his thoughts turned to Angela's funeral set for Saturday at noon, to be preceded by a ten o'clock visitation. So little time, so much left to accomplish.

His first stop at Eddie Paul's Pub had retraced one part of his life with Angela. Now, after his very public bounty on her killer, a much harder trip became necessary. He needed to return to the scene of the crime. He must return to his home in East Nashville.

Navigating the final leg of the journey to his neighborhood, Lockeland Springs, the surrealism of the short drive home hit Jackson as he passed rows and rows of hundred-year-old Victorian, craftsman, and bungalow homes that came in all shapes, sizes and colors.

The Stones' home stood out, one of three brick homes on their entire street. Neighbors took care to keep their lush lawns neat and well-watered so the August heat wouldn't burn the grass. The shade trees and full-bloom flowers were wonderful and eye-catching, but the people made it a great place to live. Jackson, who with Angela served on the board of directors for the Lockeland Springs Neighborhood Association and helped coordinate annual block parties, couldn't think of a single person in the area who might be capable of such a terrible crime.

Most viewed the neighborhood as a Nashville melting pot, drawing people of every age, color, religion, ethnicity, sexual orientation, and financial bracket.

A Korean family moved in two years ago next to the widow Edmonds, who was spending her golden years raising her granddaughter. The Waldens, a young black couple with their own insurance company, boasted four kids, two of each. They lived across the street from the Stones. A gay couple, Joe and Bob, both in their mid-thirties, lived in the purple bungalow on the corner. The Fletchers owned the corner home next to Jackson and Angela, a tasteful, peach-colored Victorian with gingerbread carvings. The Fletchers were in their mid-forties and childless, just like the Stones, so the couples spent lots of time together. The young, single teacher down the street moved from Orlando to be closer to her musician boyfriend.

Friends and neighbors like that were why this crime seemed so unreal. Sure, violent crimes still took place in 2010, but nothing like Nashville's soaring murder rate when they moved there in 1996. And now, the unthinkable had happened. How in God's name did Angela wind up way out at Percy Warner Park on the other side of town? Jackson prayed for an answer.

Wishing to attract as little attention as possible, he ducked under the yellow police tape roping off the entrance to his home and slid his key into the lock. Taking a deep breath, Jackson steeled himself and entered. Something important needed retrieval from the upstairs attic.

Angela's presence, her touch, could be felt everywhere. Almost too much to bear, it forced him to plop into the antique oak rocker. Besides Jackson, Angela's passion was antiques. She loved trolling the antique district off Eighth Avenue South and filled her house with finds. The primitive yellow pine den displayed her showcase. Against one wall stood a pine doughboy chest and atop it an original Tiffany lamp Jackson presented to Angela for their tenth wedding anniversary. They found the gold-plated andirons for their marble fireplace two years ago at the "World's Longest Yard Sale," which ran through four states from Alabama to Ohio. Before her death, an excited Angela talked about returning to the annual mid-August event that very week.

41

Jackson headed up the steps to their bedroom. On the staircase landing, a half-circle, maple-stained accent table held an ornate silver-framed picture of Angela in her wedding gown. He turned and continued up to the master bedroom. The closed bedroom door ahead of him stood guard like a towering castle drawbridge. "You made it this far," he said as he fought tears, and then pushed the door hard enough that it banged the wall.

Police had removed the blood-stained sheets from the sleigh bed, but he spotted rust-colored streaks here and there, including one ugly smear running down the wall. A lot of violence occurred here. Jackson struggled between hoping Angela didn't suffer and hoping she'd put up a fight. But investigators identified all the blood found in the bedroom as belonging to her. Jackson entered the large walk-in closet, flipped on lights, and grabbed the string to pull down the folding stairs that allowed him access to the attic storage area.

A burst of mid-August heat descended as he stepped up the first rickety rung. Two more, then he found the cord that turned on the attic light. It wasn't the brightest bulb, but it would be enough to find what he sought. He scurried across the plywood flooring, took a left at the air conditioning ducts, and fell to his knees, pushing aside the pink insulation. He found the small metallic case.

Good, the locks are still sealed. The NCSI team didn't find it. Jackson didn't know who would be after him, but sensed he must move fast. Time to get gone.

10

Thanks to the Internet, public reaction to Jackson Stone's news conference poured in, swift and passionate. The first post to the article at TenneSceneToday.com logged at 5:58 p.m., thrilling Sullivan to see responses before the television newscasts started.

GRIEVINGSPOUSE wrote: "I just wish I had the courage and fortitude to undertake the mission Mr. Stone set for himself. My husband Ralph died in a drive-by shooting two years ago and they still haven't found who did it. Maybe Mr. Stone can track down my Ralph's killer after he finds his wife's murderer."

At 5:59: p.m., NOWAYNOHOW wrote: "My advice would be to let the police handle it. Revenge won't bring back his wife."

At 6:01 p.m., I.M.ONYERSIDE wrote: "Jackson if you need help lemme know."

At 6:02 p.m., OLDSPARKY wrote: "The electric chair's too good for 'em. I'm with I.M.ONYERSIDE on this one. Let's form a posse."

At 6:04 p.m., MYSYMPATHY wrote: "Jack, I'm watching you on television as I write this. PLEASE don't go down this road. I know you're hurting but this isn't how GOD would want you to respond. Take time to heal. Let GOD punish the wicked. It will happen . . . maybe not on your timetable, but it will. I'll say a prayer for your wife. Peace be with you, brother. Amen."

I wouldn't read any of those posts until much later, and at the moment, bloggers were the furthest thing from my mind. I stood in the parking lot next to the East Nashville precinct, pen and notepad in hand, but not taking notes. I chatted with Jackson's still-in-shock brother, trying to glean the facts without pressing too much. Patrick shuffled anxiously, and it made me suspicious of his motives. I wouldn't learn until much later that the car Jackson drove actually belonged to Patrick, and he bordered on desperate to make sure his car sat where Jackson said it would be parked.

"And you didn't know Jackson's plans? How's he handled it all week?"

"It's been real tough on all of us, Mister Hilliard, but Jack kind of shut down through all this," he said, looking down at his watch and shuffling his feet. "He's been grieving his own way, I guess. But how could you expect that reaction?"

"Pretty cold," I said, nodding. "Is he the type person who could make good on this?"

"I don't think so, but maybe," Patrick said. "He'd already joined the Marines by the time I started middle school. He's never talked much about that experience. Maybe it changed him."

Reaching in my coat pocket, I took out my mini-recorder.

"I appreciate your talking with me, and there are some other people I need to see. But I'd like to get a quote from you, and I want to talk to your brother if possible."

"I don't know where he went or where he's going."

"Here's my card. How can I reach you and where is Jackson staying?"

Patrick recited his and Jackson's cell numbers, but added, "I don't know if he'll answer."

I jotted them down, then pressed the "record" button.

"This is Patrick Stone. Describe your brother's mental state. Frustration, anger, or both of the above? Will he really go after his wife's killer? And will his family support him?"

He bristled at my questions.

"Of course, we'll support him. I may not agree with him, but if something happened to my wife, I'd feel the same way. Would I go through with it? I don't know. It's the toughest thing our family's ever been through, even worse than losing our parents in the 1998 tornado touchdown. Angela and Jackson were made for each other. She was the best thing that ever happened to him, and now he's lost her. You better believe I'd be mad enough to kill if I lost my wife the way Angela died."

Patrick paused and looked skyward, swallowing hard. He wanted to make me understand Jackson's motivation.

"Terrible things happen in life, and we somehow find our way through the bad times. I hope Jackson can and we'll all be there to help him." Patrick paused again, and he smiled.

"But he sure picked a heckuva way to deal with it."

11

The six o'clock newscast took its first commercial break, and that's when Jackson's cell phone rang. He closed the front door of his house and headed to the car with his prized possession tucked under his left arm. Recognizing the number, he cursed under his breath.

"Hello, Stan."

"Are you crazy? You can't threaten to torture a man to death," Allenby, Jackson's attorney, said.

Pausing on the brick walkway, Jackson spoke with venom in his voice.

"I didn't. I promised to torture a man to death. And I meant it."

"I get you're upset, but you don't even know who you're looking for and just issued a blanket threat to all of Nashville to start a personal vendetta. Let the police do their job. They'll find him."

"There won't be any pieces left to find when I'm finished. I've got things to do. I'll see you tomorrow at the funeral," Jackson said, clicking off.

He had hoped to make a fast getaway, but Allenby's call delayed him just long enough.

Next door to the Stones' house, Sarah Fletcher still sat at her kitchen table as husband Herb cleared dishes. He had played house-husband for six months after being laid off at the glass plant. Unused to this role-reversal, Sarah picked up more hours at Saint Thomas Hospital, but wasn't comfortable as the main breadwinner.

46

Herb's ego had been battered, and he fought moderate depression. A couple of leads had come up empty, and he took it out on her. She held up her end of the shouting matches and as a result, the marital rift widened. Herb thought things had improved the last few weeks before Sarah grew quiet again after her best friend's death.

"Really weird, seeing Jack on the news," Herb said as he removed Sarah's plate. "Do you think he meant what he said?"

Sarah didn't answer, a vacant stare on her face as if miles away.

Herb strode across the kitchen and began loading the dishwasher. He glanced out the window above the sink as Jackson emerged from the front door, carrying something. Jackson ducked under the police tape and headed for his car.

"Sarah, look out here. It's Jack."

The blank stare shifted to a look of shock followed by tears. Herb opened the sliding glass doors and went out.

"Jack, hey!"

Jackson paused and turned at the greeting.

Herb sprinted across the driveway, concern on his face. "Wow, I'm glad I saw you. Look, I just wanted to say how sorry I was. We saw your press conference. Can we do anything?"

Jackson shook his head, jumped in the car, backed out of the driveway, and sped down the street, tires squealing.

Herb watched the car pull away and turn left at the stop sign. Going back inside, Herb shifted his concern from Jackson to his own wife.

Despite the arguing, Herb didn't know what he'd do if that happened to Sarah. His wife clutched a wood-framed picture of herself and Angela, taken last summer while boating on Old Hickory Lake. Tears streamed down her face. Herb sat beside Sarah and took her hand. She looked into his face and buried her head into his shoulder, sobbing louder.

"I know. I miss her, too."

12

Over at Eddie Paul's Pub, a slow business night gave Louie ample time to watch the newscast as Jackson had suggested. On the screen were those anchor people. What were their names again? He didn't watch much news. The picture cut to Stone, and Louie turned up the sound.

"I want revenge. Whoever did this to my wife—"

"Hate to see a man fall to pieces like that," said Jimmy Sheppard, one of the regulars, said after the segment ended, scratching at his beard and shaking his head.

"I'd do the same thing," Sam Borden said from the corner. "He's not crazy, Jimmy, if that's what you're implying."

"He didn't sound crazy, but he didn't sound sane either," Sheppard said.

Louie poured himself a beer.

"It sounds like he needs a friend. I sure hope he comes back."

Back at the paper, Carrie Sullivan fidgeted as she checked for my updated story. Nothing yet. My cell phone rang busy, so she fired a text message: Where RU GH? Need ASAP.

A check of my web story brought a smile to her face. She found five pages of comments comprised of twenty-eight replies from strangers communicating with each other, very similar to the debate taking place between Jackson's pub friends.

At 6:22 p.m., <u>NEKKIDTROOTH</u> wrote: "Jackson Stone oughtta be wearing one of those Tar-Jay tee-shirts with a bull's-eye on his chest. Whoever did this to his wife will now come after him."

At 6:26 p.m., <u>JONNIEREB</u> wrote: "If Stone needs back-up, me'n my boys will be glad to lend a hand. They won't find anything left of that b@$t@rd to bury."

At 6:33 p.m., <u>WYNOT</u> wrote: "Violence begets violence. When will we ever learn?"

At 6:37 p.m., <u>FEM4EVER</u> wrote: "This was a hate crime! These sick-o MEN are out there persecuting our SISTERS! Learn how to protect yourself. Click here."

At 6:52 p.m., <u>UJERK</u> wrote: "In response to <u>FEM4EVER</u>, why assume a MAN perpetrated this crime? In response to <u>JONNIE REDNECK</u>, you are freakin' scary. Go crawl back in your Neanderthal hole. Let's lock you two in a room together."

Carrie Sullivan looked at her calendar. No full moon. The loonies are out late, she thought, as she deleted the abusive posts.

Meanwhile, I sat in Commander Reynolds' office with my photographer, making small talk while waiting for Dan Clarkston's videographer and Public Affairs Officer Darrin Jensen, the Metro police media liaison, to arrive.

A squeal of brakes. A minute later, Jensen rapped on Reynolds' door, followed by Channel 11 cameraman Greg Pittard. "Look who I found, Dan. Hey, Gerry, glad you're here. We can save time this way. I know you're both up against deadlines."

After a brief meeting, we all stood and shook hands.

"Okay, I think we're set," Jensen said. "I'll talk to Chief King in a few hours and set up something for tomorrow afternoon. He's addressing a ladies' group out in Hermitage tonight, and I'm guessing didn't see the news. You can go find the Chief if you want, but Commander Reynolds can give you what you need for now."

"I can live with that. We need to get back to the station," Clarkston said.

While Clarkston and Pittard got ready for the stand-up interview, I went looking for other quotes and immediately ran into two policemen, one of whom I knew.

"Sergeant Whitfield. Good to see you again," I said.

Mike Whitfield struck me as one of the sharpest cops I'd met in years, and his superiors agreed. He had everything you look for in a policeman—intelligence, courage, confidence, compassion, and strength. He'd been on the force five years and moved quickly up the ranks.

I turned to the other officer. "Don't believe we've met."

Officer Barry Mendez looked like the old *CHIPS* television star Erik Estrada, but bigger and with a crew cut.

"I'm kind of pressed on time, but I'd like to talk to a couple of street cops about Jackson Stone. Y'all heard about his stunt this afternoon?"

"Yeah, I did," Whitfield said. "A terrible thing, what happened to his wife."

"And your reaction?" I said, turning on my mini-cassette.

"As a husband or a cop?"

"However you want to answer."

"Okay. As a husband, sure, I'd want revenge. Losing your wife . . . I don't know if I could handle that. As a policeman, I'd say let justice run its course. We'll find this guy. We don't give up. Step back and let us do our jobs."

"That's Sergeant Mike Whitfield," I said into the microphone, then turned. "And this is Officer Barry Mendez. M-E-N-D-E-Z?" A nod. "What would you say to Stone?"

Mendez leaned into the microphone, a stern look on his face. His first interview as a cop, the former college football defensive lineman at Ohio State handled a reporter like an opposing blocker. Head-on and domineering.

"I'd also tell him to back off. Like Sergeant Whitfield, my heart goes out to him. I'm not married, but my girlfriend's purse got snatched last summer at Green Hills Mall. I wanted to tear the guy's head off when they caught him, but I didn't. You can't let emotions take control of you. This is different. I get that. But Stone needs to understand he can't take the law into his own hands."

"Thanks, guys." I turned off the recorder and went out where Clarkston was interviewing Precinct Commander Mark Reynolds.

"And lastly, Commander Reynolds," Clarkston asked dramatically, "what progress has been made in solving this most heinous crime?"

"I can't divulge details, but I can reassure the public that we are leaving no stone unturned in our efforts to solve this case," Reynolds said. Clarkston didn't pick up on the unintended pun, but I did. "We've talked to neighbors and canvassed the area. I'd encourage anyone with information, no matter how insignificant they think it is, to please come forward."

Clarkston wrapped up the interview, and I walked over. "My turn."

"God, I hate this part of the job," Reynolds said.

I slapped his shoulder. "Sure you do."

"No, really. You're not so bad. You know how things work. You're out here all the time. I understand when you ask tough questions that I don't like answering. But these guys," he said, sweeping his arm, "they only come around when it's a big news story. And then they sensationalize it and justify it by saying they're just doing their jobs."

I sympathized. "I know you can't tell me everything, but I trust that what you do tell me isn't a load of bull. Okay, on the record, Mark," I said, turning on the mike, "what's your take on Stone's declared vendetta?"

"The Stones suffered an enormous tragedy. I don't blame him for being outraged and irrational right now, but if he does uncover information that is crucial to our investigation, he should bring it to us and not try to take the law into his own hands. He could get hurt or cause some other innocent person to get hurt. He needs to let us do our jobs. His wife's funeral is tomorrow, and he should focus on that, not thoughts of vengeance."

"Would you call Stone's declaration irrational or justifiable?"

"I'm no psychiatrist and won't address those aspects either way. I'll leave that to others. My job is to enforce the law and protect the public. On that note, I'd like Mister Stone to understand that any time we spend watching him to prevent him from breaking the law is time subtracted from finding his wife's killer."

I hit the "off" button, put the recorder in my pocket, and extended a hand. Reynolds made an off-the-record request.

"If you find Stone, tell him to call me. Give him my number."

I shook my head and smiled. "You know it doesn't work that way. I'll tell him you want to talk, but I can't give your number. Besides, you guys are in the phonebook."

"It doesn't hurt to ask. You could save me a lot of time."

13

Time is a precious commodity in the newspaper business, where every second counts. These are words we live by, and deadlines are treated dead-serious.

You know what a deadline is? You think you do, but it may be the one single word applied to the newspaper industry which is most misunderstood by the general public. The dog-eared New College Dictionary sitting atop my desk offers two definitions, the first of which appears written for editors and the second for reporters. I'll give the second one first: A specific time or date by which something must be accomplished, i.e. the cut-off time for copy to be accepted for publication. That's clear enough. The first definition, at least it's how I sometimes think my editors think, says a deadline is a point either inside or outside a prison that if crossed, a prisoner risks being shot.

I've lived more than thirty years under the thumb of deadlines. I've missed my share of deadlines, I'm sorry to say, and the next-morning explanations of why I missed my deadline are the closest I'll ever come to facing a firing squad. Editors want to know why I missed the deadline, what I would have done different to avoid missing that particular deadline, what steps I can take in the future to prevent missing a deadline. Sheesh.

Ultimately, the only deadline we're truly obligated to meet is whatever time it is that you wake up each morning, slip on your robe and house shoes, and stagger half-asleep out to the driveway to pick up the paper before that first morning cup of coffee.

That's our contract with you, the reader. If the paper's not there, man, it's a lousy way to start your day.

You might call to complain, get an automated response instead of a live person, and leave a message threatening to cancel your subscription if it happens again tomorrow.

There's a third, more concise definition of deadline that anyone who has ever worked for a newspaper understands— hellish! In a nutshell, here's how the newspaper that arrives at your door comes together. We all operate on different deadlines, and each one deadline affects the next person's down the line. The advertising department must finish early enough so that the amount of editorial space can be determined for the national and local news sections, business, sports, and entertainment. Section editors meet at nine a.m., noon, and three p.m., to weigh the day's news and decide what gets covered and what doesn't. Reporters and photographers are assigned to stories and must file with their editors by a pre-set time. The editor reads each story for factual and stylistic accuracy by a specific time in order to get it to the copy desk. There, various editors pull the text and art onto the pages, write headlines and cutlines and other breakout information, edit copy down to an assigned length, again check facts for style and accuracy, and then proofread copy a final time before releasing pages so that the paper can be printed, loaded onto trucks, and delivered to carriers by a certain time so that they get the paper to your doorstep before you awaken.

In theory if I'm a minute late in getting my story to my editor, that means I've given my editor Carrie Sullivan less time to fact-check/edit/rewrite my "prose" if she's to make her deadline to get it to the copy desk. And if the copy desk goes in late because five stories come to them late, it means the paper won't be printed on time, won't be loaded onto the trucks by the assigned time, and won't be delivered to your house on time.

Every reporter and editor deals with deadline pressures in different ways. We get stressed out, bummed out, and burnt out from the never-ending deadlines—and love every minute of it, even if we never admit it. I do some of my best work on deadline.

Carrie always loved a challenge and recognized the breaking news about the startling new twist to the Angela Stone murder case would be a major challenge for all of us. I mentioned stress a while back. Carrie always operates in a crisis mode and when it overwhelms her, she can get snappy with even her favorite, most trusted reporter. That explained her mood as she waited to hear back from me and start receiving the digital photographs from our photographer, Casey Leiber. Off to a fast start, getting the story online before the six o'clock television news, she didn't want us to lose momentum.

Carrie checked her computer for a fourth time before she saw the first of Casey's photographs pop into the system. Almost six-fifteen, she needed any photo for my story on the website's home page. Carrie felt the first photo lacked the raw emotion to match the forcefulness of what I'd dictated. Just good enough to post, she hoped Casey snapped something stronger for print. She downloaded it to her desktop, then called up my story and attached the first photograph, writing a cutline to describe what readers were seeing:

> Nashville businessman Jackson Stone, second from left, addresses (delete) . . . Nashville's Jackson Stone, second from left, held a press conference on Friday at the East Pricint (delete) Precinct, where he vowed revenge for the recent death (delete) murder of his wife, Angela. *CASEY LEIBER/TENNESCENE TODAY.*

She saved the changes, closed the document, and recached the article. It looked good, with the **BREAKING NEWS** caption in bright red to the left of the headline. That would do for now. She checked back to see if Casey filed any more photos—all right!

The third shot, taken moments before the conference began, captured the emotion she sought—a single tear trickling from the corner of Jackson's left eye. The fourth shot, even better, showed a look of seething hatred on his face, dry-eyed, and smoldering with anger. An outstretched hand stuck out like a pistol, his index finger cocked at the camera like a gun barrel aimed at some unknown killer lurking out there. Photo number five captured the look of surprise—and horror, maybe—on the face of his lawyer as Jackson issued his personal declaration of war. The online department would post these photos as a slideshow package.

Impatiently, she tried my cell phone number, hoping to find out how close I was to filing a website update and then my print story for first edition. But her telephone rang busy because I'd set my cell phone on speaker, and it rang and rang the number Stone's brother gave me. I listened to my tape of Officer Mendez to ensure the accuracy of my transcription. "Can't take the law into his own hands," Mendez said as I read over what I'd typed into my laptop. I went to the top of the page and scanned for typos, making one change before I saved and sent it into the system. Carrie answered on the first ring.

"The update ought to be there."

"Yeah, it's about twelve to fourteen inches. Get me a write-through within the hour."

"No problem. I still haven't reached Stone. I'd like to find him tonight if I can."

"I think we're okay if you don't. Besides his dynamite comments, you quoted three other sources. Maybe he'll talk tomorrow after the funeral. I assume you're going."

"Wouldn't miss it. This is one story I want to see through to the end."

"Can you hold it to about twenty-five inches for in the morning? Then for Sunday, we'll come back with a mainbar from the funeral and an inside piece with reaction."

"The reaction might be the better mainbar. Darrin Jensen is setting up a news conference for the police chief a couple of hours after the funeral. And there are others I'd like to talk to, and maybe chase down some sidewalk reaction. Can you put out some photo orders for me?"

"That sounds good. And look at the website when you get a chance. The photo up now isn't anything special, but Casey got some great shots, and we'll sub it out when I re-post. You were right about this story. It already has over two hundred hits. Gotta go."

Next, I re-dialed Jackson's cell phone as he drove from the city.

"Hello?"

"Mister Stone. This is Gerry Hilliard at *TenneScene Today*. I'd—"

Click.

Ring . . . ring . . . ring . . . .

"Where'd you get this number?"

"From your brother. He—"

Ring . . . ring . . . ring . . . .

"I think I've said all there is to say."

"But did you mean it, or just say that out of anger and frustration?"

Jackson's resolve came through loud and clear.

"I. MEANT. EVERY. WORD!"

Click. I smiled, then set to writing for the daily, which was basically an updated version of the online story rather than a complete rewrite. I sprinkled in a few more quotes and added a little more background. Unlike the online version, this one leaned more sympathetic toward Jackson, evoking the emotions of the past few hours. Furious as he was, Jackson still needed a news outlet to tell his side of the story. And I intended to be that outlet. I also remember thinking for the very first time there might be a book deal out of it.

I copied the online story and started a new file in case I needed to resend the original version for any number of reasons. I pressed the [F2] button, which automatically inserted my byline, then hit the "enter" key three or four times and pasted the old story before writing a new lead:

"In the two weeks since the tragic East Nashville murder of his wife, Jackson Stone's life has spiraled out of control. On Friday afternoon, three days after her body was found by searchers on the other side of town, Stone reclaimed the direction in which his fate will now take him, though the path he has chosen is fraught with peril and uncertainty.

"At an emotion-charged press conference, the 45-year-old Nashville advertising executive launched a personal campaign of vengeance for the gruesome death of Angela Stone, 35, by vowing to spend the rest of his days hunting for his wife's killer. His extraordinary promise of retribution, described in vivid detail, seemed to shock friends and family members who rallied at the East Precinct to offer their support."

I reread the paragraphs, changed "fate" to "life," then went back to "fate." I then deleted copy in the earlier version until I picked up the first quote:

"I don't want justice. I want revenge," Stone said.

14

Jackson Stone's car sped down Interstate 24 East headed toward Murfreesboro. His family farm in the Lascassas community had served as a retreat to which he and his brother escaped after their parents' tragic deaths in the 1998 Nashville tornado. Some neighbors rented out the farmland now, but the brothers still hunted on the property. They fixed up the small cabin and got a well dug. Sentiment kept them from considering offers, including two for a very nice price.

After hanging up on me, Jackson speed-dialed his brother.

"Why did you give my number to that reporter?"

"You didn't say not to. Hell, you didn't say anything after that stupid press conference. Have you lost your mind?"

The concern in Patrick's voice made Jackson ease off the gas.

"I don't know. Maybe." The words choked in his throat. "I just had to do something."

"Where are you, Jacky? Just come home. The funeral's tomorrow. You need to be with your family."

"I'll be at your place by eight in the morning. Don't worry, I'm okay. I just need some time to myself tonight. I guess you found your car."

"You should know something, Jack. That stunt you pulled is all over the news."

"Good," Jackson said, the harsh tone returning.

59

"Oh yeah? Not so good for us. The police came looking for you, and so did at least two TV stations. We turned off the phones, and Sheila sent the kids to her sister's house. I want to talk to you tonight."

"I'll explain tomorrow."

Jackson closed his cell phone and settled back as he continued down the interstate, pleased with his brother's report. It sounded like he stirred up the public reaction he wanted, but he failed to realize just how big a media bonfire he started or how fast it would burn out of his control. As the sun began its descent toward the western horizon, Jackson looked forward to getting to the cabin and settling in to see reaction on the ten o'clock news.

As Jackson's day wound down, with the toughest part of the scheme behind him, it hit high gear for me and other media outlets.

Over at Channel 11, officials mapped out the ten o'clock news to air in two hours, and producer Ellie Bligh directed traffic, expecting Clarkston and Pittard any minute.

"Nice effort at six, people, but we've got to stay on top of this story. So let's do a little brainstorming," she said, as Pittard and Clarkston walked in the door. The reporter sat between newscast co-anchors Karen O'Day and Cameron Knight, as Pittard headed for his editing bay.

"Glad you made it, Dan," Bligh said. Fellow staffers hooted. "So what's the latest?"

"We drove all over East Nashville, and nobody's seen or heard from him. Well, except for his neighbor, Herb Fletcher. He said Stone made a short stop at his house and left without saying a word. His brother wouldn't talk to us; neither would anybody down at this dive. I figured we'd been out there long enough. End of story."

"Wrong," Bligh snapped. "This story's just starting. How will we cover it?"

"We start with the funeral tomorrow," Cameron Knight said. Bligh nodded.

"And the police just sent out a release stating that Chief King will hold a press conference tomorrow afternoon," O'Day added. "That might be interesting."

"I thought I might try to profile the type of person Stone is chasing. And I want to delve deeper into Stone's background," Clarkston said.

"Everybody's going to be doing those pieces over the next few days," Bligh said. "I want something different, people. This story's got legs, and we're not going to trip over them."

Back at the paper, Carrie Sullivan downed her fifth cup of coffee since coming to work that day. She met first with Casey and photo editor Brad Moore to select the shots they wanted to run in the daily. The fourth photo—the one where a visibly enraged Stone cocked his finger like a gun at the camera—won everybody over, although Casey argued that it cast Stone in a less-than-sympathetic light. They decided to use the third shot, with Stone's eyes watering just before the media event, as either secondary art for the front cover or to run inside with the jump. Then they moved on to the design desk, where Carrie and Managing Editor Ken McGuire met with Janice Munro and her staff. They suggested several different scenarios for the front-page layout—whether to run the main photo over three columns or four. They considered page placement as either a centerpiece or a strip across the top. Should they go with a straightforward headline or a label head to convey the emotions of the story? Could they come up with any "breakouts"—informational or statistical data that are better as a chart—or "refers"—blurbs to tell readers on which pages to find related articles—to run with the story? How much space should be allotted inside for the story jump? Finally, everybody agreed, and it boiled down to making all the jigsaw puzzle pieces fit.

Still waiting for my rewrite at eight fifteen, Carrie again went to the website and noted with satisfaction the slideshow attached to our updated story had already drawn over three hundred hits with ten pages of comments comprised of sixty-four replies. She printed the most recent posts for me to check later.

At 7:59 p.m., MARYLOU wrote: "I don't know Jackson Stone, didn't know his wife Angela, but some mutual friends told me what great people they truly are. My heart goes out to Jack. I hope he won't mind my coming to Angela's funeral on Saturday at noon at Belle Valley Cemetery. My husband and I will be there to show our support for him, even though we disagree on whether he should pursue a course of vengeance. I think he should let the police find his wife's killer."

At 8:04 p.m., EARLYTOBED wrote: "I can't agree with WILDWEST. Violence is never the solution. It is A solution but it will surely land Jackson Stone in the pokey for the rest of his days."

At 8:11 p.m., JIMBOB78 wrote: "It's a bad idea. My solution would be to get"—

The telephone ring startled Sullivan. She clicked off the website, and checked the system.

"Your story's here, Gerry. Ken wanted me to ask what your plans are for tomorrow and what kind of help you need."

"I thought a little about that. Visitation starts at ten a.m., and the funeral is at noon. I just talked to Darrin Jensen. He set up a news conference for the police chief at about two or two-thirty. There's no way I can be at both if I'm writing for online after the funeral. Can somebody handle that? Then I'll wrap up both events for print with a sidebar reaction from folks after the funeral."

"Shelley Finklestein is on duty for the weekend. I'll call and get her out there. David Hill's your weekend editor. He'll be in about four."

The newspaper put to bed the state edition and then got to work on the final wrap-up. I wound up making a couple of changes in my story after all and re-filed, then drove by a couple of East Nashville bars to see if anyone had talked to Jackson. The gruff, old bartender at Eddie Paul's feigned ignorance, so I headed home, fixed a drink to go with a light dinner that Jill had put in the refrigerator for me, jotted down some story ideas, and waited for the ten o'clock news.

Jackson Stone got off at the busy Murfreesboro exit, pulled into the Golden Gallon mini-mart, and filled his gas tank. He went inside and bought eggs, bacon, milk, and coffee for breakfast, one of those heat-and-eat Hungry Man chicken dinners, plus a six-pack of light beer. He then drove past Middle Tennessee State University and out Lascassas Highway to the farm. About fifteen minutes later, he turned onto the gravel driveway and aimed the car lights toward the small cabin's front door so he could see to unlock. Crickets chirped their night song as the moon shone bright above. An owl screeched somewhere in the woods, and a bullfrog croaked. Jackson went inside and turned on lights everywhere. He put the food in the fridge and popped open the first beer of the night. The Hungry Man dinner went in the microwave.

While the mashed potatoes bubbled, Jackson took care of the main reason why he made the trek to Murfreesboro instead of returning to his brother's West Nashville residence. He needed a good hiding place for his small metallic case, and his safe house provided such. He shoved the heavy, honey-stained oak farm table across the kitchen floor, pulled up a loose board, stuck the case below, slid a weave rug over it and moved the table back to sit atop it. The microwave beeped, and Jackson got a towel to remove the steaming hot tray. He scraped the food onto a plate and took it into his bedroom. He set the alarm for six a.m., then sat up on the comfortable double bed, nibbling while he waited for the ten o'clock news.

15

Corey Adams bent over the worn green felt of the pool table and stared over the ivory cueball as he lined up his shot. "Eight ball in the side pocket."

The silent man who watched from the shadows raised his beer with one hand, grinding the pool stick into the linoleum with the other. Maude's Neighborhood Grille, a West Nashville joint off Charlotte Pike in a neon-lit strip mall, drew a rough, working-class crowd. But none of them looked as unrefined as the dark-faced stranger.

Corey thrust his stick one, two, three times and then hit the ball dead-center, sending it spinning across the table. He straightened up, already counting his money when his shot kissed the eight ball and angled it into the middle of the side pocket. He smiled. "You owe me a hundred dollars, pal."

Delmore Remus Wolfe took another slurp from his ice-cold bottle of beer, savoring the taste, then used his sleeve to wipe the trickling stream that dripped on his unkempt beard. He put down his beer before setting the cue stick back on the wall stand, then turned to the old juke box. Wolfe had grown up on the "outlaw" sound and disliked most new country music listed. He needed Merle or Cash or Hank Jr. to get his juices flowing, but Corey's smug tone penetrated Wolfe's thoughts as he fed coins into the machine.

"C'mon, dude, pay up," Corey said belligerently, holding out his hand. He stood an inch taller than Wolfe and maybe fifteen pounds heavier, and his muscular frame indicated a penchant for a good number of hours spent in the gym, so Corey didn't hesitate about throwing his weight around. He should. It's always good to size up your competition when throwing up a challenge.

Corey misjudged.

"You heard me," he said, more aggressive. "I want my money."

Corey flinched when Wolfe slowly turned from the old-fashioned Crosley jukebox and glared.

"Don't worry. You'll get what's coming to you."

Wolfe picked up his bottle and headed for the door. Corey whistled and waved to catch the attention of Bubba Nelson.

Bubba threw a twenty on the bar, and followed his fishing buddy outside.

Wolfe smiled as he headed for his rusting, faded blue 1998 Firebird.

"Hey man, where you going?" Corey closed the gap, and shouted over his shoulder to Bubba. "Rabbit's running, Bubba! Don't let him get away."

"You want your money, don't you? Come and get it," Wolfe said as he turned the corner of the building and stepped into the darkness.

"I sure wi—"

Wolfe's left fist lashed out and dropped Corey the way Baltimore Ravens linebacker Ray Lewis slammed Tennessee Titans running back Eddie George in the 2001 NFL playoffs. A crunching, steel-toed kick to the ribs followed seconds before Bubba rounded the corner. Wolfe switched the beer bottle from his right hand to his left, put his might into the swing, and connected with the just-arriving-Bubba's cheekbone, the glass shattering at the impact. Bubba's body went starched-shirt stiff and his head struck the pavement first. Neither downed man felt the savage stomping that ensued, though they would spend months recuperating from their many internal injuries and broken bones. Corey lost a spleen, while Bubba went on the wired-jaw diet and lost forty pounds.

Finally, Wolfe expended his furious energy and leaned over the two bloody pulps, emptying their wallets. "You guys owe me a beer," he said, adding a final kick.

16

Jackson Stone popped open another beer and settled back on the bed just before the phone rang. He put the beer on one of the coasters Angela bought during their last vacation to North Myrtle Beach, South Carolina, the one that promised "Sun and Fun." He looked at the caller ID, and answered, even though he didn't feel like talking to his brother.

"Hi, Patrick."

"It's Sheila. I thought you might be there."

"Oh. How's the bro?"

"Out of his mind and out looking for you. How are *you*?"

"I'm handling it, I guess. I'm not looking forward to tomorrow, but I'll be strong for Angela. That's what she'd want."

"But she wouldn't want you planning revenge in her name, Jack. Let the police handle it."

Jackson's tone grew cold. "I can't do that, Sheila. I won't do that."

"You're going to get yourself ki—" Sheila paused. "I hear Patrick pulling into the driveway now. He'll want to talk to you."

Checking his watch, Jackson saw it was almost time for the ten o'clock reports.

"Look, I want to catch the news and get some rest. Tomorrow's going to be a long day. I'll see y'all in the morning."

"Jack, I didn't—"

Jackson hung up on Sheila, then unplugged the phone, and turned off his cell phone. He picked up his beer and focused on the television, turning up the sound. The truck commercial ended, and a Channel 11 news promo came up. Cameron Knight looked up from his script and flashed a wooden smile.

"Coming up at ten, the whole city is talking about one man's plans for vengeance over the recent death of his wife. And in sports, the Titans play their second preseason game as the high schools kick off another campaign."

Jackson changed from one channel to the next—yep, lead story on all four local stations. Each news station visited his home, and two tried to talk with his brother. He switched back to Channel 11 and tightened his lips as the picture cut to a live remote.

"We're outside the Stone home with neighbor Jeannine Jones," Clarkston said. "Ma'am, what's the reaction around here since word spread of Jackson Stone's declaration for revenge?"

Stone almost laughed, because the eccentric Jeannine at this hour normally would have her face covered in cold cream, cuddled in bed with her cats at her side and one of her "stories"—a long-winded, over-written romance novel— in her hands instead of watching the late news. But Jeannine on the screen, wearing a bright red dress with a light blue sash and way too much makeup, enjoyed her fifteen seconds of fame as one of Angela and Jackson Stone's "close" neighbors.

"Well, I haven't talked with anyone except Mister Fletcher," she said, glancing toward an off-screen man on the other side of Clarkston. "But I was shocked—not like when poor Mrs. Stone died, but it really surprised me. Mister Stone didn't seem like someone so vengeful."

"Thank you," Clarkston said, swiveling to his left and followed by the camera. "This is Herb Fletcher, who lives next door to the Stones. Sir, I understand you talked to Mister Stone after he made his chilling statement this afternoon."

Jackson sat up and paid close attention to what his next-door neighbor would say.

"Well, I tried. Jack stopped by the house about an hour after he spoke. I asked what I could do to help him, but he left without saying a word."

"You personally want to help him avenge the death of his wife?"

"Well, I didn't mean it like that. I want the person punished, of course, but it's not something I could do. But if anyone can, Jackson can. I've been hunting with him."

Clarkston faced the camera and struck a pensive pose.

"Can Jackson Stone find his wife's killer? And if he does, will he turn him over to the police or actually carry out his vendetta? We'll try to learn a little more about Mister Stone over the next couple of days and what his plans are for the future. We tried to talk to him after his news conference this afternoon without success. Perhaps he will be more forthcoming after his wife's funeral tomorrow or in the coming days. Live from East Nashville, this is Dan Clarkston reporting for Channel Eleven News."

Clicking off the TV, Jackson pulled the covers up around his neck and asked himself the very questions the TV reporter posed. Could he find his wife's killer? And if so, then what? Jackson wrestled with his conscience for choosing such a dangerous path. After about thirty minutes, internal debate gave way to a fitful night of sleep as Jackson endured vivid dreams of Angela running from some unseen danger. He never quite caught up to protect her.

17

Next door to Jackson Stone's home in East Nashville, following Herb's interview with the Channel 11 reporter, a teary-eyed Sarah Fletcher chewed her fingernails ragged. She shut off the television in a state of hysteria, and scrambled up the stairs before her husband re-entered the house. Did she get her best friend killed?

Raking her hands through her hair, Sarah reeled as she got in bed, pulled covers over her head and cried silent tears. Tell Herb? No way. It would destroy him and their marriage. She couldn't confess her sins to Jackson—could she? What would she say? What could she say? She didn't know for certain what happened that night. But if he wanted to find the killer, she might hold the clue to solve this otherwise random act of violence. She squinched her eyes and prayed for guidance from God above and for Angela's soul. *Please don't blame me for your death.* Tears gave way to fitful sleep—and nightmares of the mysterious young man who she inwardly knew killed Angela. This time, he came for her.

A review of Nashville Nielsen Ratings for that night's ten p.m. time slot showed that eighty-nine percent of the homes in the Metro area tuned into one of the four local newscasts to see the latest on Jackson Stone. Most wanted to stay informed on happenings in their community, while some enjoyed watching a train wreck like Jackson's meltdown. But a small group—including me—maintained a vested interest in the Jackson Stone saga.

Flipping off the TV in the den of our Hendersonville home, I smiled inwardly. Pleased with myself that, apparently, I alone made contact with Jackson Stone after the press conference (I didn't know then about Sheila's call), I planned to stay three steps ahead on this story. Going through brother Patrick seemed the best bet, and Jackson might speak after the funeral.

As I tugged on my PJs and fell into bed, two trains of thought raced through my mind. The first was that maybe Stone lost touch with reality. I wasn't qualified to answer, but that Vanderbilt psychologist I'd interviewed last spring on a case, Doctor Erica Karnoff, she might shed light on Stone's state of mind. The other idea was far more dangerous—could I find Angela Stone's killer before the cops or Jackson Stone got hold of him? It took me awhile to get to sleep as I pondered that one.

Sprawled on the dirty, food-stained sofa in room 36 of the $29.95 a night motel on Dickerson Pike on the north-central side of downtown Nashville, Wolfe stared at the TV and opened a beer, amused by what he'd seen. Good thing he'd come on back to the grubby motel where he holed up, paying by the month at the rate of $200 per week. Wolfe drove back across town because he figured the cops would be looking for whoever put those guys in the ER. He'd kept tabs on the news since before he picked up that prowling cougar. He'd been on the hunt, too, looking to satisfy that all-consuming blood-lust.

It happened on Wolfe's third night in Music City, the latest stop on his self-styled "Tour of Death."

We now know Wolfe left bodies across the South for almost five years, and was never connected to a single death because his patterns were unusual even for serial killers. He left behind little, if any, physical evidence. He stayed on the move, going from city to city and victim to victim. In one town, he might go after elderly white women. Moving on to another city, he might target young Latino women. In the next, he might seek out a suburban wife and make it look like a home invasion gone wrong, followed by an inner city coed he attacked while jogging, followed by a model who disappeared after a night out with her boyfriend. The randomness of his selection of victims contrasted other compulsive methods: Three women over a six-month period, always. Then on to another city, often bigger ones like Atlanta, Dallas, New Orleans, Tampa, Miami, and Charlotte because the deaths were even less likely to be connected in a major metropolitan area.

Wolfe kept a meticulous journal of each and every death he caused over the years, taking great care to detail how he sized up each victim before attacking. Sometimes it required several days of stalking, other times a spur-of-the-moment decision such as the one that led to the Stone woman becoming Number 49 on Wolfe's hit parade. His now-infamous diaries cemented his legend.

His face crinkled into a sneer at Stone's first words, "I don't want justice. I want revenge." The cops never came close to connecting Wolfe to even one of his murders. *This might be fun*, he wrote in one journal entry. *So Stone wants revenge? Good luck with that one, dumb ass. Hell, I wanna be king of the world. Or a high-paid CIA assassin! Maybe I should send 'em my resume.*

Wolfe hadn't killed a man since getting rid of his aunt and uncle over a dozen years ago, when he was thirteen. He was suspected, but not connected to their "accidental" drowning when the small fishing boat tipped over. His grandmother took him in and raised him on the farm until her "accidental" fall from the tractor that ran her over when he turned seventeen. Then Wolfe disappeared for a few years before embarking on his "mission."

But Wolfe's amusement turned to anger when he saw Herb Fletcher interviewed. He intended Fletcher's foxy wife as the target that day and, well, things happened. She didn't know his true name, but could identify him. Mistakes could be rectified, as he wrote in this journal entry.

And then I'll take care of Stone. He wants revenge, huh? He wants ME? He WANTS Me??? Yeah, he's gonna get me. I'm gonna go after him. I'm gonna make him bleed. Come and get it.

That thought made him smile as he thumbed through newspapers and found an obituary for Angela Stone. At the bottom it read, "Visitation 10 a.m., Belle Valley Memorial Funeral Home and Cemetery. Graveside service at noon." The lights went off and an ever-present, smoldering rage slowly gave way to a dreamless night of sleep.

At the West Meade home of Sheila and Patrick Stone, the couple engaged in a heated argument after watching the newscast. Sheila made the mistake of telling Patrick she'd talked to his brother. "But he didn't want to talk and hung up on me."

"Where'd you find him, or did he call first?"

"No, I called him. At the farm. He said he'd be here in the morning."

Patrick cursed and grabbed for his car keys, but Sheila got to them first. "No sir, you're not going off half-cocked to Murfreesboro to face your brother at this hour. You wouldn't get there until after eleven and wouldn't get home until two. You'd sleep through the funeral."

Patrick failed to persuade Sheila to surrender the keys, and she at last convinced him it wasn't in anybody's best interest to go down there all hot-headed and confrontational.

"All right, but I'm still gonna call."

Sheila kept silent as the phone rang and rang and rang. They went to bed mad, but for different reasons. Both suffered bad nights of sleep, Patrick dreaming of punching his brother in the nose, while Sheila's dream focused on helping Jackson get some professional help.

"Perhaps he will be a little more forthcoming after his wife's funeral tomorrow or in the coming days. Live from East Nashville, this is Dan Clarkston reporting for Channel Eleven News."

Wilson King, the second African-American in Nashville history to rise to the rank of Chief of Police, turned off the TV in disgust as he watched in the den of his posh Tudor home off West End. After finishing his speech to the Hermitage Ladies Auxiliary, Nashville's top cop received a text message about nine-thirty from the Metro police spokesman. It said the Stone murder case took an odd turn, that the Chief should hurry home in time to watch the ten o'clock news and that he set up a press conference tentative for tomorrow at two-thirty, but could be changed to any time the Chief wanted. King messaged back his approval of the time. Now he might pay a little visit to Mister Stone before his wife's funeral.

"That stupid, stupid son of a—"

The telephone rang, and King grabbed it midway through the second ring.

"Did you see that nut?" District Attorney Logan Trulowicz said. "I'm tempted to issue a warrant for his arrest right now."

"Calm down, Logan. I'm going to read him the riot act in the morning."

Trulowicz picked up on the coolness and responded in kind.

"Glad to hear. It sounds like you've got this situation under control, or will soon. Sorry for the intrusion, Wil. Good night."

King hung up and stared into space, wondering if he could control the "situation." He'd set Stone straight, damn it, "and that'll be that."

After a scotch and small bite to eat (the rubber chicken at dinner left him still hungry), King and his wife turned in for the night. "This case," he explained to his wife, "could be a major embarrassment for the department if Stone worms his way into it."

Left unsaid was that it could derail the Chief's future political hopes. Then an idea came to him that would help him sleep better than a glass of warm milk. His wife purred as he lightly stroked her back. "You know, babe, if my guys can solve this one in a way that will satisfy Stone, the media, and the public, it might kick-start a run for the mayor's job in 2015." King slept hard, dreaming of little old ladies, kissing babies, and shaking hands non-stop.

The blogosphere never sleeps. So while all the major players managed to get varying degrees of rest, bloggers at various Nashville media websites continued throughout the night to churn out messages of sympathy, hope, pity, fear, concern, hatred, venom, envy, foolishness, sheer lunacy, and a gamut of other emotional reactions. A sampling:

TenneSceneToday.com: At 11:22 p.m., PAYBACK THYME wrote: "The man who killed Jackson's wife should be hunted down and shot like the mad dog he is. And if I ever climb out of this wheelchair again I'd sure help Stone track him down."

Classic Country 750-AM: At 12:15 a.m., COUNTRY CUZ wrote: "Jackson Stone is a Great American. I was stationed with him in Kuwait in 1990-91 and he saved my life. Too bad he couldn't save his wife. If he'd been there, the killer would be in the ground instead of Angela. If you see this, Jack, remember that you can call on Big Red for ANYTHING podner. I owe you one buddy."

Liberal Talk 89.9-FM: At 12:57 a.m., NOHOPE4U wrote: "What kind of whacko is this guy? I bet he's out playing golf Monday in the O.J. Invitational, trying to find the killer, when the place he needs to look is in the mirror."

Channel 11: At 1:39 a.m., JOHN DOUGH wrote: "My money's on the cops getting the killer first. Even if Stone gets to him first, I don't think he's got the stones to pull the trigger."

Golden Oldies 58-FM: At 2:14 a.m., RAY OF SUNSHINE wrote: "From each acorn springs a sturdy oak that our eyes will someday see. So move on, Jackson Stone: Stand tall and grow toward your final destiny!"

Channel 3: At 2:52 a.m., SIXGUN SALLY wrote: "I have nothing but admiration for what Stone wants to do, but he needs to understand

the consequences and be ready to live—or die—
with the choices he makes."
    Hot 100-FM: At 3:45 a.m., <u>ANNIE REXIA</u>
wrote: "This thread makes me want to puke.
Wait I just did. LOL Jack."

Links to local sites got attached to posts at national websites like Oprah, *USA Today*, Dr. Phil's self-help show, evangelist Dr. Tony Know's national prayer line, the syndicated *A.M. America* television show and to both liberal and conservative radio talk shows, and his press conference got more than a million hits on YouTube. By Monday morning Stone's quest for vengeance became a national watercooler topic. Producers scrambled to book Stone's first guest appearance. His story would be a ratings bonanza.

SATURDAY, AUGUST 14
1

The alarm clock's light buzzing began at six a.m. sharp and built into an annoying crescendo that stirred Jackson Stone from a deep sleep. He slapped the alarm and climbed out of bed. After his first complete night of sleep in four days, he awoke refreshed, if a little groggy. He made a pot of coffee, got in the shower, dressed, and then fried the eggs and bacon as he watched TV news reports. A repeat of the Channel 11 interviews played while he ate. He was in the car by seven, and pulled into his brother's driveway at eight sharp. Jackson noticed a blue-and-white sitting a couple of houses away from his brother's home.

In addition to Patrick and Sheila, his cousins arrived, but were soon leaving for the airport to pick up Angela's sister and parents, flying in from Houston. They would go to their hotel to freshen up before meeting the Stones at the funeral home for visitation. The cousins left Patrick's house at eight ten a.m., in case of traffic delays. At eight fifteen the doorbell rang.

Sheila answered and gasped, startled to see the large, bald-headed, black policeman filling the front door, regaled in his dress blues, holding his cap in the crook of his right arm. The giant man cracked a slight smile.

"Good morning, ma'am. I hope you'll pardon this interruption on such a solemn occasion, but could I speak with Mister Jackson Stone?"

"Yes, certainly, Officer—"

"Chief King, ma'am."

"Uh, yes, of course," she stammered, embarrassed. "Forgive me. I should've recognized you. One second, please." She closed the screen door, but left the front door cracked and hurried into the den where Patrick was talking and Jackson wasn't listening. He stared at his picture in the newspaper he held.

"Jack," she said, "you've got a visitor."

2

While Jackson prepared for his first—but not last—face-to-face meeting with Chief King, others also made plans.

About seven-thirty a.m., Wolfe sat at the counter of the Greasy Spoon Cafe next to the small, aging Dickerson Pike motel, sipping on his third cup of coffee as Jackson Stone stared straight at him, pointing an accusing finger. Wolfe put down the front section of the morning paper and flipped to the sports section, but he couldn't concentrate on either the story on the Titans' preseason win or the eggs Joanie placed in front of him.

"Want your coffee warmed, hon?"

"Not right now," he said, shoving the eggs away and lighting a cigarette as he picked up the paper again and stared back at Stone's picture. He studied it intensely, scrutinizing every detail—the way his arm stayed close to his body, the dangerous eyes, the snarling lips—and compared it to the image of the soft man with a tear in the corner of his eye in the picture below. Clearly, the man turned his emotions on and off as easy as twisting a spigot. So what did that mean? Wolfe pondered that very question when the waitress came back.

"Sorry, hon, I've gotta ask you to put out your smoke," she said, pointing to a sign on the wall prohibiting smoking in eating establishments, effective August 15. "Your eggs've gotten cold. Want me to reheat 'em?"

79

With the cigarette pinched between his teeth, Wolfe offered an intimidating glance at Joanie, then looked at his bill and threw six dollars on the counter, grabbing the paper as he headed for the door.

"Naw, thanks, hon. I've gotta get going. I've got a funeral to attend."

He exhaled a smoke stream and stubbed out his cigarette.

In East Nashville, Herb Fletcher awoke at eight a.m., showered, dressed, said for Sarah to get up, put on the java, walked to the corner bakery to get the paper and some chocolate-drizzled croissants, slammed the door after he returned because he still didn't hear or see Sarah up, turned on the TV in time to see a replay of himself being interviewed on Channel 11, read and reread the stories in the paper about Jackson, went to the bathroom, and looked in on Sarah again. She lay awake, but still in bed and staring into space. Were those tears?

"Hey, baby," he said, flopping on the bed. "You need to get up. It's going on nine o'clock, and visitation starts in an hour."

"I'm not going. I can't," she said, and pulled the sheet over her head.

At my house in Hendersonville, I was lying toward the center of the bed when my wife slapped me on the rump with the morning paper. "Time to rise and shine, hon," Jill said. "Coffee's made and the eggs are about ready."

I yawned, rolled over, looked at the clock, and panicked. Eight-thirty!

"Why didn't you wake me earlier? I need to get going," I said, heading for the shower. "I told you what today's going to be like."

"That's why you needed the extra rest. Don't worry, you've got plenty of time."

After an invigorating five-minute shower, I dressed for the funeral and joined Jill in the breakfast nook. My plate—

two poached eggs, two slices of Benton's bacon, and a cinnamon bagel—rested on the warmer, and the coffee was still hot.

"This is great," I told Jill through a mouthful of eggs as I scanned my front page centerpiece story.

"Are you talking about breakfast or your story?" she said.

"Both," I answered, ever the diplomat. "One's filling, and the other's fulfilling. What a great photo by Casey."

"Yeah, I stared at it for ten minutes. You can't help but feel sad for Jackson. Then I got annoyed with him for planning to go after God knows who. What do you make of him?"

"I've been trying to figure him out since last night. I think Jackson is a driven, haunted man, trying to do something right, even if it's wrong."

Jill's eyes lit up, knowing a great line when she heard one. "That sounds like either a heckuva lede for tomorrow morning or the start of a great country song."

"Yeah, I'm undecided on which to write first," I said with a grin. "I'd love to sit down and talk with Jackson. But right now I'm gonna swing by the office and then go to the funeral. Maybe he'll say something after the service."

3

Sheila ushered Chief King into the Stones' den and took a seat on the sofa to his left. The brothers sat across from him and waited.

"Mister Stone, I wanted to stop by before the services and pay my respects on behalf of myself, the police department, and the entire city of Nashville," King said. He paused and pointed at the paper.

"And if I may be blunt on such a terrible day for you and your family, I also want to try and dissuade you from setting out on this . . . quest for vengeance. I understand the sorrow and anger you must feel right now, and we'll put you in touch with some very good grief counselors, if you so desire."

Jackson listened patiently, trying to maintain control. But some of the past week's raw emotions bubbled to the surface like hydrogen peroxide poured on a festering wound.

"Sir, thank you for coming out this morning, but with all due respect, there is nothing you can say that will cause me to change my mind or my mission. Yes, mission. I am going to find the psychopath that murdered Angela and I . . . *am* . . . going to make him pay. An eye for an eye, Chief."

King locked eyes with Stone, who held his own in a test of stern wills before lowering his gaze and his defenses. It shocked Patrick because he'd never won a stare-down with his older brother. King focused all of his considerable willpower in an attempt to get through to Jackson.

"Mister Stone, do you have a gun?"

The question surprised Jackson, though it shouldn't have. That's what cops do.

"No, I don't own a pistol."

"That wasn't what I asked."

"Yes. A shotgun and a couple of hunting rifles. They're registered."

"And?"

"A hunting knife. An axe. A baseball bat. A kitchen knife. My own two hands around that animal's throat. Whatever it takes," Jackson said, rising to his feet. "How *dare* you come here and question me like this, on this day of all days. What're you guys doing to catch Angela's killer?"

The chief remained calm and shifted his position as Jackson sat back down.

"We're doing everything in our power, Mister Stone. I need you to listen carefully and understand what I'm about to tell you for your own good, even though it may not be what you want to hear right now. You need to stand down and let us handle this investigation. We *will* find your wife's murderer. We're very good at what we do and you would be in the way. Your cooperation is desired, but your interference isn't. If you break the law, you will be treated as a criminal. Every minute we spend dealing with you is a minute less spent trying to find your wife's killer."

King stood at ease, towering over Jackson.

"I'm sorry for having to speak so bluntly this morning. Go bury your wife, grieve with your family, lean on your friends and loved ones for support. But *don't* try to take the law into your own hands." He paused, relaxed his shoulders, and gave a quick nod. "Good day, sir, and again, my sympathies. Rest assured, your wife's killer *will* be found and prosecuted to the full extent of the law. And if a jury of his peers finds him guilty, you will obtain *justice* whether he receives the death penalty or life imprisonment. And that must be enough. *That's* how society behaves."

The lecture ended, and a sullen Jackson stared at the knot in the wooden floor. Chief King moved to the door, then turned back to face Jackson.

"I do understand where you're coming from, but if you're using the Bible to justify your plans for revenge, remember that vengeance is the Lord's work. Not yours."

The verbal jab stung. Jackson countered with what he thought would be the last word.

"But the Bible says nothing about what tools He might use to exact His vengeance."

The contemptuous police chief snorted and flung it back in Jackson's face.

"Don't be a tool, Mister Stone."

4

Don't be a tool. Don't be a tool. Don't be a tool.

The stinging words echoed in Jackson's mind, and he sat immobile on his brother's couch ever since the tongue-lashing by Chief King.

No more than five minutes passed since the policeman's departure. Patrick and Sheila had gone back to their bedroom to continue getting ready for visitation and the funeral. A morning of mourning was already off to a horrible start.

The doorbell rang again.

Jackson grew angry at the thought that the policeman might be returning with another sharp retort. He flung the door open. The scowl etched on his face gave way to one of surprise, then sorrow.

It was Belle Rive Baptist Church Pastor Robert Armstrong, who would soon be conducting the services for Angela.

"Oh, God, Brother Armstrong. I'm so, so sorry. I thought you were someone else."

Jackson's hateful countenance momentarily startled the preacher, but he was used to harsh, sometimes volatile emotions in these situations. Instead of inviting himself into the house, he invited Jackson out. Jackson closed the door, and they headed down the street at an unhurried pace, bathed in the sun's growing warmth.

"Maybe I deserved that." Jackson told the preacher about King's warning as they strolled. "But Angela didn't.

85

"She didn't deserve this ending. I don't understand why . . . how . . . God could allow this to happen."

Armstrong nodded, having counseled other grief-stricken members of the congregation. He knew well the difficult lifestyle adjustments Jackson would face for the next few months, perhaps even years. Many mourners would question their faith; some would turn their backs on their religion; others would grasp even tighter to their beliefs to try and hold onto their sanity.

Friends and family often were not enough for the bereaved. Armstrong recommended Jackson attend a Christian-based grief support group, and suggested several close to his home.

"Most people, even Christians, have a hard time with issues surrounding their loss and God. Where was God? Why didn't he stop this? She's in heaven? I don't want her in heaven—I want her here. In a grief group, you hear such comments. You talk to people who have suffered similar losses in their lives, find support and comfort, and learn some useful coping mechanisms."

Armstrong gave Jackson a few gentle pats on the back.

"This isn't something you have to do right away. Let's just get you and the family through the day. We'll worry about tomorrow tomorrow. And then we'll take it one day at a time. I'm here for you Jack—your family, your church family, we're all here for you."

They walked silently for a couple of minutes, Jackson deep in thought. He'd already taken his first steps down a dangerous path and knew he couldn't reveal—even to the preacher—the full depth of his plans.

So much depended on his tactics in the next forty-eight hours. This crazy scheme would never work if . . . Jackson stepped in front of the preacher, using his hardened glare to convey the truth beyond his words.

"This is difficult to explain . . . but over the next few days, you are going to be seeing another Jack Stone, one you've never seen before. The marine Jack Stone. I'm going to be doing and saying some things—I already have—that seem totally out of character for me. I have trust and faith in the Lord. I hope you'll have a little trust and faith in me. Everything I'm going to be saying and doing—there is a reason for it."

They resumed their walk, turning toward Patrick's house and moving at a brisker pace as Jackson talked at a passionate level, less than manic but above conversational. He had to make the reverend understand.

"You know I believe everything happens for a reason. I might not understand it, and while I am very angry right now, I decided a long time ago I would never blame or question God for the method He chose to call my wife home, whether it was from a heart attack, an auto accident . . ." His voice dropped to a whisper, his head slumped, and he put his hand on Armstrong's shoulder for support. ". . . or this. Good Lord. Maybe my stance, my faith, is being put to the test. I've always felt the best day of my life will be the day of my death."

Jackson stopped again, and he buried his head in his hands.

"Maybe that will still be the case. But Angela's death—saying goodbye to her? Today's the worst day of my life."

The preacher took Jackson by the arm.

"Let's get you home."

87

5

The Stones arrived at the funeral home at nine thirty a.m. to spend a few private moments with Angela's family before the visitation began. The temperature was already hovering at ninety degrees, on the way to a record one hundred and seven, but that didn't keep people away. The line snaked around the building through a queue of velvet ropes, winding down the driveway and halfway to the street. And more cars were arriving every minute. Four television trucks parked outside, with the Channel 11 van in the process of extending its antenna skyward to do a live remote.

Dan Clarkston got out of the passenger side as the funeral director ran up.

"I'm afraid you people need to leave. This is private property and a private ceremony," a dignified, well-meaning Arthur Greaves said.

"I'm sorry, but this is a news story, and we're not leaving," Clarkston said. "We'll move our van to the street and stay in the background until after the ceremony ends and everyone clears. Is that satisfactory?"

The funeral director nodded and started to speak, but Clarkston cut him off as I arrived.

"We won't tape the funeral without permission, but I do plan to attend. Also, I want to talk for a moment with Mister Stone or a family representative."

"Me too," I said. "I'm from *TenneScene Today.*"

"If you'll wait over there," Greaves pointed, "I'll find someone."

Clarkston and I both turned and watched the parking lot scene. The line of sympathizers grew longer. Cameraman Pittard shot video and a couple of anti-violence protesters stood on public property by the entrance to the funeral home. "Don't Dishonor Your Wife's Memory" read one man's sign.

"Nice article this morning," Clarkston said, making small talk to break the silence. "That photo was unbelievable. So what do you make of this guy?"

I shrugged. "He's in a lot of pain right now. But I think he's sincere."

"I think he's a nut," Clarkston said, turning to stare again at the growing crowd.

Like our confrontation with the funeral director, several others took place that hot, humid morning.

Angela's red-faced sister launched a verbal assault as soon as Jackson walked into the parlor where floral arrangements surrounded Angela's mahogany closed coffin.

"Why are you doing this? Look what's going on outside? Who *are* all these people?" his sister-in-law Christine said.

Jackson comprehended he must remain calm on an emotional day for everyone. He and Christine often butted heads, but he didn't want a scene with the cameras there to make matters worse.

"I know it doesn't make much sense right now, but please believe I'm doing this *for* Angela."

"I can't make any sense of this," Angela's father fumed as his wife Mona wiped her eyes. Jackson's brother shuffled like he needed to go to the men's room.

"Look, Fred, it's something I—"

A welcomed knock at the door broke the growing tension.

"Excuse me, Mister Stone. I hate to interrupt, but I need a moment."

"Yes, Mister Greaves?"

"There are some members of the press outside asking to speak to you or a representative of the family."

"I'll go," Patrick said, but Jackson stopped him with a hand on his forearm.

"No, I'll handle this. I'll be right back, but let's get through this day for Angela's sake. Please, all of you must believe I'm trying to do right by her. I cannot bear thinking of spending the rest of my life without her, and I need your support," he said, choking back his own tears as he again glanced at the coffin.

Several other media representatives had gathered by the time Jackson and Greaves approached. The funeral director whispered something to Jackson and left to attend to other details. Jackson spoke softly, even warmly, but his mesmerizing eyes spoke sharper.

"I don't have any comment now, but I'll speak after the funeral. I understand you think this is worthy of coverage, but please respect our family's wishes and allow us this time to grieve and say a proper goodbye to Angela. I don't want the services taped, but I'll allow one pool photographer and one videographer access to the visitation for thirty minutes. I'll allow reporters access for the first thirty minutes of visitation, and you may attend services as long as you're discreet. If any of you don't adhere to this, Mister Greaves will escort you *all* off the property. Are we clear?"

I looked around at my fellow media members, who were taking the same inventory. Clarkston shrugged his shoulders, so I nodded. Jackson abruptly departed, shaking his head at the growing crowd of two-hundred-plus people gathered outside. A woman Jackson didn't recognize called out his name. Another waved. Several people down on the street thrust homemade signs at arriving cars. Jackson expected his actions to stir the city and touch nerves, but this? Beyond anything he'd ever anticipated.

But he'd asked for it.

6

The Stones and Angela's relatives stood in a long row about ten feet away from the casket, wreaths, and beautiful flowers, greeting friends, even long-lost ones, neighbors, business associates, and many strangers moved to attend visitation after reading the morning paper or watching Jackson on television.

A wrinkled, gray-haired woman and her granddaughter approached Jackson, and the old woman clasped his hand with her tiny, arthritic hands. The young girl stood close to her grandmother's side.

"I met your wife about a year ago at the Outreach center," she said. "She was so sweet to us. So when I saw what happened I just wanted to come express my sorrow and share in your grief. I pray for her every night. I hope you find her killer."

"Thank you, ma'am. Right now, I'm just coping one day at a time."

With a few variations, the conversation repeated over and over and over. Once in a while, he recognized somebody. The whole morning sped past. Maybe he'd process it all someday.

Jackson glanced over his shoulder at the casket, looking lost when two large hands clasped his shoulders. "How are you, bud? Hanging in there?"

Jackson turned at the familiar voice of his boss, Matthew "Marty" Martin. Standing behind Marty and his wife were several of his fellow ad execs and their wives, and all as somber as Marty. Tears welled in Jackson's eyes as Marty pulled him close.

"Oh God, I don't know. I'm trying to smile and stay strong. I just don't know how I'm going to go on without Angela."

"Yeah, I can't imagine what you're going through, bud. She was a sweetheart, and we're all going to miss her."

Marty's demeanor changed somewhat as he looked around the packed room.

"Listen, bud, I know this isn't the best time to bring this up, but I was a little surprised by what I've been seeing and reading. We need to talk, okay?"

Louie the bartender gave Jackson a hug and asked him to stop by later for a toast to Angela while Pastor Robert Armstrong, who would soon be conducting the services, came by and spoke to each family member. Friends and strangers passed by to give sympathy and support for the Stone family, and a few bold ones spoke of his quest for revenge, offering unsolicited advice, either pro or con. A complete stranger said he "oughtta act more like a forgive-and-forget Christian."

Jackson finally hit an emotional wall, but in the end, all that mattered was Angela, whom he would never again hold in his arms.

7

Herb Fletcher arrived at ten a.m., surprised to see all the people lined up waiting to get inside and pay their respects to Angela's family. He walked toward the front door to look for Jackson inside, but retreated to the end of the line after several people gave him dirty looks. He was absorbed in his own thoughts—about Angela and Jack, about himself and Sarah—when a guttural voice snapped him out of his fog.

"Excuse me, didn't I see you on TV last night?"

Herb, quite pleased at the recognition from the TV interview, began telling his inquisitive acquaintance all about the Stones and himself. They chatted in the slow-moving line for about twenty to twenty-five minutes as the line grew ever longer.

"And I just couldn't believe it when I saw Jack coming out of his house the other day, not thirty seconds after the newscast," Herb said. "Almost like he teleported from the television to his driveway, know what I mean?"

"That's pretty funny," said the unsmiling man who reeked of cigarette smoke. "I notice your wife isn't with you. Is she sick or something? You said she and Missus Stone were best friends. It seems like she'd want to pay her respects."

"Sarah has been so moody the last couple of months, but since Angela died, she's been acting mighty strange. She doesn't talk, doesn't eat, doesn't even leave the house. She's always crying and looking out windows. It's like she keeps expecting to see Angela out there. I tried everything to get her to come this morning, and she just stayed in bed, all curled up and crying. I don't know what to do."

"Well, you might try to—"

"Excuse me, aren't you the Stones' neighbor, Mister Fletcher?"

Herb jumped at the unexpected intrusion as I came up behind him. Casey, off to one side snapping photos of the twisting visitation line, turned our way after Herb whirled around. The startled look disappeared from his face, replaced by a grin that gave way to a more somber look reflective of the sad occasion that brought them together.

"Yes, I am. Herb Fletcher. And to whom do I have the pleasure of speaking?"

"Gerry Hilliard from *TenneScene Today*. I saw you on Channel 11 last night and hoped we could talk about Jackson since you were the one person to speak with him. I also talked to Jackson last night. Well, I talked. He hung up."

"He's in a lot of pain, you know what I mean?" Herb said. "I wanted to get a few minutes here with him today, but this is a pretty wild scene. We're here for Angela, but we're here for him, too. Look at all these people! I don't see anybody I know."

Casey snapped a few shots of Fletcher, and then moved off to get some other scene-setting photos before our thirty-minute window ended. I got out my recorder after Fletcher agreed to an interview and held it below my notepad, scribbling his comments as we spoke.

"So were you close to the Stones?"

"We sure were," Fletcher said, beaming. "Jack and I did some hunting and fishing together, and they invited us to go out with them pretty regularly on their boat. My wife and Angela were best friends. They went everywhere together and were closer than me and Jack."

"Is your wife here? I'd like to get her insights as well."

Herb's face darkened, embarrassed at her absence. "No, this has shaken her pretty bad, and she didn't feel like she could handle it, so she stayed home."

I tried another approach, not wanting the interview to end.

"So what does Jackson do from here? Does he leave the investigating to the police or will he still attempt to find his wife's killer and avenge her?"

"Mister, you don't know Jack Stone and neither do the cops. Whoever did that to his wife should take him at face value. He's told me some war stories and I've—"

The funeral director walked up and tapped me on the shoulder. "You need to wrap it up now, sir," Greaves said before heading for Clarkston, who interviewed two young camo-dressed men holding "Stone 'Em To Death, Jack" and "A Stoning Is What Angela's Killer Deserves" signs.

"That was so cool," Herb said as he turned to talk to his new acquaintance. But a middle-aged couple now stood behind him.

The strange young man had vanished.

8

Three blocks away from the funeral home, a wild-eyed Delmore Wolfe careened down the street as he sped from the scene in a state of near-panic.

He cursed himself. "Damn me to hell! What were you thinking, going there this morning?"

Wolfe had focused on Fletcher, sizing him up and trying to get as much out of him as possible, then I showed up. As soon as he saw our photographer, Wolfe brought his visitation hour to a close. No current pictures of him existed, and he hoped he'd gotten away in time. What if it was in the paper tomorrow? The panic rose to new levels and he almost ran up on the curb as he rounded the corner, just avoiding a couple of kids on their bikes. Wolfe started to feel nauseous, the bile rising in his throat.

He pulled his Firebird to the side of the road to consider his next course of action. The hypnotic knocking of the idling engine caused him to close his eyes as he figured his next move. His head slumped, chin resting on his chest, breathing heavy. His mind raced, but he forced himself to calm the rising panic. He flexed his hands, spreading the fingers out and then closing them into tight balls again and again. Just as he regained control, a rap on the window sent endorphins spiking again. One of the kids he almost side-swiped. He rolled the window down.

"Hey mister, you okay? Want me to go get my dad?"

The freckle-faced boy backpedaled from the angry snarl.

"Get outta here, you little snot-head. And you better stay off the road. Next time, I won't miss."

Peeling out as the shaken kid scrambled home, Wolfe leered as he formulated a plan to solve most, if not all, of his problems.

9

Still curled up in bed, Sarah Fletcher prayed about the last week's haunting events. Sarah kicked herself for lacking the courage to attend the funeral, but she couldn't face Jackson over what she thought happened to Angela.

Herb and Sarah had argued for the better part of a week over his inability to land a job, any job. Herb refused to take just *any* job, while Sarah said *any* job beat *no* job. And then it got personal, making her wonder if she could remain committed to the marriage. And in that instant, Sarah's rash decision would cost first Angela and then others their lives.

Sarah liked to party back when she was in her twenties, and now she decided she needed some companionship. Months had passed since she and Herb had sex. Herb started drinking more, and she grew distant and withdrawn. Angela, a sympathetic sounding board, didn't want to offer advice that might cause either of them to blame her for what sounded more and more like an impending divorce. She hoped they could patch up their marriage. Sarah had called Angela the morning of her disappearance to see if she wanted a liquid lunch, but the phone went unanswered.

"Screw it," Sarah said. Angela always kept her cell phone close; they'd hook up later. The phrase echoed in Sarah's mind. Yeah, a hook-up sounded like a fun way to spend an afternoon. Two job interviews would keep Herb occupied until five or six. Plenty of time to scratch an itch, and Herb would never be the wiser.

So she locked up the house, jumped into her car, and went hunting across town for an afternoon boytoy who would ask no questions. Sarah ended up in Hillsboro Village, not far from the Vanderbilt campus, looking for a discreet fern bar that would not be too seedy. She wanted a certain type of man, one with loose morals and not-so-loose lips. Wolfe was prowling in the same neighborhood.

A human chameleon, Delmore Wolfe cleaned up for this occasion and hungered, but not for food. He wanted some money and a higher-class victim. Wolfe spotted Sarah going into Darlene's Hideaway Lounge, a quaint little pub off the main drag, and followed her in after a couple of minutes. She sat at the bar with her long legs crossed, dressed in a red skirt and blue top. Wolfe heard her order a mojito and smiled. He walked behind her and took a seat at the end of the bar near the flat-screen TV showing a replay of the Arkansas-Tennessee game from last season. He had shaved off his beard but not the mustache, his long hair tied back in a ponytail. The dark shirt open at the top two buttons revealed a hairy chest. He wore a tan blazer and Polo sunglasses—and an attitude that said he was the man all women wanted for a good time with no questions asked.

Wolfe ordered a scotch on the rocks and lit a smoke. Within three minutes, Sarah asked for a light; within ten minutes, they were out the door. In Sarah's blue Corvette, no chit-chat except for those first couple of minutes when Wolfe took a CD out of his blazer's inner pocket and lecherously asked if he could stick it in.

"Hey, I haven't heard that in years. Turn it up, baby. Doo doo DOOdoo doo DOOdoo doo DOOdoo dooDOOdoo doooodooooo," she sang.

Sarah "giggled like a schoolgirl," he would later write in his journal. Wolfe closed in and wrapped his muscular arms around her lithe, pulsating body. After a few minutes of heavy action in the front seat in broad daylight, Sarah wanted to go to his place to continue.

"No good, baby," he said. "I'm in town for a few days and staying with friends."

Sarah nipped at his ear and suggested a motel room.

"Wherever you want it, baby."

After a few more minutes, Sarah hit fever pitch and suggested her place. Doing something crazy, why not go all the way? Wolfe pawed at her the entire drive home and at that moment she didn't care who saw her.

Wolfe exited the car first and opened the door for Sarah, playing the perfect gentleman. He paused long enough to take his smartphone out of the front pocket and push a button. The same song that had been playing in the car started, and he planted a lust-filled wet one on her full lips.

"My favorite song," he explained. "We're the same age, both produced in 1982. It gets my juices flowing, baby."

That brought a smile to Sarah's face, and they howled the refrain to Duran Duran's "Hungry Like The Wolf" in unison as they scrambled for the house.

"Doo doo DOOdoo doo DOOdoo doo DOOdoo dooDOOdoo doooodooooo."

Inside the kitchen, Sarah began tugging at his pants as the song continued. Wolfe swept her off her feet, laying her on the kitchen floor, and he pulled at her bra. Sarah loved every second of it even if he started playing rougher and rougher by the minute. His bizarre diaries would reveal that Wolfe's pattern was working himself into a state of "bliss" that ended with his taking a life just as she reached ecstasy.

But he never achieved that moment of "bliss" in Sarah's house, because of a noise at the back door. Horrified, Sarah looked up and saw Angela's face in the window with her hand over her mouth.

Transfixed and too shocked to move, Angela realized that the glows of inhuman pleasure on their faces meant Sarah wasn't being victimized. She fled when Sarah's eyes opened and locked in on her.

"Ohmigod," Sarah gasped.

The magic spell broke, for Wolfe, as well as Sarah. Anger replaced blood-lust, followed by fear of a witness who might identify him if something happened to this woman now. Sarah crumpled on the floor crying, guilt-ridden. She felt dirty and disgusted with herself. She didn't realize the high price she would pay.

10

The cameras departed and the media honored Jackson's request to stay out of the way and act as silent witnesses to this private—yet most public—final tribute to Angela Stone. I watched the line weave through the funeral home for the visitation and recognized several people who would be staying for the graveside services. Jackson's attorney shook hands with Chief King's media relations mouthpiece, Darrin Jensen. I recognized a couple of councilmen, as well as several of Jackson's friends and neighbors I'd interviewed over the past week.

At 11:45 a.m., the funeral director announced the conclusion to the visitation and asked pallbearers to follow his assistant. Greaves gathered the family for a few final moments while media members began heading across the cemetery to the Stones' plot about a quarter of a mile from the Davis Chapel's main building. The Stones, Angela's relatives, and about fifty other people from their work, volunteer efforts, and church attended the service.

Angela's father, Fred, said it was Jackson's decision to hold a graveside service rather than over at the Stones' church, Belle Rive Baptist. Jackson thought it would be more private, Fred explained. The sun beat down, and everyone sweated as the crowd gathered. The limos arrived and the Stone/Crosby clan filled the rows of plastic seats under the makeshift tent. Jackson was flanked by his sister-in-law Sheila on one side and his mother-in-law Mona on the other, each holding a hand. Tears streamed down the women's faces, but Jackson's eyes remained dry.

His gaze never left the casket as pallbearers ushered Angela's coffin to her final resting place.

"God, have mercy," Jackson whispered.

At noon, Reverend Robert Armstrong stepped forward to shake hands and offer encouraging words of faith to Jackson and each family member, then addressed the crowd.

"Friends and neighbors, we are gathered to say farewell to our beloved sister, Angela Stone. Join me in saying The Lord's Prayer. 'Our Father which art in heaven, Hallowed be thy name . . .' "

As a rule, reporters act as observers, not participants in a story, but this sorrowful time seemed the exception to the rule. I bowed my head and prayed with the others. For Angela.

11

Delmore Wolfe's senses were edgy as he made his way across town to East Nashville. At approximately 11:45 a.m., he parked three blocks away from the Fletchers' house and crept from house to house peering into windows to make certain of no witnesses. It seemed all the closest neighbors attended the visitation. The loud, buzzing mower made him grin again. That noise would drown out any screams.

Upstairs, Sarah remained curled in bed, lost in her thoughts about that day Angela caught her cheating.

Wolfe slipped on Latex gloves, jimmied the backdoor lock, and stepped inside.

Sarah thought about that day she was with "Chuck," the man she was almost certain had killed Angela. She knew she should have gone to the police, but couldn't bear the shame. She had to drive Chuck back to his car, then he wanted money. She recalled driving him to the ATM and withdrawing three hundred dollars, how he asked about her friend, wanting to talk to her to smooth things over.

"No," Sarah shouted as they pulled into the parking lot at Darlene's. "Just get out Chuck. NOW! And don't let me see you again!" Wolfe eased out of the car. "Later, baby."

Sarah had hurried back home, showered, and tried to compose herself. She needed to talk to Angela, whose car remained parked out back. Sarah tried calling, first on the home phone, then to Angela's cell phone. Angela's voice answered both times: Please leave a message. But Sarah desperately wanted to look Angela in the eye and somehow explain her inexplicable actions. She'd pounded on Angela's front door, crying for her to please open it. No answer. Finally, Sarah went home weeping. Getting late, with Herb due to return anytime, she'd try talking to Angela tomorrow. But tomorrow would never come for Angela.

Those next few hours were horrible. Herb had gotten home and innocently asked what she'd been up to all day. She'd felt dirty and guilty, staying silent through dinner. Thinking she was still mad at him, Herb had given up trying to talk to her and said he wanted a beer and to watch a ballgame. She'd gone to bed. He had thoughts of staying up and watching the news, then maybe some Leno and Letterman, after the game. He noticed blue lights flashing out the window. He looked outside and counted five police cars, with another roaring down the street. "Something's going on next door," he'd yelled up to Sarah.

Now her best friend was being buried, and Sarah was, again, in bed. She snapped out of her thoughts and back to the present when she heard raps on the wall down the hall. She froze when Chuck, looking very different, stepped in her bedroom. He smiled viciously, remorselessly.

"Hello, baby."

What was Chuck doing here? A terrorized scream died in her throat as she cringed. The grandfather clock in the hall chimed noon, and Wolfe closed in for the kill. Sarah began reciting The Lord's Prayer, her last rites. "Our Father which art in heaven, Hallowed be—"

His well-timed, left-handed chop to the throat snapped her trachea, and she died instantly. Step one proved easy enough, but staging it like an accident might prove harder.

"What could be suspicious about next-door neighbors mysteriously dying within weeks of each other? Get a grip, Delmore," he wrote in his diary entry.

Maybe he'd make it look like she fell down the steps and broke her neck or banged her throat against a stair edge. Wolfe always solved messy details and worked out a solution. He hovered over the body and studied the scene and the layout of the bedroom before finding his way around the house. He made a ham sandwich and turned on the TV.

12

The brief, emotionally wrenching funeral service concluded with a loving and eloquent eulogy from the pastor, and each relative laid a white rose on Angela's casket before it was lowered into the ground. Brother Armstrong said a closing prayer, and friends closed in to say a few parting words to Jackson before going back to their own busy lives.

I took it all in and headed back to the funeral home where I compared notes with fellow *TenneScene Today* reporter Shelley Finklestein, who would write the online story and handle a sidebar for print.

"I felt so bad for Stone and his family," Shelley said. "That preacher made me feel like I'd known Angela all my life. Very touching."

"And very compelling. Let that come through in your story. You want to evoke emotion," I advised her.

"So now what? Sorry I got here late and we didn't get a chance to talk before the visitation. I saw you talking to a few people in line and did the same. I corralled Casey and got her to shoot some of the people I spoke with."

"Great. Stone said he would talk with the media after the funeral, but I don't know if he's going to do it now that we're here or will want to hold off awhile. I'm going to find Greaves and see what he knows."

Jackson had remained under the tent staring down at Angela's casket for a final time, searing it into his memory. He looked up as a heavy hand closed over his left shoulder.

105

Herb, tears streaming down his face, pulled dry-eyed Jackson into his arms. "Oh man, I am so, so sorry."

Jackson returned the genuine bear hug.

"You're a good friend," Jackson said. "I just can't believe this happened. It's unreal."

"I know what you mean." Still embarrassed for having to explain his wife's absence, he added, "Sarah sends her love, too. She's still too broke up to make it this morning. You know how close they were."

Jackson understood. He didn't like funerals himself. "No problem. We all handle grief in different ways. We'll come visit Angela whenever Sarah thinks she can handle it."

"She'd like that. So what are you doing the rest of the day? Angela wouldn't want you to be alone right now. C'mon home with me."

Jackson looked around the sun-splashed grounds, feeling Angela's presence in the serene setting.

"Thanks, Herb. Maybe I'll see you guys later. The rest of the family's headed over to Patrick's, and I'm going over a little later. Right now I'm going to talk to the press. If I'm going to find Angela's killer, I need to keep this in the news. Maybe somebody will see or hear or read about it and divulge something they wouldn't tell the cops. Say, why not pick up Sarah and come over—if she's up to it, that is."

"I'll check—if she's talking to me, that is." He hesitated, then continued. "I guess Angela told you we'd been having some problems."

Jackson nodded.

"Well, it got pretty nasty a couple of weeks ago . . . it was right after that last trip with y'all out on Old Hickory Lake. You remember," Herb said, "We all probably had too much to drink. All but Angela, that is. Well, we got home, and Sarah started right in on me for not trying very hard to find a steady job. You know what this economy's like. But I was half-drunk and overreacted. I swear, I almost felt like hitting her."

The last sentence felt like a death sentence for his marriage, and his shoulders slumped. Jackson put a hand on

106

his shoulder to say something sympathetic, but Herb beat him to it.

"Aw, man. I'm feeling sorry for myself and look what you're dealing with. You're a rock, Jack. You inspire me. Life's too short. I'm going home and talk to Sarah and straighten this mess out right now, if it's the last thing I do."

13

Jackson Stone recognized Clarkston, several other reporters, and me in the visitation room. I flipped through the registration book. Reporter Shelley Finklestein and Casey the photographer were on the other side of the room. The TV station cameramen took strategic spots about a dozen feet in front of the lectern where their microphones were scrunched together. Shelley and I added our microcassette recorders to the pile, all aimed at Stone as he stepped forward.

"I know this isn't something the media hears very often, but thank you for the professional manner in which you all conducted yourselves during the visitation and services. It was a fitting, emotional, and proper farewell to my darling wife, Angela, whom I know I'll see again someday in heaven. Our family has suffered through a tragic week, and my comments yesterday reflected that nightmare. Clearly, none of you—nor my attorney, nor the police, nor my fellow Nashvillians—expected that reaction, and I didn't anticipate some of the backlash I've encountered."

His anger rose close to the level reached when Chief King visited earlier that morning. He pondered calling out King in his press conference and decided against it. As he needed the media, Jackson might someday require the help of the cops—and didn't wish to alienate them.

But that was in the future, and for now Jackson focused on the next phase of his plan.

The idea to use his advertising skills to honor Angela had popped into his head earlier that morning.

It was a peaceful drive back from the cabin to West Meade and the perfect time to think about acting as a force for good in her memory. He thought Angela might approve of that use of her name, even if she disapproved of the method he used to keep the spotlight focused on her death. Jackson looked around the room. He had the media hanging on every word, waiting to hear his next outlandish statement. We didn't wait long.

"I said it yesterday, and I'll say it again now. I'm not interested in justice. I will find the animal that killed my wife and burn his eyes out with a hot poker."

In that instant, no trace of the fog-headed, sympathetic widower remained. Only a cold-blooded, ruthless avenger. Menace hung in the air.

"A quick death won't happen, whoever and wherever you are. Preying on defenseless women, does that make you feel like a man? Let's see how you do against me. You know where I live, tough guy. Anytime, anywhere. Gutless." He spat out the last word before changing his tenor. "Now I've saved some money and if anybody out there has any—"

"Ladies and gentlemen," Allenby shouted from the back of the room as he strode to the lectern and all but pushed Jackson aside, "you must forgive Mister Stone for his emotional outburst. He just buried his wife and is under great strain. I hope you all take that into consideration when you file your stories. But this press conference is over. Now."

"That's bull," Jackson shouted as Allenby grabbed and pushed him toward the door. Allenby, a Navy officer thirty years ago, clamped his iron grip on the nape of Jackson's neck and pulled him down nose-to-nose and whispered in harsh tones. The fight left Jackson as he obeyed marching orders and calmed down. It made, as they say, for great television.

Away from the microphones, the shocked reporters viewed a heated dressing-down from the bulldog lawyer and angry gesticulations from Stone. In the back of the room, Darrin Jensen flipped open his cell phone and speed-dialed his boss, who'd just sat down to lunch. "Chief, you won't believe what's happening."

Allenby approached the microphones as the transfixed media waited to see what transpired next. Jackson straightened his tie and smoothed down his hair. Looking disheveled and acting crazy would not do. His rage had gotten the better of him, and despite the way Allenby treated him in front of the cameras and reporters, Jackson appreciated his being there. The fit of anger evaporated, and it might make him a more sympathetic figure to the public, Jackson thought, going into his spin-doctor advertising mogul mode. Allenby took off his glasses and wiped at smudges before beginning.

"Since I don't know all of you, let me introduce myself. My name is Stan Allenby, and I am Jackson Stone's attorney . . . and his friend. Against my advice, Jackson wants to continue this press conference. I can't stop him, and I can't tell you what to write or say." Allenby paused and glanced at Jackson before addressing the media as if addressing the jury instead. "But it would be a mischaracterization to paint Jack Stone as some obsessed, revenge-minded, Rambo-type lunatic whose stated desire to find his wife's killer makes him a public menace. An upstanding citizen, Jack has served his country proudly and his community well. A terrible tragedy has now taken place, and he is grieving and expressing his anger. Does he want to find the person who killed his wife? Of course. Would he take the law into his own hands and resort to torture if he were to find the murderer? Of course not. Jackson is a law-abiding citizen who respects the police and wants to see his wife's killer caught in a swift, timely manner and then prosecuted to the fullest extent of the law."

The persuasive lawyer then turned all his oratory skills on the media, addressing each of us as if we were jurors, not journalists.

"Mister Clarkston, have you ever lost a loved one to a horrific crime?" he asked. "How about you, Mister Hilliard? Or you, Ms. Jones? Or any of the rest of you? Have any of you ever arrived home late one night to discover no one home, then go upstairs and find your bedroom splattered in blood?"

Jackson chewed at his lower lip and visibly shook as his attorney continued.

"I pray to God none of you ever walk in Jackson Stone's shoes over such an act of violence. Unfortunately, it happens every day somewhere across the U.S.A., and everyone deals with tragedy in his own way. Jackson is emotional right now and has every right to be angry."

Allenby sipped at a glass of water. He hoped the media would swallow his explanation and continued closing arguments in the media versus Jackson Stone.

"I'd be worried about him if Jackson wasn't upset, grief-stricken, outraged, and to a certain degree vindictive," Allenby said. "The difference is that most citizens don't call a press conference to express that outrage. Jackson has done so, and struck a raw nerve with the media, the police, and his fellow Tennesseans. I'll now turn this over to Jack, who gives me his personal assurance that he will cooperate with the police in every step of this investigation in every way."

As Allenby moved back to his right and Jackson stepped to the lectern, nobody noticed the police spokesman in the back of the room talking into his cell phone.

"Yes sir, you heard that okay? This is Stone," Jensen said, taking a seat on the back row and holding aloft his cell phone so Chief King could listen in on the press conference.

14

Wolfe worked up a good sweat while dragging Sarah's body down to the basement. The stairs creaked and groaned with every step. She's going to commit suicide, the poor thing, he giggled. Her husband said she'd been depressed since the death of her best friend. Herb could testify to her recent mental state. It sounded like he might even be happy she disappeared. Wolfe threw the piece of rope over the old plumbing pipes near the washing machine, looping the end around again and fashioning a noose. He figured a broken neck and a rope around her throat would cover up the way she died. He grunted as he lifted the body, so he could slip her head in the noose. That's when he heard the back door open and close.

"Sarah, I'm home. I hope you're not still in bed. We need to talk," Herb said.

Wolfe lowered her body to the floor and crept up the basement steps, cracking open the door into the kitchen.

"Sarah?" Herb's voice echoed from the bedroom or maybe the bathroom. He tried a gentler tone. "Where are you, hon?"

Footsteps approached from down the hall, and Wolfe ducked out of view on the far side of the refrigerator.

"What great timing. I decided his death would be what drove Wifey to commit suicide," Wolfe would write in his diary entry of Fletcher's last trip home.

Herb re-entered the kitchen and looked around. The lid of the mustard jar lay on the granite counter, the twist-tie to the loaf of bread on the floor. He saw the basement door ajar and wondered if she might be downstairs doing a load of laundry.

"Sarah, you down there?" he said, opening the door and flipping on the lights.

Wolfe squatted and waited until Herb reached the door before rising, then tapped Fletcher on the left shoulder. Expecting to see Sarah, Herb got the shock of his life, or what remained of it. The odd man in the visitation line stood right behind Herb in *his* house.

An evil smirk touched the wide-open, gleaming eyes. "Have a nice trip, Herb."

Wolfe gave Herb a hard, two-handed shove down the steps.

He thought it comical the way Herb's eyes popped open so wide and his arms flailed like windmills as he tried to balance to no avail. Tipping over backwards, Herb's head cracked hard on the edge of the fifth step and bounced off the next three before splitting open on the concrete floor. Just like a small melon smacked with a mallet by that half-crazed comedian Gallagher. Momentum had carried heels over head in a bizarre death somersault.

Wolfe's hands shot over his head, holding an imaginary sign.

"A perfect ten." His laugh bordered somewhere between hysteria and insanity. "Way to stick that landing, Herbie."

Wolfe worked fast. He turned and grabbed a carving knife out of the utensil drawer, then headed down the stairs. Neighbors could return home from the funeral any minute. After several minutes, he stood and surveyed his handiwork. Herb's twisted body lay at the bottom of the stairs with the knife sticking out of his back between the third and fourth ribs. The bloody knife bore Sarah's fingerprints all over it. Sarah's body hung limp in the noose. Her dress was torn in several places and deep scratches marred the left side of his face. Red fingernails, but not from polish, and damning evidence caked under them. Wolfe grinned.

Now for the coup de grace.

He slipped out the back door and used the shrubbery wall to cover his swift trip next door to the Stones' house. He picked the back lock and entered the same way as when he assaulted Angela eleven days before.

Light on his feet and careful not to leave traces of his second visit, Wolfe made his way to the upstairs bedroom and took three pairs of Angela's underwear from the lingerie drawer. He then slipped back downstairs and out the back, relocking the door and leaving no evidence of his brazen daylight panty raid. Wolfe put one pair in Sarah's purse in the upstairs den, then went to the master bedroom and put a pair in Herb's sock drawer, stuffing them in the back where investigators would be certain to find them. The third pair he took back downstairs with him. He bent over Herb's body and shoved the bikini briefs into Herb's mouth the way an angry, humiliated, jealous wife would after she discovered indisputable evidence of her husband's torrid affair with her best friend.

Wolfe imagined how the investigation would all play out. Sarah confronted Herb with her suspicions. He denied all accusations until shown what she found. Wolfe could hear Sarah asking if he killed Angela. And Herb lashed out! He struck Sarah and chased her through the house, knocking over a lamp and other items. In the kitchen, Sarah got hold of the knife and stabbed Herb. And then she pushed the staggering man down the stairs. Finally, in her moment of despair over just what she'd done, Sarah hung herself. Yes, that's just how it happened.

Wolfe slipped out the back, and made his way to his old car. At the fleabag motel, he took a long hot shower then tossed his blood-splattered shirt and the Latex gloves in separate garbage bins.

15

Jackson Stone looked embarrassed as he cleared his throat, peered at the skeptical faces of the media before him, and plunged ahead with his press conference, trying to lighten the atmosphere.

"Now where was I? Oh yeah. I asked my attorney if he had my back," he said, a half-grin on his face. Allenby laughed and puh-shawed.

"The video shows I grabbed you by the back of the neck. But it can't be admitted as evidence." Several media members chuckled, but Jackson didn't. Ole Stone-face again.

"But seriously," Jackson said, "there's nothing to add to earlier comments except to say that Stan's assessment of me is one hundred and ten percent accurate, and I should add that I stand behind my comments and convictions. If I could get my hands around that killer's neck right this second, I would choke the life out of him right here in front of you in front of all these cameras."

Allenby winced as Jackson's emotions once again ran the gamut for the next few seconds, from helpless rage to being on the verge of a breakdown. After a pause, he gathered his strength and composure.

"My wife meant everything to me, and I lack the vocabulary to tell you how much I loved her, how much I miss her now and will for the rest of my life. If you're happily married like we were, you know. We shared everything—the same politics, the same traits, the same tastes in food and fashion, the same love of sports, the same love of life, the same sense of humor.

"One thing we didn't share," he said, choking back tears again and then half-laughing at a precious memory, "was the same sense of direction. Even before GPS, she managed to find her way all over town without following directions. If she turned onto 15th Avenue and tried to get over to 17th . . . well, you'd get there eventually."

He tightened his lips, shook his head, then continued.

"Whenever she drove, I'd always be digging out the city map or saying, 'turn left here' or 'turn right there.' It became a running joke for us, the pilot and her navigator. I always told her 'you'd be lost without me.' But the truth is I'm lost without her. I'm lost without her love."

His tears flowed, and Allenby took a step to support him. Jackson waved him off. Dabbing his eyes with a handkerchief, he regained his resolve and voice.

"That's why I'm doing this. Yes, I want revenge. And if it's in the form of a conviction and a trip to the electric chair, my wish would be to pull the switch. That jackal—not a man and less than an animal—who did this must be found so nobody else will suffer at his hands and so their husbands or wives and children and family won't suffer the way we are suffering. That's why today I am announcing a one-hundred-thousand-dollar reward for information leading to the arrest of Angela's murderer. I'm setting up a toll-free hotline and starting a website in her memory. If you saw anything or know someone who might have seen something, please contact me or the police. If you call the police, there will be an arrest and a trial. Call me, and I'll be the judge and jury."

Allenby coughed a little too loud, and Jackson felt sorry for him having to stand there while his crazy client ranted again. Time to save the attorney from further embarrassment.

"That's it. I'll take just a few questions and then join my family."

Hands shot up, and the press conference ended about twenty minutes later with no further outbursts or revelations. Shelley headed to the newspaper to begin writing her online story, while I zipped over to the Criminal Justice Center for

Chief King's news conference. If half as wild as Jack's, we'd put out a fantastic front page on Sunday morning.

Shelley arrived at the paper at two o'clock, and anticipated posting a story by two-thirty. No problemo. She opened a new Word document, typed in her byline, and took a straight-news approach. She would polish the lede for the print edition. She began:

Jackson Stone, who on Friday shocked the Nashville community at large by saying he wanted to avenge the murder of his wife, bid a tearful farewell to Angela Stone at her funeral on Saturday in Belle Rive and then announced he is offering a $100,000 reward for information leading to the capture of her killer.

Shelley deleted the redundant phrase "he is offering," then replaced the phrase "saying he wanted to avenge the murder of his wife" with "vowing revenge for his wife's murder."

Admittedly not great prose, but it was accurate.

16

Still in his dress blues, Chief King waited as everyone arrived from the Stone funeral. When I got to the CJC, the chief stood off to the side away from the microphones, getting an update from his P.R. chief, Darrin Jensen. Cameras and lighting in place, the smallish conference room filled to overflowing. Stepping forward, Wilson King, an imposing figure even when relaxed, wanted all of Nashville to know his position. Through the media, the chief gave his city the same stern lecture he imparted to Stone.

"Thank you for coming out this afternoon," he said in his usual brusque, no-nonsense manner. "I know you've all been to the services for Angela Stone this afternoon, and let me add my sympathy in the wake of this unspeakable tragedy. I wish to assure everyone that the police are pursuing every lead to find Mrs. Stone's killer.

"Like you and all of my fellow Nashvillians, I was shocked by the statements her husband made yesterday. I met with Mister Stone this morning for two reasons. One, I wanted to offer my personal condolences to him and let him know where the investigation stands. Two, I wanted to let him know that I understand the grief and the rage he is feeling, but I urged him to recant his public desire for revenge. When he failed to do so, I explained to Mister Stone why he needs to step back and let us handle this investigation without interference. I further informed Mister Stone that the police department is doing everything in its power to solve this crime. The Tennessee Bureau of Investigation has also taken an active role.

"In addition, we are being assisted by cooperating law enforcement agencies in surrounding counties and, if need be, from across the state."

King paused, recalling the confrontation that morning, and shook his bulbous head.

"It wasn't what he wanted to hear, but I cautioned Mister Stone against trying to take the law into his own hands should he indeed continue on this quest and somehow find the murderer before the police." A terse look came over King. "Mister Stone seems to believe that revenge is a synonym for justice. No sir!" A fist slammed the lectern.

"Revenge is not justice. And justice . . . true justice, swift justice . . . is not about revenge. Our society seeks justice, not revenge. Society does not condone such actions. I made it quite clear to Mister Stone that any criminal behavior on his part could result in charges being filed against him. He would be treated like any other criminal."

Then like a light switch flipped off, the chief's anger melted. Thinking of Stone's outburst made him reflect on his own family's tragedy. His rare display of humanity would draw more people to his opinions than promises of retribution if Stone crossed that uncrossable line.

"I can understand Mister Stone's desire for revenge . . . or justice, I should say . . . and I empathize with him. My grandfather was murdered in Memphis in 1982, and it killed *me*. I was just twelve years old when his best friend shot him during a poker game. They'd been drinking and he laughed because he stole a two hundred dollar pot with a *stinking* pair of *threes!*"

King pounded the lectern with his fist, and it made members of the media jump at this very private individual's very personal revelation.

"So, so angry, I wanted to punish the man who took Grampy from us. A year later, my mother moved us to Nashville. That angered me, too, and she made me talk with some counselors after I got into several fights at school. I got past my anger, or so I thought till today. But I never forgot what happened, and it was a major reason why I chose to go into law enforcement. I've never spoken about this and do so

119

now to let Mister Stone know that *I* know the kind of pain he is suffering and that I *will* do everything in *my* power to bring his wife's killer to justice. I'm aware of Mister Stone's comments this afternoon, and I applaud his decision to post a reward for information leading to the apprehension of this menace to society. I trust Mister Stone will turn over any information he may receive to the proper authorities, who can be reached at 1-800-555-COPS."

The chief's candor impressed, but he wasn't finished.

"I again caution Mister Stone not to attempt any acts of revenge," King said with that same stern tone. "Time spent dealing with Mister Stone is time taken away from trying to catch Mrs. Stone's killer. I met Mister Stone for less than ten minutes at his brother's home. From that brief encounter I would characterize Mister Stone as a decent, honorable man who will choose the right path and work with the police in our manhunt, not go off on his own and become a killer himself. I do not believe that is the legacy Mrs. Stone would want to bequeath to her husband. Questions?"

A dozen hands raised. We peppered Chief King for the next thirty minutes about the Stones, his background, and the general direction of the investigation. Finally, the Chief asked for one more question. Clarkston started to speak as my hand shot up and caught King's eye. He nodded in my direction, leaving the Channel 11 reporter fuming.

"You make a compelling case for why Stone should stop searching for his wife's killer and even threatened him with arrest if he should cross a line," I said, turning aggressive. "But who draws that line and is it an arbitrary line set by you or one of your officers? How far can he go to find Mrs. Stone's murderer without crossing that line?"

King's gaze focused on me like lasers burning through steel.

"You pose an interesting question, Mister Hilliard. The simplest answer is the law is the law," he said, speaking in a harsh but measured tone. "If you break it, you are in trouble. If you refuse to obey it, you are in big trouble. If you flaunt it, you are in deep trouble. If you cross it, you are going to wish you hadn't.

"Now there's nothing against the law in setting up a website to seek information or establishing a reward for that purpose. But if you use that information in an attempt to harm or injure another person, whether it's physical or mental or cyber-bullying, you are breaking the law. If you make an illegal purchase of a weapon to commit an act of violence against someone you suspect of this crime, you are breaking the law. If someone supplies you with a weapon to commit an act of violence, that person is an accessory to breaking the law. See how it works?"

Immense fists drove home his point, and he at last broke eye contact with me. He looked around the room.

"Our job is to enforce the law, not make it or set its boundaries. But our officers retain the right to use a certain amount of discretion in interpreting when the law is being broken. If Mister Stone had made a direct threat against another person, he would be in custody right now. That's not quite the case . . . for the moment, but we will be monitoring the situation. We would welcome any information that any citizen might be able to provide us to help solve *any* crime, not just this one. And while a person may invoke a citizen's arrest when he sees a crime being committed, I would urge anyone not to attempt to do so. It puts you in danger and could endanger the lives of others. Call the police, and we will handle the situation as it may warrant."

Clarkston jumped in with a quick follow-up question. "So you're concerned that if Stone succeeds in finding his wife's killer, others might try to copycat his brand of vigilante justice?"

The chief's nostrils flared. "You bet I am."

17

After the funeral and brief press conference, Jackson made a quick trip to East Nashville to see if the police had finished their investigation and when he could move back into his home. As he rounded a curve, an old blue car came barreling at him, the driver slowing down just enough to make the turn with his tires squealing.

"Crazy sum—Hell's only half-full; you'll get there," shouted Jackson, not knowing how prophetic or accurate his admonition would turn out. Three turns, and he was home.

Putting the car in park, he got out and stared at the brick cottage. So normal. No yellow police tape to remind him of the horror. He could almost see Angela, on her knees by her flower bed digging at weeds encroaching on her petunias. Hopeful that he would somehow, some way, get through this ordeal without losing his sanity, Jackson fell to his knees and cried out loud.

"Lord, help me understand. I want to believe everything happens for a reason, but I can't fathom why this happened. I know Angela is with You now. I know I'll see her again someday in heaven, but, God, I miss her. Help me. Grant me peace now. I want her here, now. You know my heart. You know my intentions are pure, even though it looks like I've lost my mind. Help me find Angela's killer, Lord, let me be the one who brings him to Your justice. Amen."

Rising to his feet, he decided to head to his brother's house. It was time to put into motion just *how* he would find the murderer. Glancing around the neighborhood, he noted both of the Fletchers' autos were in their driveway next door, so he guessed that Herb failed to talk Sarah out of her funk and would not be going to Patrick's.

Jackson was pleased with his announcement of the Angela's Angels website and foundation at the press conference, despite the blow-up with Allenby. Jackson had argued like a lawyer himself until he won over the attorney.

"It's a good cause, Stan, one that'll do a lot of invaluable work in the community. And it gives me a platform to stay active in searching for the killer."

The inspiration for Angela's Angels came out of the blue as he drove back to Patrick's from the cabin. He was listening to the oldies radio channel, and between songs, the station aired a public service announcement for the National Center for Missing and Exploited Children. Founder John Walsh, the host of the television show *America's Most Wanted*, delivered the message.

The Walshes' six-year-old son, Adam, disappeared from their Miami area home on July 27, 1981, and his remains were found soon after, though the killer never was. John and Revé Walsh began their own foundation in Adam's memory so his death would not be in vain. Their movement gained national attention, and their success over the years has resulted in the arrests of thousands of criminals.

Twenty-five years to the day after Adam was abducted, President George W. Bush signed the American Child Protection and Safety Act into law.

Jackson had never met John Walsh, though his firm handled some ancillary work for Walsh's NCMEC foundation. Jackson vowed that after the dust settled, he would reach out to Walsh for advice about setting up the foundation, setting up a tip line, and how best to go about solving crimes. Perhaps feeling pangs of conscience over his vendetta, Jackson wondered if Walsh ever considered pursuing a similar path of being the one to mete out his own brand of justice. If they ever talked, that would be one of the first questions Jackson would ask.

18

After his shower, Wolfe dressed and drove across town to a little hole-in-the-wall he spotted near the park just off West End. He was always ravenous after a hunt, and the nineteen-fifties atmosphere of Rotier's reminded Wolfe of the old home place back in Arkansas where he had gorged on his first meal after his first kill as a teenager. Since then, it became another bizarre ritual, almost cannibalistic in nature, to visit a meat-and-three in that city and chow down following a fresh murder. He gobbled down a cheeseburger on rye bread with those crinkle-cut fries and a soda. Two kills in one day were a rare treat, so he ordered a slice of chocolate ice-box pie.

"Thanks, hon," he said to the cashier, brushing crumbs from his mustache, and then off his pants. He took a final slurp from the fountain glass and followed with a loud carbonated belch before throwing a ten and a five on the table and leaving. He crossed the street and walked to Centennial Park, where he took off his shirt and plopped on the lush grass, ogling the vast array of college coeds who were just returning to Nashville for the start of the fall semester.

When the heat got to him, he drove back to the Dickerson Pike motel. Wolfe opened a beer, flipped on the old color television and turned on the baseball game. The bottom of the ninth, and Los Angeles led two to one with the middle of the Braves' batting order coming up. Back-to-back strikeouts, and a long fly ball to center field. Game over.

"Damn. C'mon, dudes." Wolfe lit a smoke and turned off the television in disgust. He opened an old suitcase and grabbed his newest journal. Pulling the faded chair from under the rickety desk, he switched on the lamp and sat down. He needed to get busy writing.

Wolfe turned the TV back on as the six o'clock report began. He was so focused on his writing, a minute passed before the news broke his concentration and got in on the middle of a sentence: "One-hundred-thousand-dollar reward for information leading to the arrest of his wife's killer." Clarkston continued, "But Stone also made it clear what he would do with that information if given the chance." The camera cut to Stone behind the lectern, staring into the camera that slow-zoomed to a close-up shot. "If you call the police, there will be an arrest and a trial. Call me, and I'll be the jury."

It struck a raw nerve with Wolfe, who slapped his beer bottle off the table and screamed at the screen. "You're *next!*" Mumbling under his breath, he added, "I don't care what it costs." And he meant it.

He turned back to his journal as Chief King's image came on screen. Clarkston spoke again. Wolfe ignored them both and resumed his choppy writing, which he would continue for the next couple of hours before taking a dinner break. "She begged . . . ."

With the six o'clock telecast finished, Dan Clarkston enjoyed an hour dinner break before preparing for the ten p.m. broadcast. He invited other crew members to join him at his favorite barbecue shack/pool hall, Cue Tips. His cameraman declined, wanting to re-edit footage from the two afternoon press conferences. "But take this ten," Pittard said. "I want the large, smoked turkey sandwich with slaw and sweet potato fries. And bring extra sauce and napkins."

Clarkston listened to the auto race in Bristol, Tennessee, as he made the ten-minute drive to kitschy Hillsboro Village, a small retail area catty-cornered from the back side of the Vanderbilt campus. Cue Tips shared its Belcourt Avenue location in a refurbished house with Darlene's Hideaway

Lounge. Clarkston had frequented Darlene's in his younger, wilder days when the station hired him straight out of college. Now his photo hung on the recently repainted wall along with other, real Nashville celebrities.

"Hi Dan. The usual tonight?" asked Kitty, his favorite Cue Tips waitress. He glanced over Saturday's menu scratched out on a faded chalkboard behind her and shook his head.

"Think I'll go with barbecue on cornbread tonight instead of the bun. And hold off on the fries. I've added a couple of pounds. Just slaw on the side."

"It looks good on ya, Danny boy," Kitty said, winking at the excellent tipper.

"My wife doesn't think so. And neither does my producer. Oh yeah, I also need a to-go order. But keep it warm till I'm ready to leave."

He sat and watched the short-track race on the big screen as Kitty shouted orders to her father, the cook. She returned with his cup of sweet tea and a few minutes later, brought his barbecue plate. She sat on the hard bench across from him.

"I saw your pieces about Jackson Stone, Danny. That policeman made me mad."

"You mean Chief King. He came off a little strong, except when talking about his grandfather. He's just doing what he thinks is right. So is Stone, I guess. I haven't quite figured him out yet."

Two tables behind Clarkston, Wolfe's ears perked at the mention of Jackson Stone, and he tried to act nonchalant while sipping his beer. He'd remembered the gaudy Cue Tips sign from that day he picked up the Fletcher woman, and decided to eat here, arriving about ten minutes before Clarkston. He recognized the television reporter, but couldn't quite put a name to the profile he could see from his angle. When he heard the waitress say "Danny," he matched it to Clarkston.

Wolfe drained the rest of his LandShark and left. He smiled and watched and waited.

19

I zipped to the paper and wrote a twelve-inch mainbar from the police chief's press conference. Then I read over Shelley's story on the funeral and reward announcement with photo slideshows from both the visitation and two news conferences attached. It was all posted by four p.m. The weekend editorial staff gathered in a conference room to consider story play on Page 1A and inside the front section.

My story at TenneSceneToday.com ignited reader reactions and I finally got an opportunity to check a few. By four-thirty, there were seventeen posts. By five, it zoomed to forty-eight, and by the six o'clock TV news, the hits spiraled to one hundred sixty-three.

At 4:08 p.m., JUSTICE 4 ALL wrote: "The cops will railroad you, Jack, so you might as well catch the next train out of town and start over somewhere else. That topcop King must think he's the king of Nashville, the way he talked. That scum you're looking for is the real criminal and they spend all their time talking about you instead of trying to catch him. Good luck Jack."

At 4:42 p.m., GRETTA LIFE wrote: "Copycat vigilante justice? Yeah right. Like everybody's gonna go shoot everyone who ever wronged them. The chief is a dope. Maybe he's on dope."

At 5 p.m., HAPPY HOUR wrote: "The death penalty should be enough justice for Jackson Stone. Otherwise there can be no justice. There is a right way and a wrong way to do things and Jackson's way is just plain wrong."

At 5:29 p.m., T.RIGGER wrote: "The death penalty is a burden on our taxpayers that we can do without. Go for it Jack. Save us some money."

At 5:46 p.m., PROVIDENCE wrote: "What if you track down your wife's killer and a year later find out you gunned down the wrong guy? Could you live with that on your conscience, Jack? Didn't think so."

At 6:15 p.m., GALLATIN GAL'S PAL wrote: "I don't know who killed Stone's wife, but for $100K I'm sure going to find out. When's his website going up?"

After the TV news, media outlet message boards all across the city started buzzing with more of the same pros and cons, taking both sides, dissecting the police, and questioning Stone's motives. The blogging never ceased or ceased to amaze.

I began rewriting for Sunday morning's final edition and finished about eight o'clock, then took on the inch-thick stack of background material I'd printed out about Jackson. First, I ran a search and scored hits on articles about his 2007 advertising awards, campaigns for noteworthy causes to which he contributed personal time and effort, a 2004 sports story on a ten-point trophy buck bagged near his Lascassas farmhouse, and a mention of his home being featured on the 2005 East Nashville Christmas Caroling Tour, where for ten dollars, visitors walked through the close-knit community and oohed and ahhed over twinkling holiday decorations and were treated to cookies, cocoa, and a visit from Santa.

The last article mentioned Stone's involvement with the annual Iroquois Memorial Steeplechase at Percy Warner Park. The steeplechase, now a major fund-raiser that benefits the Monroe Carell Jr. Children's Hospital at Vanderbilt, is one of Nashville's largest amateur sporting events, drawing crowds of twenty thousand or more to the lush, green hillside of the spacious park. Held the second Saturday of May, it's as much social as sporting event. The Stones' involvement with the Iroquois consisted of volunteering to help plan entertainment for the official parties. Angela's connections inside the music industry landed some big-name performers, while Jackson handled publicity.

I noted the Steeplechase course's proximity to the section of the park where Angela's body was found. I scanned printouts from the Nexus search. It contained information on Jackson's USMC career, the honorable discharge after being injured, their 1996 wedding announcement, public information about how much the Stones paid for their house in 1998, how much their taxes were, and how much the house was worth today.

Yawning, I took off the reading glasses and rubbed my tired eyes. Hoping for a call-back from the Vanderbilt psychologist, I'd just about given up and began tidying the desk before heading home, when the phone rang.

"*TenneScene Today*. This is Gerry Hilliard in the newsroom. How can I help you?"

"Good evening, Mister Hilliard. Erica Karnoff here, I hope it's not too late. We went to a movie and I just saw your message."

I switched the phone to my left hand, grabbed a notepad and a pen, and scribbled "Doctor Karnoff," underlining her name twice.

"Not at all, thanks for calling. I'm covering the Angela Stone murder case and it's taken a fascinating twist the last few days with the desire for vengeance comments from her husband. I recalled your insights last spring during the East Nashville rapist case and thought you might shed some light on Stone's current state of mind."

"I'm honored that you thought of me," she said. "Yes, I'd love to sit down with Mister Stone and chat. It sounds like he has some real anger issues, but I know very little about his background . . . just what I've read and seen on television. We're off the record, right?"

"Yes, but I would like to quote you at some point," I said, scribbling "OTR" but continuing to take notes of our conversation. "It sure has Nashville buzzing and it seems like as many people hope he carries out his plan as there are people against the idea of taking the law into his own hands."

That wasn't a question, but the good doctor answered it as one since most media-types loved to throw out observations to "experts" and gauge their reactions.

"Yes, it could be very divisive, for example, on the gun-control issue. Anyone who has ever been a crime victim might vicariously attach themselves to Stone's quest for revenge. And it would also be a hot-button issue for those who are either for or against the death penalty. Yes, indeed, it has become larger than Stone."

"So would you call Mister Stone's declaration for vengeance irrational or justified?"

"Both, and a little egocentric, perhaps stemming from the obvious anger and probable depression issues with which he is dealing. From the outside looking in, revenge has no place in modern society and such behavior cannot be condoned. But from the inside looking out, these feelings for revenge—or at the very least, helping find the man who murdered his wife—may be all Mister Stone's got right now."

Karnoff cleared her throat and continued.

I tried to scribble all this down and absorb what she said, trying to respond in an intelligent manner. Tired, I stifled another yawn. I hoped my questions didn't sound too foolish.

"And this applies to Stone how? I see the anger, of course; we all have the last couple of days. And the emotional roller coaster of depression has been apparent."

"Stone's stated desire for vengeance goes well beyond the clear anger he has shown, and this may well be something new. For example, when Dr. Elisabeth Kubler-Ross hypothesized—"

Karnoff's husband said something that I missed, and the doctor cut me off before I fired off more questions.

"Yes, I can. Excuse me," she said, pulling the telephone away from her mouth, then she spoke back to me. "Forgive me, Mister Hilliard, but I must run. Perhaps we can talk again next week. I am fascinated by Mister Stone and look forward to your articles."

I said a cordial goodbye and stared at the phone. I tried going down the path upon which the doctor led me, but the bridge washed out and mental roadblocks made it too late for deep thinking.

I perused the biographical sketches of the Stones, and then glanced at the first edition front section of the Sunday morning paper that had been laid on my desk while I talked to the psychiatrist. Distracted, I paid scant attention to the perfect headline for my story, and then flipped to the jump on page 10-A. My eyes focused on the four-column picture of Reverend Robert Armstrong at the visitation, talking to Jackson and his brother. The mahogany casket was behind them. The preacher's right arm was wrapped around Jackson's back while talking to Patrick. Jackson was staring up at the imposing preacher as if seeking understanding and guidance in the worst of times. I hated admitting it, but the raw emotions that photo would convey to readers were far stronger than any thousand words I could write. I glanced at the nebulous cutline information:

Belle Rive Baptist pastor Robert Armstrong, center, comforts Jackson Stone, right, and Patrick Stone at Saturday's visitation at Belle Valley Cemetery. *CASEY LEIBER/TENNESCENE TODAY*

Studying the photo made up my mind. I realized where the saga's next twist would take place. I logged off my computer, grabbed my notes and first edition sports section, and headed to my car.

"Looks like I'm going to church in the morning."

20

Most of the visitors at Patrick's house after the funeral were fellow church-goers, and they'd all shared kind words and promises to pray for Jackson, especially the aging organist who'd accompanied Angela during her choir solo the previous Christmas. But it became more difficult for him to hold his tongue as everyone opined on how he should proceed in his quest, or that he should end this nonsense now, or that he wasn't acting as a faithful follower of Jesus Christ should, and on and on and on throughout the evening.

"I'm just trying to do the right thing," he said. "It's something I *have* to do."

The flow of familiar faces continued to stream by until about eight-thirty and by nine dwindled to just a dozen or so stragglers. Jackson sagged into the couch where Chief King sat just twelve hours ago, though it seemed more like twelve days. He closed his eyes and prayed.

"God, I could use some sleep right now. Keep me strong, Lord." His eyes popped open, and he started upright as a large hand clasped his shoulder. He looked up into the smiling face of his pastor, Reverend Armstrong.

"Hope I didn't startle you, Jack."

"Not at all, Brother Bob. I prayed for guidance, and here you are. There are no coincidences."

"I've been working on my sermon for tomorrow morning. I hope you'll be in church. I've changed from the topic I'd originally planned to speak on, and I think you'll find it very enlightening."

21

Wolfe grew impatient and looked at his luminous watch. It was ten thirty p.m.

"Dammit, where is he?"

He had followed Clarkston back to Channel 11 after he emerged from Cue Tips at seven thirty, parking in the drugstore lot so he could eye the television station's front door and lobby. Three long, hurry up-and-wait hours had passed. He was anxious to get back to his journal, but more eager to see where Clarkston lived—just in case. He watched and waited some more.

After Pittard had downed his sandwich, he and Clarkston spent an hour reviewing footage from the morning visitation and both afternoon press conferences, then spent a half-hour with weekend director Joan McCall discussing the gist of Clarkston's ten o'clock report. Joan wanted Clarkston to do a stand-up introduction plus cutaways to walk viewers through a chronological summation of the day, but Clarkston balked.

"This is my story and since Ellie's off this weekend, I'm calling the shots," Clarkston said, flexing his muscles as the station's top investigative reporter. "It's going to be a lot sexier if we lead with Chief King putting this kook in his place. And who knows—it might even help Stone win some support or sympathy."

Joan didn't like it, but didn't protest much. The A-team rarely worked Saturday shifts, and she didn't want him acting all prissy on *her* newscast. After a few questions, she nodded approval.

133

"Sounds good, Dan. We'll run through a thirty-second intro to the day's news, then you've got the next three-and-a-half minutes. Maybe four, if it's good enough. Get cracking guys. I want to see something by nine fifteen."

Clarkston grinned. At nine ten, Pittard finished his final re-cuts the way he and Clarkston discussed. Joan arrived, and Clarkston handed the director his script. She scratched one phrase. "Would that work better?"

"Perfect, Joan. Give us five minutes and we'll be ready."

After feeding copy into the teleprompter, Clarkston took his position on the set and awaited his cue from weekend anchor Luis Reyes. "Our Dan Clarkston has spent the day following the extraordinary twists and turns this case has taken."

"Thanks, Luis. Yesterday, Jackson Stone threw down the gauntlet to Metro police, challenging them to find his wife's killer before he did. Today, no less than Chief King delivered a response no one expected." Clarkston swiveled to camera two. "Just hours before Angela Stone was buried, Nashville's top cop informed Stone in no uncertain terms that he could face charges if he continued his quest for vengeance. Then about an hour after Stone announced a one-hundred-thousand-dollar reward and a website in his wife's name, Chief King explained to the media what penalties Stone could face if he takes the law into his own hands."

"Cut to video one," Joan said in the control room. King's commanding presence filled the screen. "The law is the law. If you break it, you are in trouble."

Clarkston watched the rapid-fire report he and Pittard put together on the studio's large monitor. Clips included Stone's confrontation with his lawyer, the Chief's recollections of his grandfather's murder, and interviews from the visitation. One particular scene caught Clarkston's attention, one he failed to notice on Pittard's smaller editing unit. During a wide pan of the visitation line outside the funeral home, he noticed Stone's neighbor Herb Fletcher talking to a young mustached man behind him. He'd seen that face before, but where?

At ten forty, Clarkston exited the station, tapped the keyless entry system numbers on the driver side's door, got in his Audi and sped off. Wolfe, tired and half-asleep, almost missed him.

Cursing, he peeled out. There wasn't much traffic at that time of night, so Wolfe hung back. When Clarkston made a right turn on Belle Meade Boulevard and drove through the highest end of Nashville's high-end communities, so did Wolfe. When Clarkston went through the four-way stop at the upper-crust country club, so did Wolfe. When Clarkston turned left onto Harding Road, so did Wolfe some ten seconds later. But the light turned yellow some five seconds after Clarkston's turn, so Wolfe stomped the pedal and ran the red light as a car on his right honked.

Clarkston heard the horns and saw in his rearview mirror the old car barrel through the light. But he didn't make much of it until he turned right, crossed the railroad tracks, and eased through the four-way stop, then realized the old car behind him made the same maneuvers. A paid observer of life, Clarkston paid attention to the inner alarms going off and drove past his normal turn. Two streets later, Clarkston swerved right, hit the gas, and then made a hard left and whipped his car into the driveway of a vacant, tear-down house for sale. He shut off the car and waited. Some five seconds later, an old car—blue, he noticed in the streetlight's harsh glare—roared down the street and sped out of sight. He waited for another half-minute before backing out of the driveway.

Puzzled, Clarkston headed home for real. Who's the stalker?

SUNDAY, AUGUST 15
1

A beautiful morning spread its way across the Nashville skyline. The day began with a variety of reactions as those connected with the Angela Stone murder eagerly fetched their morning newspapers. Our outside sales for that Sunday edition were the highest since the Titans went to Super Bowl XXXIV in Atlanta.

Jackson Stone woke up about a quarter to nine, feeling refreshed after an emotional, exhausting Saturday. His first thoughts were of Angela. He hoped they always would be.

He showered, dressed, and joined Patrick and Sheila in the den, where they drank coffee and read the Sunday paper. A steaming cup of extra bold roast awaited Jackson as he sat. Patrick leaned over and handed him the folded front section.

"You better look at this."

I woke up from a dead sleep at nine and joined Jill in the breakfast nook. She sat at the table with her right leg folded under her, enjoying her steaming first cup of fresh coffee. I looked over her shoulder at the front page. Wow!

"Morning, babe," she chirped. "You were late. Sorry I couldn't wait up. I loved your story. And that headline! Perfect."

"Thanks. Wish I'd written it," I said, filling my mug. "What a day. And today might be more of the same."

"What now? I thought we'd go to the Nashville Sounds ballgame tonight. It *is* my birthday you know," she said, preening in her flowery sun dress.

"Happy birthday, hon. That would be fun and relaxing. I hope I'm home in time. But first I'm curious to see what kind of reaction Stone gets in church this morning."

Jill's jaw dropped. It had been at least five years since my last trip to church.

Monica Clarkston had awakened her husband, Dan, at nine-fifteen, setting her cup of espresso on the bedside table and leaning over to plant a wet kiss full on the lips. It was his regular day off, so the Channel 11 star reporter ignored the outside world as much as possible, meaning he didn't see the newspaper until later that afternoon. They spent the rest of the morning in bed, finally going to brunch in Green Hills, followed by a movie at their favorite art house.

When they finally got home, Dan cursed when he read the main headline, wishing he'd used the catchy phrase in his report the night before. Up until that moment, his day off had been enjoyable.

The Kings arrived home at nine-fifty from Midtown United Methodist Church, and the giant policeman's mood had soured rather than having been lifted by the early worship service.

He thought the headline in the paper stated his point perfectly and expected a good response at church. Just the opposite, King drew one sharp comment after another from fellow worshipers. Few appreciated his stance.

"That poor man just lost his wife," Edna Edmundson said shrilly to the chief on the front steps before services. "How could you talk to him like that? I hope he finds the killer before you do."

"Now, ma'am, you know two wrongs don't make a right," King said, keeping his cool. "Believe me, no one is more sympathetic to Mister Stone's plight than me, but nobody can take the law into their own hands."

138

A few church-goers paused to watch, and Joe Davenport added his two-cents worth.

"I think the police are afraid he's going to find the killer before they do," Joe said, and others nodded in agreement. "It's going to give your department a black eye."

"No it won't," Marvin Kripkey said, standing a few feet behind the Chief. All eyes turned to him, including the Kings'.

"If Stone catches up with his wife's killer, do you think he'll call another press conference to announce it? Angela's death will remain an unsolved mystery."

The Chief stared dumbfounded at the crowd for a few seconds, then took his wife's hand and led her into the church. But King grew so irritated and frustrated that he barely heard the sermon, which centered on the theme, "Do Unto Others." King didn't want anyone doing anything to anybody in his city.

About ten a.m., Patrick Stone, sitting on the sofa, watched his brother re-reading the extensive newspaper coverage of Saturday's events.

"Jack, you okay? What'd you think about the Chief's statement? He tore into you, didn't he?"

Jackson looked up, took a half-sip of his now-cold coffee.

"I know what he meant when he said he understood what I was going through. But he didn't understand me when I said I *had* to do this."

Jackson stood and looked at his watch. "How come you're not dressed? Give me fifteen minutes, and I'll be ready to leave for church. I feel a need to be there."

At ten-fifteen, Chief King began thumbing through the morning paper again. The television blared, but his thoughts centered on Jackson Stone and just what to do about him.

"My department's not going to take the blame if Stone gets himself killed," King vowed as his wife set a fresh cup of coffee at his side. "Or somebody else, God forbid."

139

Mechelle King could always read her husband's thoughts, even when he didn't talk about his problems or seek her opinion. And while she didn't always offer solutions, she'd been a good sounding board.

"This is one fight you can't win, Wil. You've got to figure out some way to stand up for what's right without coming down too hard on Stone. Don't make him a martyr."

After she left the room, King puzzled over his wife's advice. Right, as usual.

But how would he help Stone without hurting him?

Both the Stones and I left for Belle Rive Baptist Church at about ten-thirty a.m. With three times as far to travel from my Hendersonville home, I should have left by ten, but thought I'd still get to the church on time.

"Are you sure you don't want to go?" I asked Jill after a final kiss at the door. "I'll be glad to wait."

Jill straightened my tie and shook her head.

"I don't want you to have to bring me home before you head to the office. Just don't make a scene at church."

I smiled and headed for the car.

"There may not be a story. If nothing else, an hour in church won't hurt me."

The Stones arrived at ten forty-five and took their customary seats seven rows back on the right side of the church, near the center aisle.

I've always been on the right side, Jackson reflected as the organist played her prelude music. *Am I now?* He looked up to the large wooden cross on the wall behind the purple-robed choir that filed in and took their seats, and he prayed for guidance. He shifted and found Brother Bob's eyes upon him, a curious smile on his face. Jackson nodded.

Sitting between Patrick and Jackson, Sheila held each brother's hand. She worried about Jackson and considered trying to get him an appointment with her friend Judy's teaching psychiatrist, a Doctor Karnoff at Vanderbilt.

At eleven sharp, the church music director stood, the choir members rose, and the congregation joined the singing of "Jesus, Lead Me to the Cross."

I arrived at church about five after eleven. The wreck at Trinity Lane had reduced traffic to one lane, or I would've been there on time. The choir's voices greeted me as I opened the church doors, and a deacon handed me a program, whispering "Welcome, Brother." I nodded my thanks, smiled, and took a seat on the next-to-last row. I got out my pen, notepad, and microcassette recorder from jacket pockets, then laid them on the empty pew and glanced at the program. After the church welcome, hymn, Offertory prayer, and choir special would come the Pastor's Message. I wondered if that message would be directed at more than one member.

Back at his squalid Dickerson Pike motel, Delmore Wolfe woke with a start at about eleven-fifteen, grabbed a tallboy out of his mini-fridge and lit a cigarette.

"What a wasted night. Good thing I got wasted," he growled, scratching himself.

Enraged that he failed to find out where the TV reporter lived, but certain that he'd find out eventually, Wolfe decided to play it carefully. After he had finally zig-zagged out of the West Nashville neighborhood near midnight, Wolfe drove around downtown until he saw the young guy in a darkened alley. He drove around the block three times before he hit the brakes.

"So whaddya got?"

"You coulda stopped the first time, man," the dirty teen-ager said. "Ain't no problems here. I can get whatever you want and more. This is our corner. Need some weed? How 'bout some speed?"

"Got any Gold?" Wolfe handed him a wad of bills.

The youth took the money and handed him two plastic bags full of pills and pot.

"Not here, but check back tomorrow."

141

Wolfe's head still buzzed Sunday morning. He slipped on his jeans, a tee-shirt, and his sneakers, and opened the door. The heat beat down on him, and the bright sun burned his eyeballs. He ducked back into his grungy room, put on his wraparound sunglasses, and crossed the road to the 1960s-themed diner. Outside the door, he popped quarter after quarter into the newspaper vending machine and got the last one. The diner's air conditioner, set on high, couldn't fully counteract the heat from the grills.

"It's hot as hell in here," he barked at the short-order cook, who retorted, "Get used to it, pal."

Wolfe took the table at the far end of the diner and stared at the paper. Plastered on the front page were pictures of Stone grappling with "some old fart and a burly, mad cop," as he later wrote in his journal of that incident. The bold headline hit a home run.

I'll be damned!

Police to Stone:
Thou shalt not kill

Nashville man warned that quest for vengeance won't be tolerated

By GERRY HILLIARD
TenneScene Today

Nashville advertising executive Jackson Stone could face severe consequences — at least second-degree murder charges — if he were to succeed in his premeditated quest for vengeance stemming from the Aug. 3 murder of his wife, Angela, 35.

That was the stern message police Chief Wilson King delivered Saturday morning to Jackson Stone just hours before Angela's funeral at Belle Valley Memorial Cemetery. King reiterated that message at a press conference shortly after Stone made more headlines by announcing a $100,000 reward and the imminent launching of his "Angela's Angels" website and hotline.

"Our society seeks justice, not revenge. Society does not condone such actions," King said during an emotional recounting of the 1982 shooting death of his grandfather in Memphis that he said led him to a career in law enforcement. King added that "any criminal behavior on (Stone's) part could result in charges being filed against him. He would be treated like any other criminal."

Stone could not be reached for comment on the possibility of facing charges for what King called "vigilante justice."

The chief said he was concerned about a copycat
>>CONTINUED ON PAGE 10A

"You ready to order yet, hon?"

Wolfe ignored the waitress, thumbing through the paper to continue reading. But instead of picking up the story on 10-A where it jumped from the front page, his eyes went to several photos on the facing page that accompanied an article on the Stone visitation and funeral. One, a vertical, showed a close-cropped picture of Herb Fletcher. Behind him, one could see the right shoulder and a few strands of hair on the head of a man with his back to the camera.

Delmore Wolfe sighed in relief.

143

2

The choir soloist sang "Find Victory Through Jesus." Deacons brought offering plates full of bills, change, and envelopes containing checks to the front of the church, then placed them on the Communion table before walking down the aisles to sit with loved ones. At eleven thirty, Brother Armstrong rose to deliver his message of hope and faith—and more.

The bald preacher, strong in both physique and spirit, walked to the pulpit and unbuttoned his navy sport coat. He withdrew several sheets of paper from an inner pocket, which he held up for the congregation to see.

"Brothers and sisters, welcome on this glorious morning for a divinely inspired message that will touch far more people today than I ever will with these words," Armstrong said from the pulpit, putting the notes back in his pocket.

"I just wanted you all to see the sermon I'd planned to give this morning. After yesterday's services for our sister, Angela Stone, who has gone on to a better world without pain and strife, I went home to write a message specifically for today. While many of you were bringing comfort and solace—and food, lots of food—to brothers Jackson and Patrick Stone and their grieving families, I went home to the solitude of my garden to find the proper words of hope, healing, and salvation that I thought Jackson needed to hear this morning. I spent hours writing and rewriting that message and now . . . now I'm putting it away. They are good words, but will save for another day."

Brother Bob smiled at Jackson, nodding as he spoke.

"Or perhaps I will share them in a private moment with Jackson and his loved ones. You know that I—and your church family—always will be here for you, Jack."

The preacher's eyes didn't lock in on Jackson again. Instead, he held up four fingers and then pointed at the congregation.

"Today's divine message consists of just four of the Lord's most important words for troubled man, and they are out there today for all to see. Did you see them?"

Armstrong looked around and smiled at the puzzled faces before he continued.

"Surely you saw the message. In bold type in this morning's newspaper with inch-high letters. Did you see it? Surely, it jumped out at you. It went out over the Internet on the paper's website with the potential to be seen by millions. And while the message was a clever attempt to get readers to buy a paper, these four words stand among the Lord's *holiest* of words. God delivered the message to Moses thousands of years ago, one of the Ten Commandments that God gave to mankind as instructions on how to live your life on Earth. Did you see the message? I pray at least one man saw it, one brother who needs to understand that message and embrace the Lord's Sixth Commandment—Thou shalt not kill."

No one in front of him or to either side turned to look, but Jackson felt as if every set of eyes in the congregation were upon him. His face reddened as he looked up at the choir and saw eyes dart in another direction. He glanced over at Sheila and Patrick. Their expressions were impassive, but their dancing eyes followed the preacher.

Jackson was unable to concentrate on the rest of the sermon. The preacher continued to expound on the "Thou shalt not kill" theme for the remaining twenty-five minutes. Jackson would later recall hearing the preacher say he should turn the other cheek, that the best revenge would be the act of forgiveness.

In the back of the church I scribbled notes, just glad I brought my recorder. Talk about being in the right place at the right time. I looked around the congregation as I wrote, hoping something dramatic might happen—as if the preacher's words weren't enough. But there were no "amen" shouts, no movement throughout the sermon. It surprised me as much as anyone that the newspaper's clever headline became the sermon's main focus. Fascinated, I watched an impassioned Reverend Armstrong hammer home his point, moving back and forth across the pulpit, using his hands to deliver points of emphasis. Now, he pounded his right fist into his open left palm.

"The Sixth Commandment is very clear on this matter; you shall *not* murder. There is *no* ambiguity. It's a straightforward message. No matter the circumstances, do *not* take the law into your own hands. 'Vengeance is Mine,' saith the Lord. If you believe in the Lord Almighty, take Him at *His* Word. *Believe* that all accounts come payment due on Judgment Day. This message isn't just for Jackson Stone. I am not singling him out because of his reaction to the tragedy that has befallen his family. It's a message that all of us in the Christian community must embrace. In this wicked world, terrible things happen to good Christians every day."

Reverend Armstrong continued to pound away on the theme, knowing full well it would be a topic of discussion for many days to come and could cause friction within his middle-class congregation. But until he saw me ducking out a side door as the choir finished the closing chorus and Benediction, Armstrong didn't know his message would reach the world at large. My notepad and cassette were obvious giveaways.

Armstrong walked to the back of the church where he would shake hands with his departing flock, hoping he'd get a chance to speak with me. He would, but not right away. As I stood outside, I wondered how Jackson would react to being called out by both the police and his own preacher. I watched and waited.

The Stones remained seated in the pew as those around them rose to leave.

"Bye, Mister Stone," one young voice said as his mother shushed him down the aisle. Jackson felt drained, as if he'd just survived a ten-round fight. His conscience waged a battle, knowing the preacher's words rang true but what he must do also felt right. Supported by Sheila and Patrick, who rose when Jackson did, they made their way to where Brother Bob waited. He thrust a hand at Jackson.

"Hope I didn't rough you up too much. I was—"

"I know. Doing your job," Jackson said coldly and left without shaking the preacher's hand. Patrick apologized and said his brother didn't mean it.

Jackson emerged from the church, and I plotted an intercept course, cutting across the parking lot to re-introduce myself.

"Hello again, Mister Stone. Gerry Hilliard from *TenneScene Today* and—"

"I know who you are. What do you want?"

"I played a hunch you would be in church today and since I couldn't reach you by telephone yesterday, I wanted to give you an opportunity to respond to Chief King's comments about possible charges you could face if you continue to pursue this vengeance thing. And I'm curious about your reactions to the reverend's sermon this morning. I sat in the back and watched. I half-expected you to get up and walk out." I grinned at that last line, and it seemed to be the ice-breaker in our chilly, budding relationship. It also caused a turnabout in Jackson's attitude.

Jackson chuckled as his brother arrived, red-faced as if he'd just eaten the tongue-blistering medium quarter breast at Prince's Hot Chicken Shack. "Yeah, the thought crossed my mind. Wait here a minute, and I'll be glad to talk. Maybe you can join us for lunch. Talk to my kid brother."

Jackson sprinted back into the church, where he found Brother Bob. He met the preacher with true humility.

"I want to apologize for the 'just doing your job,' line, Brother Bob."

"No offense, Brother Jack. We'll talk about it soon."

"This is all still . . . raw emotion right now, but I promise I'll explain everything someday . . . soon, I hope."

Jackson came out of the church and got in the backseat of Patrick's car. I followed them to Patrick's house in autopilot mode as I thought about where I wanted to steer our conversation. Sheila heated leftovers as the brothers led me into the den. We chatted a minute, then got down to business. I opened my notepad, turned on the recorder, and set it on the table between us.

"Sunday August fifteenth. Jackson and Patrick Stone. So what's going through your mind after that sermon?"

"Honestly? I'm kind of numb. I loved the headline, but I sure didn't see that coming. But I'm even more determined than ever to find Angela's killer. I anticipated some harsh reaction, that not everyone would agree with or condone what I am trying to do."

"Describe your meeting with Chief King."

"Without getting into all the details, you heard the same basic spiel at his news conference. I didn't know about *that* until I picked up the paper this morning."

Jackson shrugged his shoulders in a what-can-you-do fashion, adding, "I can't say I'm surprised by the Chief's reaction. He's got his job to do."

Jackson paused, reflecting that he made the same comment to the preacher. He still felt bad about that and chose his next words with care.

"I don't hold any animosity toward the chief or the police. I've supported the police on many levels and became acquainted with several at the East Nashville precinct before this happened. I sincerely hope they find Angela's murderer. He's still out there somewhere and has to be stopped. If they can't stop him, maybe I can. Someone has to. Might as well be me."

"How about possibly facing criminal charges? As the chief noted, it *could* be considered premeditated. Did you ever consider not going public with your mission, as you've called it?"

Jackson shook his head.

"The answer to both of your questions is no, I didn't. Criminal charges are one thing. A conviction is another. I've got a good lawyer, and I think any jury would be sympathetic to what this monster has put us through. He deserves to die."

Jackson scooted forward and looked me in the eye to make sure *I* got the message.

"The second thing is I can't do it alone. I *need* the public's help to find this psycho. I've put up a hundred thousand dollars of my own savings and as soon as we get the paperwork complete, the public will be able to make donations at my Angela's Angels website. All contributions will be used to: one . . . find Angela's killer, and . . . two . . . increase the reward money as necessary, and . . . three . . . solve other murders and help other victims' families long after we've found Angela's killer."

"What makes you think you can solve this crime if the cops can't? I read your bio, so I know about your military training."

My follow-up question caused Jackson to stiffen and cross his arms, almost belligerent.

"I'm not going to answer that, because I've got some definite leads that I want to check out and you never know who will read this—maybe even the gutless coward who killed an innocent woman and I'm guessing has killed before. I want to stop him before there's another victim. I don't know why, but I feel he's still in Middle Tennessee somewhere. I'll track him around the globe if that's what it takes and spend the rest of my life in that pursuit until he's found."

I hunched over, scribbling in my reporter's notebook in case the recorder fouled up.

Sheila brought in a tray of sandwiches, part of the cornucopia of food brought over by caring friends and neighbors.

"Oh not for me, thanks," I said and stood. "I need to get to the office and start writing. Deadlines, you know."

Jackson walked me to the front door, and I dug a business card out of my wallet, writing my home information on the back. My turn to lecture, just like the police chief and the preacher.

"You're in the ad game and know how to manipulate the media. But if you're honest with me, I'll be fair with you. You're hot news now, but the day will come when the next big story bumps you off the front page. I won't be your mouthpiece, but if you've got something you think I need to hear or know, call me anytime. That's day, night, at the office, at home, or on my cell. I can help you get your message out. And I would rather see you face-to-face than at a news conference. I'll be glad to converse off the record, and we'll talk about what is on the record. But you can't say something and then say 'that's off the record.' No take-backs. And I'll keep my editors in the loop on every conversation. Fair enough?"

With the ground rules established, I stuck out my hand, and Jackson accepted it.

3

Scenes from a gorgeous Sunday afternoon:

Sally Thompson grew frustrated. The Channel 11 general assignments reporter left message after message for every phone number Clarkston left her while he enjoyed a beautiful Sunday at the lake or wherever he was. She couldn't find Jackson Stone or his cell number, just an email address for his office. Patrick Stone's voicemail asked her to leave a message. Darrin Jensen's pager went unanswered, and she dared not call the police chief without going through his PR flak first. She looked at the latest blogs on the station's website and other media sites for inspiration. She found it. A sampling:

Classic Country 750-AM: At 11:57 a.m., BACKSTABBED wrote: "Jackson Stone better watch his back because somebody might plant a knife in it. And if the killer doesn't get him first, the cops will. You're a dead man walking, whacko Jacko."

Channel 11: At 12:22 p.m., CAROL177 wrote: "Great headline in the paper this morning, bet you guys are jealous. Your coverage has been pretty good, but it seems like the media has been leaning too much toward the police. Treat Jackson fairly and don't judge him too harsh."

TenneSceneToday.com: At 12:45 p.m., EXCOP replied to CAROL177: "Stone is planning

to play Judge and Jury and you don't want him
judged too harshly? You're a fool and so is
Stone if he thinks he can get away with using
his wife's death as an excuse to take the law
into his own hands. Murder is murder any way
you cut it."

That settled Sally. What did average Nashvillians think
about Jackson Stone's plans and the police's reactions? She
speed-dialed her weekend videographer. "Grab your camera.
We're going to Centennial Park."

What a good idea, she thought as she climbed into the
passenger seat of the newsvan. Even if it didn't pan out to be
a great story, just hanging out at the park would be great.

Sergeant Mike Whitfield didn't like working weekends,
but with everybody—from the mayor's office to the chief to
the media to the public—watching how the police handled
the Stone case, pressure intensified to solve the case.
Detectives handled most of the workload, but relied on
Whitfield's street-smart instincts to determine what forensics
couldn't. He'd played a major role in finding the East
Nashville rapist last year.

"There's gotta be a clue here, somewhere." Another
report flew across the desk littered with a stack of papers
detailing physical evidence, none pointing to the killer's
identity. Fingerprints in the house belonged to the Stones
and their closest family and friends. The city-wide manhunt
for Angela began in East Nashville and slowly fanned out
over a twenty-mile radius. It took more than a week for the
search party to reach Warner Park, but once they did, police
dogs discovered her body less than a half-mile from the golf
course. A couple of volunteers swore they combed over that
area less than twenty-four hours before the call went out that
a search dog sniffed out her shallow grave. No trace of her
car.

The autopsy revealed the cause of death as
asphyxiation, and the ribs broken by something swung—a
metal rod or a tire iron—indicated a left-handed killer. Neck
and facial bruises showed Angela was unconscious before

she died, which meant the murderer didn't rush. Sexual abuse, but no semen. No flesh underneath her fingernails, no bloody shoeprints, no tell-tale traces, no muddy tire tracks at the scene to help identify the killer.

"Nothing, dammit," he said in frustration as his phone rang. "East Precinct. Sergeant Whitfield."

"Good afternoon, Sergeant. Chief King here."

"Yes sir," Whitfield said, straightening in his chair. "What can I do for you?"

"You can tell me you've found something to crack the Stone case."

"Sorry sir. There's nothing useful. But that suggests we're dealing with somebody who knows how to cover his tracks."

"Not surprising. What else?"

"Detective Williams rechecked the FBI database for comparisons to other cold case files and ongoing investigations around the South, with no hits. There's a missing connection. I'm going back to the crime scene tomorrow."

"Send somebody else," the chief ordered, "and be in my office at ten a.m."

After leaving the Stones' house, I sped to the paper about one-thirty. I sent a budget line for my story to the weekend editor, wrote a ten-inch website version about Stone's visit to church, and got it posted. I then copied that story, opened a new Word document, and began writing for print. I re-read my notes and listened to the recorder once to make sure I accurately typed a quote. Then I called Reverend Armstrong, apologized for not sticking around after church, and told him the gist of my story.

"I think I've said enough," the reverend said when I asked him about the quote, "but I look forward to reading the article."

Quickly, I filed a twenty-inch story on the day's events, left the paper, drove twenty minutes on I-65 North to pick up Jill in Hendersonville, and turned right around to drive back downtown to Greer Stadium, just ten minutes from the paper. Ordinarily, I'd be ticked, but not on Jill's birthday. She'd been a good sport about my working on a regular day off.

I sat my large beer in the cup holder, stood with Jill, and removed my ball cap as the young woman belted out the national anthem at the Nashville Sounds' Class Triple-A game against the Salt Lake Bees. The paper could find me if news broke or an editor raised questions about the story, and I'd tucked a printout of my story in my pocket.

The Sounds scored two runs in the bottom of the first inning on Eddie Smith's two-out, two-run double, but the right-fielder threw him out at third base trying to stretch it into a triple. The Bees threatened in the top of the third when my phone began vibrating. I couldn't hear because of the loudspeakers and cheers of the fans at the first out. I tapped Jill on the knee. "Be right back. Want anything?" She shook her head.

I left the box seats and flew up the concrete steps two at a time until I reached the concourse. I found a sheltered site and flipped on the phone. The missed call came from the paper, and I dialed the weekend editor.

"David, you rang?"

"Yeah. We got a little tight for space, and I wanted to go over a couple of changes. We'll run your story full on the website."

"Hang on a second," I said and pulled out my printout, reading along as he went over the proposed changes in the copy about halfway down.

"Finally, in that paragraph where the preacher is talking about the sixth commandment, I paraphrased the last part to say that his Sunday message was for all Christians, not just Stone. It picks up with the quote, 'Terrible things happen to good Christians every day.' "

"That's fine, Dave. 'Preciate the call. Anything else?" There wasn't. "Tell Lex to frame that headline. Inspirational," I added, then got in line to buy a couple of small plastic souvenir helmets filled with ice cream. Vanilla for me, chocolate for Jill. They'd reached the top of the fourth inning when I got back to my seat. The Sounds were leading 4-2, but eventually lost 5-4 on a three-run shot in the bottom of the ninth by Boomer Malone.

Delmore Wolfe spent the afternoon in a daze after reading the morning newspaper at the diner. Pushing the cold, tasteless cheeseburger away from him, he rose to pay the bill and took the paper with him back to the motel. He showered and tried watching the game, but his mind kept going back to that blaring headline **Police to Stone: Thou shalt not kill**.

Wolfe tried to write in his journal, but couldn't concentrate. Growing impatient, he tore the front page off the paper, got out his pen, and blacked out the words **Police to** and **not**. That left the headline reading **Stone: Thou shalt kill**.

He flashed an evil smile—*I think I will*—as he slashed a big X through the picture of Stone, marking the crossing diagonal lines over and over until he obliterated Stone's features.

The cackling laugh finally ceased when Wolfe's appetite roared. Pushing six o'clock, he headed downtown for food and some good, country, butt-kicking music.

Wolfe stopped in at a couple of the Printer's Alley lounges and strip clubs before heading down to lower Broadway for a quick stop in Tootsie's Orchid Lounge. The world-famous bar built its reputation in the 1950s and '60s when some Grand Ole Opry members would slip in for a cold one between sets on Friday and Saturday nights at the Ryman Auditorium. He downed a couple of Pabst Blue Ribbons, then wandered into Robert's Western World, once a clothing store converted into a bar that served one of the best burgers in town. Its claim to fame: Helping launch the career of BR549, a band which took its name from an old *Hee-Haw* running gag. That was the telephone number of country comedian Junior Samples' used car dealership.

Wolfe pulled up a stool at the counter and ordered a longneck and a rare cheeseburger. Bobby Ray's Bumpkins were just taking the stage for their first of eight sets that would run until about two in the morning. The new house band completed its soundcheck as Wolfe's food arrived. Before stepping to the mike, Bobby Ray leaned behind an amp and picked up a big tin can which he sat on a stool. Taped to the can, a picture cut out of the newspaper. A sassy Angela Stone on stage at the 2009 CMA Country Music Festival, looking Pure Palomino.

"Don't know if y'all saw the paper the last couple of days, but you probably know that Nashville's Jackson Stone is starting a website to raise money to find the guy who killed his wife Angela," Bobby Ray told the dozen or so tourists seated around the bar/boot store. "Our drummer's wife met Mizzus Stone at the outreach center earlier this year, so we talked it over and thought we'd contribute tonight's tips to this good cause. Hope y'all pony up on the way out."

Wolfe sat there for a minute as the music started, then threw a ten on the counter and left. He'd lost his appetite. He didn't put any money in the tip jar.

After checking with the precinct to see if he could return to his house, Jackson got home about four, unpacked the car, and took the first steps to putting his shattered life back together. Going into the bedroom proved the hardest part. The police had confiscated the sheets and mattress pad for testing, and he saw other signs of disturbance. He vacuumed, made the bed, and put his clothes away, then heated some of the leftovers that Sheila had packed for him.

At five-thirty, he drove across town to Belle Rive Baptist—the church where he grew up, where he found Jesus, got married, developed lifelong friendships—to attend evening services. He didn't expect a repeat of the morning service from the preacher and didn't get another lecture. But the fallout from that sermon continued, pro and con. Everyone spoke to Jackson about his plans, some harshly.

After services, the Keanes and Blakemores cornered Jackson before he could get away.

"How are you?" Mary Keane said. "I mean, really."

"I sure didn't expect Brother Bob to go off on me like that this morning. I'm just going to try to focus on work and help find Angela's killer."

"That's what we wanted to talk to you about," Joan Blakemore said. She opened her purse and handed him five one hundred dollar bills. "This is in memory of Angela."

Surprised by the amount, Jackson accepted it humbly.

"Joan, Wally, it's too generous, but thank you very much."

"Nonsense. We loved Angela and—"

"Don't take it, Jack," Mary Keane interrupted. "That's blood money. You should take to heart what Brother Bob said—Thou shalt not kill. Forget this foolish talk."

Joan turned on her sister, saying she could spend her inheritance how she saw fit. Jackson didn't like being the cause of a squabble, but Wally Blakemore said the sisters wouldn't be happy if they weren't arguing over something.

Their words, the preacher's words, all the opinions of strangers that he saw on Channel 11's ten o'clock newscast kept echoing in his brain that night as he lay in bed. Finally, about midnight, he turned to the power of prayer as a sleep aid.

"Lord, please help me get through the night. I need sleep, God. I need to be able to go to work tomorrow. Oh God, please give me guidance and direction. I'm trying to do the right thing. Please give me a sign. Amen."

Jackson finally slept, dreaming of a wild date with Angela at the long-gone Opryland theme park. They were riding the Screaming Delta Demon roller coaster.

MONDAY, AUGUST 16
1

The bedside alarm began screaming at seven sharp. Jackson jumped up fresh and alert, showered and dressed, turned on the coffee pot and put a couple of slices of bread into the toaster, then went to get the newspaper.

He noticed that both the ad-filled Sunday and the lightweight Monday papers were in the Fletchers' driveway where their cars were parked.

There were no lights on inside the house, but Jackson thought nothing of it. Sarah worked second shift, and Herb remained jobless.

Jackson considered taking the papers to the house and knocking on the door, but he didn't want to be late for work.

Jackson poured coffee and sat at the breakfast table to check the headlines, anxious to read the story about him.

"Oh, Lord." He hadn't foreseen this.

Yes, the veteran advertising executive was both surprised and satisfied with the jaw-dropping coverage he'd generated. It was the "top-trending story" on both TV and the web, and newspaper sales soared.

Former readers who canceled subscriptions because they didn't like the paper's political leanings scrambled to find a copy of Monday's paper. People who discontinued subscriptions because their companies dropped them from the payroll clambered to find a copy of Monday's paper. Online readers caused a near meltdown with hit-after-hit and post-after-post on my article.

Gospel truth: Headline inspires pastor's message

Reverend Armstrong aims
his 'Thou shalt not kill'
sermon squarely at Stone

By GERRY HILLIARD
TenneScene Today

Taking his cue from a headline in Sunday's editions of *TenneScene Today* that referenced the Bible's "Thou shalt not kill" Commandment, popular Belle Rive Baptist pastor Robert Armstrong's sermon delivered an impassioned plea to revenge-minded congregation member Jackson Stone that he heed the Good Book's advice.

Stone, a 45-year-old Nashville advertising executive, made headlines last week when he called a press conference to vow vengeance for the Aug. 3 murder of his wife Angela, 35. Those comments stirred a firestorm of controversy, with some praising him and others—notably Police Chief Wilson King—offering harsh rebukes.

King, in fact, went so far as to call his own media conference just hours after Angela Stone's funeral to denounce Stone's "premeditated plans" and said Stone could face possible jail time if he tried to take the law into his own hands.

That comment led inspired copy editors at *TenneScene Today* to come up with the clever headline—"Police to Stone: Thou shalt not kill." And that headline prompted Reverend Armstrong to toss aside his planned Sunday sermon in favor of a lecture on the Sixth Commandment.

"The Sixth Commandment is very clear on this matter: You shall not murder. There is no ambiguity; it's a straightforward message," Armstrong told about three hundred church-goers—including Stone—who were attending the 11 a.m. service.

Armstrong, who among other things told Stone that he "should turn the other cheek," said he was inspired to switch his sermon because it was a

160

Commandment everyone needs to be reminded of from time to time.

"This message isn't directed at just Jackson Stone," Armstrong said. "I am not singling him out because of his reaction to the tragedy that has befallen his family. It's a message that all of us in the Christian community must embrace. . . . Terrible things happen to good Christians every day."

>>CONTINUED ON PAGE 10A

Stone put down the toast and flipped to the jump. He paid attention to the quotes, trying to remember exactly what he said.

"I loved the headline, but I sure didn't see that (sermon) coming," Stone said in an exclusive interview with *TenneScene Today* after services ended. "But I'm even more determined than ever to find Angela's killer. I anticipated some harsh reaction, that not everyone would agree with or condone what I am trying to do."

Jackson's watch beeped. Time to leave for work. He needed to get his mind off Angela, to regain some semblance of normal, though deep down he knew nothing would ever be normal again.

He turned off the coffee pot after refilling his mug and left the paper on the table. He would finish reading it when he got home.

2

I learned at a young age, on the ballfields of Atlanta, that life is all about competition. Nothing thrilled more than staring down the pitcher and then lining a shot over his head through the gap between the shortstop and second baseman into centerfield to drive in the winning run. And in high school, nothing to this day stung more than seeing East Douglas tailback Robbie Wilcox bolt through our defensive line just out of my reach, break two tackles and sprint into the end zone for the winning touchdown in the Class 3-A championship game. That game still haunts my dreams from time to time.

When I went to Georgia, wanting to be a sports writer since I wasn't a good enough athlete to play at the collegiate level, I discovered how the competition intensity ramped up in the classrooms and within myself. My first two submissions to the student newspaper for my Introduction to Journalism 101 class were so bad that I didn't even recognize them after they were rewritten. I thought of changing majors. I soon improved to the point that I joined the *Red and Black* sports staff.

It's curious how your life can be headed in one direction and change in an instant, or in my case, two instances. That happened for me the first time during my sophomore year during summer sessions. Junior cross-country runner Marcus Dean Jones, whom I got to know through several stories I wrote on his award-winning career, was driving home late one summer night near mountainous Dahlonega, Georgia.

162

Sadly, he fell asleep at the wheel and bounced down an embankment. M.D.'s death wasn't front-page news, but I wanted readers to know what a terrific young man we'd lost. The profile got great reader reaction and soon even more non-sports features came my way.

The second piece, the one that turned me away from sports journalism for good, occurred in my senior year. I'd crashed at my high-rise dorm that cold December night when fire alarms began screaming for us to all get out. False alarm, we thought, until somebody yelled "Fire!" and we all emptied onto the snow-covered lawn. Smoke poured out of a window three floors above my first-floor dorm room. While we stood around and froze, awaiting the arrival of the fire trucks, a window burst out and two coeds shrieked for help. I'd grabbed my notebook and a pen on the way out of my room, but I cast them aside, ran back to my room, yanked the thick bedspread, and scurried outside. Other students grabbed hold, we pulled it tight, we got as close to the building as possible, and shouted for the two scared girls to jump. My first-person account of that harrowing night won first place in the collegiate division of the Georgia Press Awards, and I knew I'd spend my career writing hard news.

The competition I faced growing up barely prepared me for the cutthroat world of modern American journalism, which reached fever pitch with the advent of the Internet and other social networking tools. It put more pressure on old media to get news out faster—but a greater responsibility to first get it right. When you accomplish both, as I did that Monday morning, it's a great rush—nothing like it in the world. After losing so many recent scoops to the electronic media, I slammed a winner, and all the television stations tied for second place. The euphoria wouldn't last long, but I enjoyed it while I could.

I got a round of applause from editors at the nine-thirty news meeting, led by Carrie Sullivan raising her arm for a high-five, which I delivered.

"Ger-reee," she said, grinning. "Man of the hour. Everybody is talking about your story this morning. Did you hear the radio? You're getting a lot of buzz."

I tried to act nonchalant, but I glowed, and it showed.

"Yeah. Some of the calls were pretty funny, the posts, too. Did you see the one about—"

The phone interrupted and Sports Editor Biff Nelson answered, then looked panicked.

"It's Reverend Armstrong," he said, extending the telephone.

I winced and hoped to avoid bad news. I felt certain the preacher wasn't seeking a correction or clarification.

"I enjoyed your article this morning except for one small issue," he said.

"I'm sorry to hear that. I know I didn't misquote you. I recorded the sermon."

Sensing my displeasure, Reverend Armstrong tried to mollify me.

"No, but I would call it a mischaracterization to say your paper's headline *inspired* me. The Lord inspires; the newspaper just reminded me that it would be a well-timed message."

"I see your point, Reverend."

The mood lightened as Armstrong continued. "Like Jack, I also enjoyed the headline. And I thought your article hit just the right tone."

That gave me the opening I needed to steer the conversation in another direction.

"Let's talk about Jack. Is he going all the way on this?"

"Is this on the record?"

"Preferably, but I'd like your insight either way."

"I believe I've said enough for public consumption. It's pretty clear where I stand on this matter. They say revenge is sweet, but Jack is bitter right now. He's not acting like the man I've known the last five years I've been at Belle Rive."

Wow! Ka-ching! Jackpot! What a great quote, if he'd let me use it.

"I think not, Mister Hilliard. I don't want to alienate Jack, just guide him to follow the Lord's teachings as he's always done until now."

"Well, if you change your mind." As I hung up, I hoped no more surprises were in store.

3

Channel 11 editors, writers, directors, and producers squirmed as they awaited Ellie Bligh's arrival for the morning news meeting. At nine o'clock, the feisty station manager burst through the door, and stormed to her seat.

A rolled-up copy of *TenneScene Today* held in her right hand slapped against her left palm with each short stride. *Thwack! Thwack! Thwack! Thwack!* Eyes averted as she stared from person to person, and the newspaper unfurled when she tossed it on the large oak table.

"Did everybody see what we missed? Why wasn't our crew at church Sunday morning? On Friday, didn't we talk about staying on top of this story? Then I pick up this rag to see we got beat on *our* story. Where was Clarkston? Why were we at Centennial Park?"

"Sally's piece wasn't that bad, and you know it," six o'clock news director Sam White said. "Everybody's talking about Stone, but the only public reaction came on blogs and radio talk shows. The paper didn't run that story, did they? Okay, Clarkston took his regular day off. You know corporate's cracking down on us to stick to forty-hour work weeks. He left Sally a list of contacts, and nobody called back, so she went out and dug up something fresh."

"Yeah, but *the* story was in church and *we* got our butts kicked," Bligh said. "We *should* anticipate that story . . . *every* story. *How* do we keep it from happening again?"

Reading between the lines of the morning paper, Clarkston had anticipated a ton of grief from Ellie.

165

His eleven-thirty swing shift began with Sam White again stomping out of Bligh's office, shaking his head.

"Someday," White said, settling into his office chair as Clarkston closed the door and took a seat across from him. "I swear, she's gonna give me a heart attack."

"Good story either way. Film at ten," Clarkston grinned.

"She's not happy with you either. Keep your distance." In his best high-pitched imitation, White squealed, *"Why wasn't Clarkston in church?"* They shared a brief laugh and turned to business. "Seriously, Dan, what's next?"

"I'll call Stone to find out what kind of reaction he's gotten, but it may be a nothing story. Maybe he'll say something about starting up his website. Not sexy stuff."

Clarkston went back to his office, logged on to his computer, and opened his email. The first one to pop up told him the direction of his next Stone story.

> Sent by: Victoria Highsmith. On: 08/16/10 at 7:15 AM
> To: Dan Clarkston
> I am a producer for the *Ed and Tara* show, which airs on your station. We're always looking at hot topics for future shows and at our production meeting, Mr. Warren mentioned a clip on your segment concerning Jackson Stone. After seeing it, Ms. Bradley concurred that Stone's story was the type of story we want to bring to our audience. We hope to get Mr. Stone up to New York for a live appearance with you as the local point man. Getting the first national interview with Mr. Stone would be a feather in our cap. We look forward to working with you.
> Regards, Victoria

Clarkston read it a third time. He'd clear it with Ellie, but if it didn't pan out, it would be good cross-promotion. Another thought unnerved him.

"I bet every show's trying to book Stone. I've got to get to him first."

4

At ten o'clock, Sergeant Mike Whitfield grew impatient outside Chief King's door. He'd arrived at nine-thirty with all his case files. At last, the chief's aide buzzed him in.

"Sergeant, thank you for coming," King said without looking up as he signed documents.

Whitfield surveyed the chief's private office. One wall was covered with photographs of the chief at several stages of his career and with various Music City celebrities, notably George Jones and Garth Brooks. He smiled at the numerous plaques, awards, and commendations King had received.

Whitfield noted that King's desk was as messy as his own, covered with various case reports and paraphernalia. He scanned to his left, and the smile vanished.

Sitting front and center on the desk was a copy of the paper, with the "Gospel truth" headline facing Whitfield. Chief King pointed.

"You saw this?"

"Yes sir. Quite a story. It sounds like the pastor failed to reach him any more than you did. Mister Stone seems very determined."

The chief stared out his window across the Cumberland River toward the Tennessee Titans' football stadium.

"Did you know Stone before this case?"

"Just by reputation. He did some pro bono ad campaigns for the precinct's annual youth league fund-raisers," Whitfield said, uncertain where the interview was headed. The chief didn't call him in to gossip. "I met his wife once. They seemed well suited."

The chief mulled this. The silence made Whitfield twiddle and pick at his nails. When King finally leaned forward on his desk, a sly smile crossed his face.

"So how would you like to be . . . Lieutenant Whitfield? Here's my plan . . . ."

5

Jackson turned on his radio as he backed the car out of the driveway, on his way to work and an eleven o'clock meeting with his boss and old friend, Matthew "Marty" Martin. Preset to NewsTalk 990-AM, the radio blared. Right-wing radio host George Dunkirk hit his stride, taking pot-shots at politicians and breaking down breaking-news topics.

"And I applaud Jackson Stone, who has suffered an immense tragedy, in trying to find his wife's killer," Dunkirk said. "That's what's wrong with this great country. Not enough people out there are willing to do whatever it takes to get these scumbags off the street permanently. Pushed too far, he's pushing back."

Jackson switched to the more liberal-minded Howard Baldwin on Hot 100-FM.

"And what I can't figure out is why Chief King doesn't just go ahead and throw this Stone in jail and throw away the key. He's a menace to society, if you ask me. I sure don't feel safe with him on the streets gunning for who knows who. Do you feel safe, Nashville? Let me know at six one five four two—"

Jackson switched to Golden Oldies 58-FM, dismayed to hear more of the same.

"And I'd like to dedicate the 5th Dimension's 'Stoned Soul Picnic' to Jackson Stone, a great American," the caller said.

"Okay, cat," drive-time deejay Howlin' Bob Smith screamed in his trademark raspy cigarette voice. "Stony, this one's for youuuuu!"

Jackson cut off the radio and drove to work in silence.

Everyone acted sympathetic when Jackson arrived at the office just before nine a.m., but they yammered all day about the controversy he'd stirred. His secretary brought in a pile of mail and messages, not to mention he had backlog of emails to go through after his two-week absence. An hour later, he sighed and returned another call.

"Good morning. The Ellen DeGeneres Show. This is Michelle Albright."

"This is Jackson Stone. I'm returning a call."

The perky voice took on a pleased, but urgent tone.

"Thank you *so* much for calling, Mister Stone. I'm a producer for Ellen, and we've all been reading about your wife's tragic death and your bold stance. We would love to schedule you this week."

"Oprah's people called too. And so did producers from Maury, Leno, Letterman, along with *Today*, *The View*, and *60 Minutes* and all the rest. I'll tell you the same: I'm not yet ready to do a national show. Tell Ellen I would love to be on her show in the future, but things are moving too fast right now. Today's my first day back at work."

"Fine. I'll check back with you in—"

Jackson hung up as new email arrived.

> Sent by: Marty Martin. On: 08/16/10 at 10:38 AM
> To: Jackson Stone
> Welcome Back Kotter! Can you join me in five?

Jackson replied:

> Be right there.

He put on his jacket and walked down the hall. Marty gave him a hug.

"Good to see you. You doin' okay?"

Jackson shrugged. "It's been pretty crazy."

"Yeah, that's what I wanted to discuss. I can't imagine what you're going through, but you've got to know this isn't the kind of PR we need in a tough business climate. I put out fires all weekend, but our clients hate the negative publicity you've generated and how it might affect their products."

Jackson raised an eyebrow—and his voice.

"Are you firing me, Marty? Because on my desk is a stack of messages from producers for Oprah, Doctor Phil, Katie, Ellen, Jay Leno, *60 Minutes*, the *Today* show, all fighting to book me on their shows. I put them all on hold for now. But hey." He shrugged.

They talked several more minutes without any clear-cut understanding and agreed to meet again after lunch.

Two hours later, an impasse still existed, and the meeting ended on a sour note. Marty remained convinced that clients would start bailing if Jackson stayed on the front page much longer. Marty didn't want to fire his best friend, but felt he might be forced into it and cussed Jackson for putting him in that position.

"All I'm saying is just cool it for a while. Let all this die down. Otherwise . . . the firm might have to distance itself," Marty blurted, embarrassed.

Red-faced Jackson stood his ground, determined to find Angela's killer before the cops.

"I'm sorry you feel that way. I'm not quitting. My job or my search."

They decided to talk again the following morning, and Jackson left for home. He'd hoped returning to work might restore some sense of normalcy, but no.

Driving with the air conditioning on high calmed him.

The more Jackson thought about it, the more leaving the firm appealed. He'd go hunting.

6

Sheila Stone woke up early with the kids, fixed them breakfast and waited until nine to call Doctor Karnoff's office. Sheila explained that the appointment wasn't for her, but her brother-in-law, who made a big splash in the newspaper and on television over the weekend.

"You mean Jackson Stone?" The polite receptionist had overheard Doctor Karnoff talking about him, and knew she would love to sit down with him and peer into his mind.

The receptionist informed her that the doctor wasn't accepting new patients.

"Well, I'm sorry to hear that," Sheila said. "Perhaps you or the doctor could recommend—"

"Tell you what. Let me pass this information along, Mrs. Stone. That's the best I can do," the receptionist said.

At ten fifty, Erica Karnoff called, cordial, but obviously excited at this opportunity.

"I would be happy to talk with Jackson. I understand your concerns, and normally, we would not be having this conversation, but I recognize this is an extremely unusual case. All I know is what I've seen and read in the media."

They chatted several minutes, then Karnoff said she must get to class and wondered if Mrs. Stone could bring Jackson in Tuesday about two thirty.

"Thank you ever so much, Doctor," Sheila said, relieved. "He'll be there."

Getting Jackson to the appointment would take some ingenuity. A woman's touch.

172

Sheila called him about three.

"Hi, Jack, I wonder … can you give me a ride to Vandy tomorrow afternoon? Say about two? I've got a doctor's appointment."

"I'd love to, but—"

"Great, I really 'preciate it. Patrick put my car in the shop, and he'll be in Lebanon. If not for you, I'd have to rent a car because I'm not about to call a cab or take a bus or—"

"Fine," Jackson said, cutting her off. "I'll be there unless something comes up. See you then unless you want to go to lunch first."

"I can't. The appointment should take about an hour, and you'll have to wait unless I can get Janie to pick me up."

Jackson assured her he could do this for her after all she'd done for him. Sheila got a little teary-eyed for lying to Jack. But he needed to talk to somebody, and she hoped Doctor Karnoff could help.

About that same time, Sheila wasn't the only person close to Jackson Stone discussing him with a third party. Reverend Armstrong returned to his office after having visited three Nashville hospitals and two nursing homes. The church secretary had left several messages at his desk.

The last came from Mark St. John at *The Witness*, the Baptist bi-monthly publication circulated nationally and in fifty-four countries.

Curious, he dialed the main number, and got transferred to St. John, a senior writer and editor.

"We've read about you, and your ministry to Jackson Stone," St. John said. "We'd like to interview you on the subject of owning and carrying a gun versus the stance you've taken in church. You delivered a *powerful* message Sunday, and the gun control issue is a divisive subject among church members, pitting those who want guns for personal protection and the Biblical message you presented."

Erica Karnoff looked forward to the session with Jackson Stone. She finished up her final class at five and stopped by her office before heading home. She sat down

173

and punched in the cell phone number of her New York agent, Katherine Robinson, who often worked late. The call went to voicemail so Erica left a message that she expected to be returned as soon as the agent heard it.

"Katherine? It's Erica. Listen, I've thought it over and I believe I can do that next book you wanted after all. How much were we talking about? Give me a call. Ciao."

Erica was working her way through her inbox when the telephone rang. She recognized the number and smiled.

"You've just made my day," Katherine said. "Tell me all about your next bestseller."

Erica laughed, but struck a serious tone.

"There's a fascinating story developing in Nashville. I must get clearance, but have you heard of Jackson Stone?"

7

Monday went fast for all except Delmore Wolfe, who slept till noon. On his last trip past Stone's house in East Nashville, he'd spotted a coffeehouse he wanted to check out. His head pounded like a bongo drum, and he needed a caffeine fix, as well as some other stimulants, to get through the day. Wolfe made the short drive over, ordered a dark roast coffee and rare roast beef sandwich.

While waiting for his order, Wolfe surveyed the mostly empty seating area. A middle-aged woman picked at her salad as her husband read the newspaper. When Wolfe saw the "Gospel truth" headline over the guy's shoulder, he clenched his teeth to keep control.

His order came, As the couple got up to leave, Wolfe leaned toward the man with the folded newspaper.

"Can I look at that, if you're done?"

It was more statement than question. The paper stayed.

Wolfe didn't like what he read, not one bit. All his past crimes generated much media coverage, but none like this. All because of those whiny, pitiful cries for retribution—"I don't waaant justice, I waaant revenge."

"Stuff happens, dude," Wolfe said to no one but himself as he took the newspaper with him and drove back to his room. He decided to hole up for the day and catch up on his journal, writing down all these feelings and more. He might get out after he saw the news.

Wolfe unlocked two suitcases filled with his collection of rambling journals, detailing his transformation from a kid with a mean streak into the rage-filled monster whose diaries

175

would mark a trail of unsolved homicides across the South. They would later enthrall FBI profilers who had failed to connect the dots to the murders he claimed.

He never knew his parents, drug-abusers who met in high school in Tupelo, Mississippi, the birthplace of Elvis Presley, the "king of rock 'n' roll." When Wolfe's journals came to public light, some pundits referred to him as the "king of rot in hell." The nickname stuck.

Relatives took in Wolfe, raising him on a farm in northeastern Arkansas, near Memphis. His earliest victims were field mice and other barn pests. Wolfe not only liked killing things, he excelled at it. But when he started torturing the cats and "accidentally" killed the family dog, Delmore's life changed forever. In one of his earliest journal entries. Wolfe wrote:

"Ole Harry's gonna pay for that someday. The mark of the beast is upon me and this Wolfe will bite back."

Apparently, Uncle Harry gave him a horrific beating to show him how it felt, leaving nasty scars on his back and butt and uglier scars on his soul. Aunt Vera ignored it, not saying a word and didn't take him to the hospital to treat a fractured arm and likely head injury. Wolfe needed three months to recover physically, but never recovered mentally.

On the one-year anniversary of his horrific beating, a farming "accident" claimed the lives of Aunt Vera and Uncle Harry. At age thirteen, he went to live with his maternal grandmother. Wolfe wrote little about that four-year span, but unearthed clues indicate a period even more torturous than his childhood. He lived off the inheritance after his grandmother's "accident" and drifted through the South unnoticed because he didn't need a job. When he worked, it consisted of menial labor, skills picked up from his uncle on the farm. He wanted cash, which employers also preferred. He acquired several drivers licenses, none in his true name, paid no taxes, and had no criminal record.

The monster became the invisible man.

8

It was pushing four o'clock, and I hoped to accomplish something before calling it a day. Like Channel 11's Dan Clarkston, I considered the next twist in this bizarre story. Nobody returned calls, and Jackson must've gone into hiding. His secretary said he'd just left for lunch the first time I called. Not yet back the second time I called. Finally, after the fifth time I called, the exasperated but courteous secretary said Mister Stone wasn't expected back until Tuesday morning. About to tell my editor of no new news, a ding alerted me to new email. Instead, I messaged that I'd file a short story, or at least a local note, involving Stone. Police spokesman Darrin Jensen sent a terse press release to several of us at the paper, plus Clarkston and other media outlets. It raised several questions—but not the right ones:

> The Metro Nashville Police Department today indefinitely suspended with pay Sergeant Mike Whitfield of the East Precinct, pending an internal investigation.
>
> "Our highest standards must be met, or the public will lose confidence in our ability to protect and serve," Chief Wilson King said. "Sergeant Whitfield has an outstanding reputation in the community and has been instrumental in solving a number of major crimes to make Nashville a safer place to live, and that is why I am disappointed to make this announcement. But I expect Sergeant Whitfield

to be back on the streets soon and that he will
be able to put this behind him."

The email cited Whitfield's years of service, awards, and accomplishments and said his current duties on the Stone investigation would be shared by several other officers. I immediately called Jensen for an explanation.

"Everybody's being kinda hush-hush, and you can't use this," Jensen said. "Mike has a bit of a drinking problem that got out of hand at home and his wife called his supervisor. He goes into treatment tomorrow."

Hanging up, I muttered, "That seems out of character for the Mike Whitfield I know."

At Channel 11, Clarkston's day mirrored mine, accomplishing little. After a series of meetings with editors, directors, station management, and telephone calls to New York, Clarkston got word that both he and videographer Greg Pittard would work with *Ed and Tara*, provided that any footage shot appeared on Channel 11 at least twenty-four hours in advance. In exchange, the station would receive on-air credit for its aid in the story. Clarkston spoke with Tara Bradley, who thanked him for agreeing to help and said she looked forward to working with him. Now to convince Stone to do his first national interview on *Ed and Tara*. Clarkston felt that would be no problem. He called Jackson's office, and an irate secretary lit into him. Clarkston's first call came after my five.

"I don't know where Mister Stone is or when he'll be back," she said. "It won't be today. Please don't call again."

Clarkston ran with the story. If Jackson saw the six o'clock newscast, he would learn of the offer that way. A two-minute rehearsal primed Clarkston. "Channel 11 has learned that the syndicated *Ed and Tara* show hopes to land the first national interview with Jackson Stone for an upcoming segment," Clarkston said, then swiveled to camera two. "There's no word yet on when the segment would air on this station."

After wrapping up the rehearsal with a recap of the story to date, Clarkston went back to his desk before they went live and looked at his email for any late news tips. In his inbox, the same note about Sergeant Whitfield arrived. Like me, Clarkston called the police spokesman and learned off the record about Whitfield's alleged drinking problem. At the end of the live telecast Clarkston turned back to camera one.

"And in an unrelated development, an officer working on the Stone investigation has been indefinitely suspended for a violation of the department's personal conduct policy."

The subject of that late-breaking report, Sergeant Mike Whitfield, drove back to the East Precinct after his downtown meeting with Chief King, cleared his desk, and packed up personal items in his locker. Like wildfire, word filtered through the station grapevine that Whitfield drew a two-week suspension for getting drunk and getting physical with his wife. Officer Mendez came by, and Whitfield confirmed the time off to deal with "a personal issue." They shook hands and Whitfield left for his Antioch home. He wanted to explain to his wife before it made the news, but Interstate 24 was backed up almost to downtown, because of an accident. He tried to call, but his battery was running low.

Marti Whitfield heard the garage door open and ran to greet her husband, tears running down her face. She flew into his arms.

"What is going on? I just saw on the news that you'd been suspended."

"Shhhh," he said, smiling at her concern as he wiped away a tear. "Let me explain, then I'm taking you to dinner."

9

Jackson parked outside Eddie Paul's Pub and entered the ancient watering hole, hoping to re-establish some of his old routines. He waved to several drinking buddies. Louie, the bartender, nodded as Jackson approached the bar.

"Good to seeya. I didn't know if you'd be back since you and Angela spent so much time here."

Jackson wondered, too, if he'd ever return until after the unnerving series of meetings with Marty at the office. Had his "mission" jeopardized his career? With much to think about, Jackson needed a drink. He wasn't ready to lay all this on Patrick yet. Maybe he'd pick Louie's brain. He smiled at the bartender, knowing he'd listen to his troubles.

"Think I'm going crazy. This is like a second home to me. It might become my permanent home," Jackson said as Louie handed him a beer. Jackson rolled the sweaty bottle in his hands and contemplated his future. "I might crawl in this bottle and never come out."

Jackson didn't hear the concern in Louie's voice when he said, "C'mon, Jack, don't talk like that." He moved to "Angela's booth" and tuned out his surroundings, the world.

He and Angela had spent so many hours here over the years that it did indeed give him a sense of security. Following that 1995 fund-raiser for one of Al Gore's projects, they worked on his unsuccessful 2000 presidential campaign, hammering out many details over drinks at the pub. The laughs at Eddie Paul's poured like the beer, booze, and wine. Jackson had brought friends, family, and clients to the neighborhood eatery; they'd cheered at the annual Super

Bowl party and other major sporting events; they gathered for wakes for friends who passed, for wedding receptions, for young couples just starting out, and for holidays and birthdays.

Louie brought a second beer. Friends kept coming over for a few minutes to express sorrow, then moved to another table after Jackson choked up or retold a story about Angela for the second or third time. He sat alone, sipping his third beer when a promo for the six o'clock news caught his attention. His picture was being shown on the big-screen television, but Jackson couldn't hear the report over the 1970's rock music playing on the sound system.

"Hey, Louie, turn that up."

The barkeep complied. "Coming up on the six o'clock report," co-anchor Cameron Knight said, "which starts right now."

After reports on a possible Metro tax increase and an apartment fire in the Hermitage area that displaced three families and injured a fireman, the news anchor introduced Clarkston's next piece. Jackson watched without comment. He didn't remember getting a message or talking to anyone from that show. His interest perked up when the segment ended with Clarkston's late-breaking add-on about the suspension of one of the cops working his wife's case.

"That's going to slow down the investigation. Bad for them, good for me," Jackson told Louie, who turned the music back up.

As Jackson headed for the bathroom, he wondered what the cop did.

When he returned, he got his final surprise of the night. He could ask the cop in person why he'd been suspended.

Being seated two tables away were Sergeant Whitfield and his wife.

Jackson re-introduced himself, not surprising the policeman in the least. In planning a run-in with Jackson, Mike had asked around and learned of his affinity for the pub. He figured Jackson would show up there eventually.

"Come sit with us," Whitfield said, introducing Marti.

"Sure I'm not interrupting?" Jackson asked, not wanting to let on what he'd just seen on television.

Whitfield laughed, and Marti flashed a weak smile. "Nah. You didn't hear this from me, but I'm off duty tomorrow. And a few days after that."

As he retrieved his beer from the bar, Jackson silently reflected that he might also be off duty tomorrow. And a few days after that.

The evening's major shocks were over for hunter Jackson. But not for the hunted Wolfe.

He thought about trying to tail the TV reporter again because he saw the six o'clock report about Stone being sought for a national talk show. Agitated by that revelation, Wolfe felt better after seeing the segment about the cop getting suspended.

One thing that kept Delmore Wolfe from being caught all these years was that he learned all he could about potential adversaries. Once he saw a policeman's name in the paper he found out everything he could about who might be hunting him. He would go to the library and read local papers about their past cases, their successes and failures, and tried to think like they did to stay a step ahead. So far, that paranoid strategy had worked.

Instead of going after Clarkston, he decided to check out his true quarry in East Nashville.

He drove past the Stone and Fletcher houses—all quiet and no lights on at either house. "No bodies home. Stop, yer killin' them," the comedian later wrote in his journal.

As Wolfe cruised around East Nashville, a series of powerful growls rumbled through his stomach. He pulled into the tavern's packed parking lot and went inside.

He never liked being startled, not since that little jerk back in high school—he forgot his name but remembered the twerp never tried that again—snuck up behind him and pushed him down the hill. Wolfe straightened him out good that day and—Rudy, yeah, that pint-sized pissant—Rudy exhibited the scars, mental and physical, to prove it.

But Wolfe received one of the most unexpected astonishments of his young, twisted life at the popular but quaint restaurant called Eddie Paul's Pub.

He went straight to the bar, ordered a scotch on the rocks, and asked for a menu. He swiveled around and saw Jackson Stone sitting at a table about a dozen feet away, talking to a young blond-haired couple. He didn't know either person, but studied them. The guy looked familiar, but he couldn't place the face. Then it dawned on him—*what's he doing here talking to him?*

Wolfe downed his drink, left a ten on the bar, and left as quickly as possible without making a scene. Deep in conversation, neither Jackson nor Mike Whitfield noticed Wolfe or saw him exit the building.

But the security cameras did.

TUESDAY, AUGUST 17

1

The insistent alarm clock made his head throb harder. It felt like it took forever to crawl from the bed and stagger across the room to shut it off. Yawning, Jackson made coffee, and took a Goody's powder to fight off the hangover. He flipped on the TV and slumped on the couch, rubbing his face and trying to remember last night. "How many beers did I have?"

It took him a few minutes to remember how he got home. Oh yeah, Mike and his wife followed after he insisted on driving his car.

"He probably would have given me a DUI if he still wore his badge. He's all right," Jackson mumbled.

Because of his cover-story suspension, Whitfield had asked Jackson to call him Mike and not sergeant. They'd talked for hours at the bar, and it got plenty deep.

Jackson learned where the investigation stood, and about the lack of physical evidence. They chatted about why Jackson went to the media like that, where he thought he might find Angela's killer, and what Jackson would do to the murderer if and when he found him. Perhaps because of the beer, Jackson found himself opening up to Mike. He said he'd start by cutting the guy's heart out. Mike said he should start lower, a non-chemical castration with a straight-edged razor. Jackson laughed and said he would hold him down if Mike would do it. When Marti shivered and said to cut it out, Mike laughed and said that's just what they'd do. Jackson snorted so hard, beer spewed down his chin.

They talked about the suspension. Mike admitted plans to check into rehab for a week and wanted a night out with his wife before then. Jackson said to let him know how it went because he'd started thinking he might face similar issues. They cussed and discussed Chief King and why he came down so hard on Jack. Mike said the chief didn't make the laws, just enforced them. Jackson understood, but could live with prison time if it meant Angela's killer died.

But the conversation didn't run as deep as Mike believed at the time.

They argued the morality and ethical issues of Jackson's quest, and the more they debated it, the more suspicious he became of Mike's motives. Jackson had just ordered his fourth beer, but he was never thinking more clearly.

Mike might be on suspension, but he was still a cop. And he was asking a lot of questions, Jackson thought.

When it turned into a verbal sparring match, Jackson decided to employ the rope-a-dope tactics used with such great effectiveness by Muhammad Ali in his 1974 "Rumble in the Jungle" match against George Foreman. In the ring, the strategy was to let the opponent come out swinging and tire himself out by either missing or landing ineffective punches. Jackson's plan was to dodge and weave, and maybe win over the policeman.

Mike fired the first shot. Right between the eyes.

"So if you find this guy and carry out . . . whatever . . . do you think you'll go to hell for this?"

Jackson squirmed, and hoped he wouldn't be the one to come off looking like the dope, but decided the best way to keep investigators from learning his true motives was to respond with part truth and part what they expected to hear.

And a shoulder shrug.

"I'll beg God's forgiveness and pray I'm with Angela for the rest of eternity."

"Instead of begging God's forgiveness for hunting down another man, perhaps you should listen to Reverend Armstrong and forgive your wife's killer."

186

Jackson shook his head. "I only hope God forgives me, but I won't do that. I just can't. How horrible do I sound? I know I'm not setting a proper example of a Christian, but I've got to do this. I'm doing the right thing for me."

"Are you hearing yourself? Ex-Marines should know when to stand down. This is one of those times. Hopefully, my suspension will be over soon, and I'll be back on the case. Tell you what, if you stop acting so loopy, I'll keep you in the loop till we find this guy. We will get him."

"Not if I find him first. There won't be anything left to find."

"That's a heavy load, all that hate you're carrying."

Mike paused, took a swig and switched tactics.

"Have you directed any of that anger toward God for taking Angela from you? Do you blame God for anything?"

Jackson gave an emphatic "no" head-shake. "Let me amend that. Of course I've been angry, but it's because I don't know or understand God's plan for Angela . . . or me. I just know things do happen for reasons we can't comprehend. And they happen on God's timetable, not ours.

"We're all here for a finite time before moving on to our eternal home. My best friend, same age, twenty pounds less than me, a runner, died last year of a stroke. Why him? Why not me? My parents died in the 1998 tornado that roared through Nashville. They were planning a trip to Miami that April, but decided to delay it a week because mom wasn't feeling well. If they'd gone to the beach as planned, they might still be here today. We had an accident one time when a kid ran a red light. If we'd been at the intersection five seconds earlier, or five minutes later, we'd have avoided that mishap. Or he might have been five minutes later, and the crash still would have happened.

"Do I blame God for any of those incidents? Was that fate, or destiny? Was it coincidence? Just plain bad timing? I don't know."

Jackson was sitting on the edge of his chair, and both Mike and Marti were amazed by the change that had come over him in the last few minutes.

"Am I saying that God had a plan in place for Angela's time to be up and the means of her death? Absolutely not," Jackson said. "That would be falling into the blame-game trap. I admit I don't have answers, but I have faith. I accept what happened to Angela."

"If you accept that," Mike said, "why can't you accept your preacher's message? You know . . . those parts about 'thou shalt not kill,' and 'vengeance is mine saith the Lord.' You heard that, didn't you? Preacher to Jack. Come in, Jack. Roger that, Jack."

Everyone laughed, a break in the building tension. But Jackson turned serious again.

"All I can tell you is that I feel so strongly, as strong as I have ever felt about anything, that I'm doing what I'm supposed to be doing. I accept Angela's death, and I accept that I am destined to play a key role in catching and punishing Angela's killer."

"Maybe so, maybe so," Mike said. "Whatever happens, I hope someone's watching out for you. Or over you." He paused. "Do you believe in guardian angels?"

"Yes. Mine is named Angela."

Mike smiled, and ordered another round.

Like Stone, others were having trouble getting going that morning. Chief Wilson King rose before dawn, as usual. But instead of putting on his uniform and fighting West End traffic to go downtown to work, King donned a lightweight jogging suit that would get rid of the excessive sweat that poured off his large frame and laced up his size 18EEEE running shoes. He headed for the new public park in Antioch on the southeast side of Nashville near Percy Priest Lake. The first golden rays of the morning sun showed few people out using the jogging trail. King stretched his calf muscles as he watched the runner approach, rounding the last curve before hitting the front straightaway. King studied the man coming at him. There was something different about him, about the way the sun glistened off this guy's hair. The familiar build, but a shock of brown hair, a dark, bushy mustache, and he wore darkened glasses.

2

Up early myself, I flipped through the paper as I stirred creamer into my coffee. My twelve-inch bylined story on Whitfield's suspension had been whittled into a four-inch lead item that topped the local briefs package on page 5B. I skimmed the national news, read the editorials, and then the comics. I saved the sports section for last, a habit developed as a teenager when playing high school football, basketball, and baseball.

The new K-Cup Kona coffee I selected hit the spot, and I reminded myself to ask Jill to get that assortment pack again. I took another sip and turned on my laptop, clicking onto the paper's website, then clicked on local briefs. There were eight comments.

At 6:10 a.m., GOOBERS wrote: "They'll never catch Angela's killer now. This Sergeant Whitfield was supposed to be the finest of Nashville's finest."

At 6:22 a.m., SNITCH wrote: "The sarge is a lush. My brother's friend has a pal whose uncle knows a cop who works out of that precinct and he says Whitfeld goes into rehab today, that he got caught drinking on the job and failed a breath test."

Horrified, I didn't bother reading the rest. Instead I picked up the telephone and called the office. The receptionist transferred me to online, but nobody, no answer. They didn't get in until eight o'clock. I cursed and left a message. That is what's wrong with this system, as message board posters can say anything, whether inaccurate, a half-truth, or a half-lie.

"This is Gerry Hilliard in news. I'm calling from home at seven-thirty. I'm leaving now, but as soon as someone gets this, please take down a comment from Snitch on the local news section. The headline says 'Metro suspends veteran policeman.' It contains potentially libelous information that could get us sued."

I dressed and prepared to head out the door, when Jill got up for a kiss 'bye.

"I made your coffee," I said. "It's waiting by the paper. I'll try to be home by five unless something comes up."

I turned on NewsTalk 990-AM to hear who George Dunkirk would skewer that morning. I'd met Dunkirk on several occasions since the right-wing radio talk-show host began writing a semi-regular column for *TenneScene Today*. Even though we disagreed politically, I got along well with George. The "bump music" lowered as his pounding voice crackled.

"We're dedicating this morning's show to Nashville advertising executive and recent widower Jackson Stone, whom many of you are now calling Stony, thanks to Howlin' Bob over at our sister station," Dunkirk said. "Our crack research team uncovered a few details about Stony's sparkling service record for our glorious country, and I'll bring on a special guest who will tell us why he thinks Jackson Stone *will* track down his wife's murderer. So if you're listening out there, Stony, give us a call. We would love to talk with you. We'll be right back on the B-I-G network."

Jackson got in his car and turned on the radio, preset to 990-AM. Backing out of his driveway when Dunkirk's voice came up after the break, he hit the brakes and listened for a minute, then drove to work in another daze. If not so distracted, he might've noticed the newspapers really starting to pile up on the driveway next door.

Dunkirk boasted the Nashville morning drive-time's top-rated show, so Jackson, myself and thousands of others listened, enthralled by every twist and turn in the murder investigation.

Not gonna be much fun at work, Clarkston thought as he drove to the television station. Telephone lines lit up at the radio station. Attorney Stan Allenby shook his head while he sat in line at the gas station, wondering if his client and friend would wind up in jail. Marty Martin almost wrecked as he drove past the power station, wondering if he'd ever really known Stone.

The commercial ended and Dunkirk came back on the air. Jackson smiled as he recognized the familiar, one-of-a-kind accent of his old "country cuz" war buddy from Lynchburg, Tennessee. Jimmy 'Big Red' Boyle possessed such a distinctive Southern drawl that Jackson often joked Red was the only person he knew who turned a one-syllable word like "Jack" into a three-syllable cadence that came out something like "Juh-aihh-uck." Even to life-long Tennesseans, the country accent tortured ears at first, then it just fit Big Red, whose shaggy hair might best be described as copper-colored. After a few minutes, listeners warmed up to his Tennessee twang inflections.

"We're talking this morning with Jimmy 'Big Red' Boyle, who served in the Marines during the Gulf War in the 1990s," said Dunkirk. "I want to read you an email that Jimmy posted over the weekend at our B-I-G sister station, Classic Country 750-AM. I quote, Jack Stone is a great American. I was stationed with him in Kuwait in 1990-91 and he saved my life. Too bad he couldn't save his wife. If he'd been there, the killer wouldn't have had a chance. Jack, if you see this, remember that you can call on Big Red for anything, partner. I owe you one, buddy. Unquote.

"Jimmy . . . I'm just going to call you Big Red . . . you need to work on your spelling, but I think we all get the gist of your message. Like so many others, I am fascinated by this public war that your old friend Jackson declared against his wife's murderer. Based on your personal experiences, what makes you certain he'll avenge his wife?"

"Shu-ucks, Muh-isst-uhr Dunkirk, I would not be here talking to you today if it wasn't for Jack. He sure saved my

life over there, just like I wrote. I never expected to talk
about him with you, though. I listen every morning, and it's
a real honor. Could you sign a picture for Big Red and send
it to me after we're finished talkin'?"

I laughed as I drove. Like most TV/radio personalities,
George scarfed up the compliments the same way he
devoured those little square Krystal burgers—by the sack
full. But he did come across the radio sounding humbled.

"The honor is all mine, sir," George said. "And thank
you for your service to our wonderful country. My secretary
here at B-I-G headquarters will send out a photo this very
afternoon. But let's talk about Jack. It's quite a tale, I'm told,
and all of our listeners would like to get to know Mister
Stone better."

For the next five minutes, Big Red's recollections and
the warm sunlight streaming through the car windows did a
number on Jackson as he drove toward work. His mind
wandered as reflections from the sun-splashed car in front of
him took Jackson's mind off present problems to the life-
and-death ones they faced together in January 1991.

Their Marine unit hit the ground just outside of
Rybadashi that morning during Op Payback. Seventeen U.S.
sailors died aboard the USS *Roughrider* when it struck a
mine and drew fire from an Iraqi warship. *Roughrider*
responded by blowing the Iraqi gunboat out of the water
while U.S. missiles shot down two Iraqi jets. Bunkered Iraqi
forces faced relentless shelling by two other aircraft carriers
patrolling the Gulf.

Saddam's Red Brigade tried to stem the tide of
advancing forces by conducting an all-out assault that would
push the ever-growing coalition forces out of his claimed
lands. It would fail, but not before more U.S. and Coalition
lives were lost. Big Red and Jackson were almost part of
those casualties. Tank shells sent bodies flying, and Greek
General Calathis was one of the first losses. Then the ground
surge began and the Coalition forces stemmed the Red
Brigade tide.

Jackson flashed a grim smirk as he drove across Victory Memorial Bridge into downtown, recalling how he and Big Red got trapped behind the advancing Iraqi forces after everyone else fell back. The Iraqis took them prisoners, and wanted information, and wanted it quickly. That meant inflicting inhumane, unbearable torture to learn what they could. Jackson blamed himself for their getting caught. With some of his men pinned down, he refused to fall back when the order came, and Big Red stuck by his side. His men escaped to safety, but not he and Red.

Fortunately, they were held at an advance outpost, well ahead of the Iraqis' main surge, and there were just three guards and their inquisitor.

"So," Jackson whispered to Red, "if we get out of this, we can get back to our guys. If we can't, I'll see to it they don't get anything out of us." Red nodded grim approval.

Jackson expected to die that day, by his own hand if necessary, and often dwelled on the incident. Once you've stared down death, life's other problems seem easy.

The torture session began with drugs pumped into Big Red's body, but he fainted during the savage first beatings. The Red Brigade captain wanted information about the size of the Coalition forces, their positions, and ordnances the Iraqis faced. The Red Brigade captain knew that such information lay not in the head of Corporal James Collier Boyle, but felt certain that Second Lieutenant Jackson Lee Stone, serial number nine-one-eight-one-four-three-zero-zero-zero-seven-five-five, held such key data. The guards made Jackson watch, expecting his tongue to loosen from the fear of seeing what would happen to him if he didn't talk. But they underestimated both Jackson and Big Red. They were Tennessee tough.

"Oooof."

The whooshing escape of air from Red's lungs was followed by a series of harsh, weakening coughs. The largest Red Brigade guard again had buried his large fist deep in Red's gut as Jackson watched unblinking, trying to maintain a stoic composure. The following series of forceful, back-handed slaps flushed Red's cheeks brighter than his close-cropped hair, then the guard paused and looked questioningly at his captain.

"Why do you let this continue? Tell us what we want to know. What are your orders? To where do your ground troops head?"

The captain directed his interrogations at Jackson, not Red. A lick of parched lips was the only sign that Jackson heard the questions. Eyes front, he watched the guard resume wailing on helpless Red. He smashed at his ribs, chin, and kidneys, then moved behind Red and brought mammoth forearms down on his collarbones.

"Yiiieee—"

Red had gritted his way through the first series of blows, but the bolt of pain that shot from his shoulders to his toes elicited a scream of agony and then silence as Red fainted. The captain smiled as Jackson stared in horror, hoping Red's bones weren't broken. The captain didn't care about breaking Red's bones; he intended to break Jackson's spirit.

"You can spare your friend . . . and yourself . . . further pain by telling me all you know," the bearded Red Brigade captain growled in broken English, through broken teeth.

Jackson shook his head, and the captain snarled. "Oh, you'll talk, my friend."

The guards revived Big Red with a bucket of water so he could watch Jackson's brutal lashing. Jackson took it all. His jaw purpled and swelled from the guard's heavy, well-timed series of punches. Jackson tried rolling with the deliberate, overhand blows, but being strapped into a chair he could soften them just so much. Blackness, thankfully, descended . . .

. . . "ohohgodhohnoooOOOOOGODNOOOOOOO!"

The ever-increasing, blood-curdling scream lifted Jackson from the muffled veil of darkness. Jackson recovered full consciousness in time to witness the end of the second round of torture. Red's left hand remained

194

wrapped in bloody bandages, the index finger taken off at the second knuckle on the table in front of him.

Red blubbered, shaking spasmodically. Large beads of sweat, mixed with tears, ran down his face. One drop fell from his nose and he glared defiantly at the guard.

"You . . . I swear you'll pay—"

The guard smiled through yellowed teeth. And brought his flattened palm down on Red's gauze-wrapped hand.

The agonized screams disturbed Jackson most as the bearded Red Brigade captain and his guard turned their attention to him.

"See, my friend, what happens if you don't talk? Spare yourself—and your friend's other fingers—and tell us what we want to know." A defiant Jackson never got a chance to answer, spitting blood as he took another beating from the angry, powerful guard who enjoyed punishing the American pigs. Jackson's awareness of pain ended when he passed out again, but it didn't halt the beating . . .

. . . Darkness approached when Jackson came to, and the Iraqis celebrated a forward push. Jackson's father had taught him well, first as the troop leader in the Boy Scouts and then as his position coach on the Hillsboro High School football team. So Jackson steeled himself for the challenge ahead. Strip-searched, of course, but Jackson didn't need a weapon to deal with the likes of these, he decided. It would be over tonight one way or another.

Two huge guards came to take Jackson for another torture session, and when the first one pulled Jackson to his feet, he used the momentum to spring into the second guard. The element of surprise and anticipating his opponent's reactions served him well. Two clubbing blows loosened the second guard's rifle grip so that Jackson could grab hold of the gun and flip the stunned guard into the first one as he brought his weapon to bear on Jackson. A sharp chop with the gun butt broke the first guard's neck. Jackson then swung the rifle like a 44-inch baseball bat and cracked it against the second guard's head.

Jackson took one dead guard's long knife and stealthily approached the front of the tent. A glance through the flap sent a surge of adrenaline through his body. Jackson sprang into action. Big Red, being tortured by the other two Iraqis, caught a hazy glimpse of the heavy fist flying directly at the bridge of his nose. It never connected, and the blood that spattered Red's uniform wasn't his own.

"Git 'em, Jack!"

Just like gutting a deer. In less than five seconds, two more members of the Red Brigade were dead, the knife buried to the hilt in the captain's chest. Jack pulled out the knife and sliced through Red's bonds. Red struggled to his feet and rubbed gingerly at the left hand with the severed finger as Jackson checked to see if any of their captors had heard the scrap. All clear.

"C'mon, buddy, we've still got a long way to go before we're safe."

"One second," Red said, taking the knife from Jackson.

Big Red turned and hacked the left index finger off his chief assailant, blood again spurting and turning the canvas tent floor wet red.

"An eye for an eye and a finger for a finger," Red said, flashing a wicked grin that Jackson returned. "Now let's go."

Jackson took the captain's Soviet-made Tokarev .30-caliber sidearm, and they escaped under cover of darkness, walking fifteen miles in the desert as U.S. bombs pounded Iraqi positions. Clearly, the Red Brigade had bigger problems than the escaped Americans. Jackson buried the gun a mile from base camp for later retrieval.

Jackson wheeled his car into the company parking lot as the memories faded, and Marty pulled in at the same time, glancing at Stone before entering the building. Jackson listened a few minutes longer. Dunkirk thanked Big Red for coming on the show. Red assured him he'd be proud to take orders from his old Marine platoon commander.

"I would do anything for Jack," he said. "*Anything!* You listening, Jack?"

Jackson was.

And so was Dan Clarkston, almost to the station when he made a sharp U-turn and headed up Franklin Road back toward the SoBro downtown district. Fascinated by Dunkirk's interview, Clarkston kicked himself for not having tracked Boyle down beforehand. On the seat beside him, a story dated 2001 that mentioned both Boyle and Stone attending a ten-year reunion of Gulf War veterans at the ornate, five-star Hermitage Hotel.

The radio interview ran five minutes, and Boyle expounded on how Jackson had saved his life during the Gulf War and staged their escape. Maybe Jackson would fill in some gaps in the story if he ever returned a call or answered email from Dan.

"We're going to a break, folks," Dunkirk's voice came over the radio, "but don't cut away because we've got a very special guest on the next segment—Jackson Stone!"

Dunkirk's interview with Red decided Jackson's course of action. He went to his office and locked the door. He clicked on the station's website and found the number for the call-in line. Busy, so he hit redial.

"Good morning! This is the B-I-G network! How may I direct your call?" the pleasant secretary said.

"This is Jackson Stone. Patch me through to Dunkirk."

"Uh, one moment please." She put him on hold.

Dunkirk's show went to a commercial break, when the studio line buzzed.

"Leslie," Dunkirk growled, "you know not to use this line during the show unless it's an emergency."

"There's a man on line three who says he's Jackson Stone."

Dunkirk slopped steaming coffee on his hand as he punched the line to his producer.

"Pick up line three and make sure this is the real Jackson Stone, not just some crank call."

The call-screener asked how and Dunkirk screamed.

"Just *do* it. We'll go to him after the next break if it's really Stone."

The producer asked several questions and gave the thumbs-up as Dunkirk espoused on what was wrong with America in general and Nashville in particular. They cut to commercial, and Dunkirk picked up line three.

"Mister Stone, thanks for calling our humble show. Did you hear my interview with Big Red?"

"That's why I called. I wanted to set the record straight on a few things."

"The floor is all yours," Dunkirk said. "Hang on, we're about to go back on the air in three . . . two . . . one.

"We're back," Dunkirk said to his audience, "and with us now is Jackson Stone. I would assume, sir, the reason you called this morning is because you heard our conversation with your old war buddy Big Red Boyle. He's quite a character."

"Yes, he is, but Red's got a tendency to exaggerate stories sometimes. That's why I'm calling. I didn't do anything special, just what was necessary."

"We'll get back to that in a moment, but first my vast listening audience and I would like to know how you're doing since Angela's funeral. Have you made any progress in tracking down your wife's killer? How goes the hunt?"

"I started back to work yesterday. I'm at the office now. I'm meeting with some folks later today to get the website going. I would ask that anyone with information on Angela's murder, please hold off on trying to reach me at work and wait till our eight hundred number is up and running."

Dunkirk steered the conversation back to the Gulf War. Jackson revisited the incidents Big Red discussed, giving a toned-down version.

"Don't be so modest, Mister Stone," Dunkirk said. "The commendations you received are well-documented. I would venture to say that your exploits over there answer any questions of whether you have the *cojones* to find your wife's killer."

"I'm doing what's necessary," Jackson said, then spoke to the as-yet-unknown killer. "If you're listening, I'm coming for you."

Delmore Wolfe wasn't listening. On his back, he snored in a deep, drug-induced sleep.

Clarkston wheeled into the advertising firm's parking lot as Dunkirk quizzed Stone about reactions from the police chief and his pastor. He shut off the engine and went inside. He strode to the receptionist's desk and tried to impress the secretary who at nine o'clock was already tired of the unwelcome media intrusions.

"Good morning. Dan Clarkston, Channel Eleven. I'd like to see Mister Stone."

She pointed without looking up. "Get in line."

Clarkston turned, crestfallen. I sat in the corner of the lobby, flipping through a late-July issue of *Sports Illustrated*.

3

Marty Martin didn't know Jackson called the radio station for the follow-up interview with George Dunkirk. Until his secretary buzzed, Marty didn't know a couple of reporters waited in the lobby. But first thing, as soon as he pulled into the parking lot and saw Jackson, Marty made up his mind. He spent the next hour putting together a generous severance package, certain the firm would take big public relations hits for canning a man who just lost his wife. But the possible long-term repercussions of lost business outweighed the short-term recriminations if he left. Marty knocked and entered. Sitting in front of his computer, Jackson hit the print button and faced his somber boss.

"Hey, I was just coming to see you. This isn't working out, and I shouldn't have tried to come back so soon. I'd like to take a leave of absence."

While they hammered things out upstairs, Clarkston and I engaged in a cat-and-mouse conversation about Jackson, picking each other's brains without revealing how much we knew ourselves. The secretary's telephone beeped.

"Yes sir," she said, then looked our way, glad to be rid of us. "You can go up now. The conference room is the second door on the left."

Dan, the runner, hit the steps two at a time. I followed, a tad slower. Marty and Jackson sat at the far end of the long cherry table. Clarkston called his cameraman, who was five minutes away. Jackson didn't want to wait, but agreed to a standup interview later if he failed to show in the next ten. I got out my notepad, recorder, and cell phone, and snapped a couple of pictures of Jackson and Marty sitting together while they waited. After I emailed those images back to the paper, I used the delay to text my editor, Carrie Sullivan. I let her know to expect a story, but said I wasn't sure of the angle.

Channel 11 cameraman Greg Pittard blasted through the door and took another minute to set up his equipment and lighting. Jackson straightened his tie and handed out a press release. Marty had approved it after a brief review, a call to his co-partner Mark Robbins, and a few amendments Mark suggested, and Jackson accepted.

"Thanks for attending this impromptu press conference. Since you guys were already here, I assume you heard my interview on the George Dunkirk show this morning," Jackson said. "Effective immediately, I am taking an extended leave of absence from Martin and Robbins. I don't know how long I will be away, but everyone knows that I am committed to finding my wife's killer. I want to honor her memory by setting up the Angela's Angels website, where people can leave tips and information and make contributions to help other crime victims' families and track down criminals."

Jackson paused as the finality hit full force. First he lost Angela and now his job. He never thought of it as a job so much as a labor of love, and it pained him to walk away even if on his terms, not Marty's. But Jackson resolved to move forward with his plans and not look back with regrets.

"Achieving those goals will require my full attention for the time being. I thought I could do both and do my job also, but I was wrong. It would be a disservice to my boss and long-time friend Marty Martin, the firm Martin and Robbins, and my colleagues to remain here for the immediate future. I brought undue attention and scrutiny to the firm, which was never my intention, and I want to thank Marty and all the rest for their generous support and encouragement throughout this ordeal."

Marty took over. "This has been a terrible time for Jackson and all of us here at Martin and Robbins. We support Jackson one hundred percent in this decision."

Clarkston hung around a few minutes after the impromptu news conference to tell Jackson of his involvement with the *Ed and Tara* show in New York and how much they wanted him on as a guest in the next few days. Jackson declined, saying he wasn't quite ready to hit the national talk show circuit yet, but he'd keep it in mind. Clarkston's panicked reaction amused Jackson when he mentioned that representatives from major network news magazines left messages.

"All I can say is I hope you'll give me the first chance," Clarkston said, regaining control of his emotions. "We've been telling your story since day one."

After we left, so did Jackson. Marty Martin sighed, relieved at how well it went. Fearful at being portrayed as the guy who made Jackson a victim twice, now he looked magnanimous for being so supportive and sympathetic.

Marty promised Clarkston and me that he would hold off on the press release with Jackson's statement until noon, which gave us time to post breaking news stories. TenneSceneToday.com posted its story with my cellpix of Stone one minute after Channel 11 got its video "exclusive" online. Clarkston won that round.

4

Jackson's spirits felt bouyant as he drove to his meeting with whiz kid Chris Webber at imMEDIAte Assistance to discuss getting the Angela's Angels website up and running ASAP.

"I think I've got a pretty good idea of what you're looking for, Mister Stone. No problem," the pimple-faced twenty-something said. "Give me a couple of days and I'll show you some ideas."

They shook hands, and Jackson drove out I-40 West, getting off at Charlotte Pike. A red F-150 truck far behind him also exited. But Jackson didn't notice as he headed to pick up Sheila for her appointment at Vanderbilt. Jackson called her from the car.

"I'm gonna grab some lunch and thought I'd double-check to see if you could get away and join me," Jackson asked as he waited at the red light.

"Thanks, but I haven't finished my chores yet. The appointment's at two-thirty, but I'd like to get there early."

"We'll be fine."

Sheila hung up, went back to the kitchen counter, and lifted the Panini-maker lid. The sandwiches were almost ready.

"So what was that about? I thought I was taking you to the doctor," Patrick Stone said as he sat at the table awaiting his lunch. Sheila chewed on her lower lip.

Jackson swung his car into the parking lot at Maude's Neighborhood Grille and went inside. After several minutes, the red pickup pulled into the gas station across the street where the dark-haired driver could keep an eye on things.

Taking a seat in the no-smoking section of the restaurant, away from the bar side, Jackson got out his smartphone and checked the newspaper website.

My story, up for an hour, had already drawn sixteen comments. Titled "**BREAKING NEWS: Jackson Stone granted leave of absence**," it ran four paragraphs long with the picture I'd taken of him next to Marty Martin. Below the "Return to TenneSceneToday.com for the latest news" tagline, Jackson read some of the posted comments.

At 11:14 a.m. <u>GEMINI</u> wrote: "Good move on Stony Soprano's part to take a leave of absence if he's serious about finding his wife's killer. It's hard to be in two places at once, unless you've got a twin. I don't see how he's gonna be able to do the website thing AND be a bounty hunter at the same time. Good luck Stony!"

At 11:38 a.m., <u>SCORPION</u> wrote: "His firm should have just fired Stone. He was an embarrassment to them and he's an embarrassment to Nashville. The national media is having a field day with this. SHUT UP ALREADY and GET A LIFE. You're not the first man to lose a wife or child to some senseless tragedy!"

At 12:07 p.m. <u>SHANGHAI SUE</u> wrote: "My husband and I planned a trip to Nashville this fall to visit the capital of country music, which has a growing following here in China. But now I don't know. Are all Nashvillians running around with guns? Will we be safe? This Jackson Stone sounds dangerous. I sympathize with his loss but more violence is not the solution."

At 12:26 p.m., <u>MARGE</u> wrote: "The man should really listen to his preacher. Thou shalt not—"

"Here's your sandwich," the waitress said, setting the fiery salsalito chicken hero with a side of roasted red pepper potato salad before him. "Want another beer?"

Jackson looked up at the harried waitress working too many tables at the popular watering hole. Her nametag identified her as Marge.

"No, I'm driving. I just read a post from a woman named Marge. Not you, I'm guessing."

"You kidding? Yeah I'm back there textin' and emailin' and *all* that stuff," Marge said as she picked up her tip at the table across from Stone, cleared dishes, and went to the kitchen.

Jackson watched the baseball game on TV as he ate. About ten minutes later, Marge asked if he needed anything. Told no thanks, Marge started to leave, but lingered and stared. Finally, she realized who he was. His picture appeared on the front of the paper at the table she just cleaned.

"Scuse me, but aren't you that fella they're callin' Stony on the radio?"

"Call me Jack," he said, grinning. "Good sandwich Marge. I'll remember this place."

"First visit, huh? Sure, come on back, Jack. Tell all your friends. We don't get many celebrities here. It's pretty tame, although we did have a bad incident out in the parking lot a coupla nights ago."

Before leaving the restaurant, Jackson dialed the cell phone number he'd gotten from George Dunkirk. He smiled at Big Red's familiar drawl. They'd talked only twice since that ten-year Gulf War reunion in 2001, but picked up the conversation like they skyped on the computer every other day.

"Jack? I just talked about you on the radio."

"That's why I'm calling. I'm taking my sister-in-law to the doctor, but I wonder if we could get together for dinner tonight. I'm heading to Murfreesboro after I run her home."

5

Patrick Stone didn't need to shout. The brooding silent treatment, just sitting, sulking, and staring as his wife tried to explain her actions of the last few days said plenty. But the more she talked and explained why, the more he relented and finally agreed with her plan.

"I'm worried about Jack and all the stress he's under," Sheila said, pacing the kitchen as Patrick put up the food and loaded the dishwasher. "*I'm* stressed out. I know he's your big, tough brother, but this is getting way out of control. Who knows what he's going to do next? If he's not careful, this could cost him his job. I mean, how's he going to keep working while starting this website he's talking about *and* tracking down Angela's killer? And all this media coverage and the police and Brother Armstrong—my God, Patrick, look what's happening to us."

"And so you decided to go behind Jackson's back to get him to see this doctor? Why not do an intervention or just have him committed?"

"That's not fair. You know he would never agree to see a psychiatrist."

The younger brother grew quiet again, mulling over the statement. He wanted to stick up for his brother, but backed down.

"You're right, and I'm sorry. Jackson's sure not listening to us. Okay, I'm in."

Patrick drove downtown where he would be waiting for their arrival.

Minutes after Patrick backed out of his driveway, Jackson pulled into it. He arrived in plenty of time to get Sheila to the appointment. Jackson noticed the red pickup in the rearview mirror, but thought nothing about it. He would later recall also seeing a beat-up old blue Firebird that earlier barreled past him in East Nashville, but wouldn't make a connection that time, either.

Sheila, dressed in a floral print, was ready to go when Jackson pulled into the driveway. She got up from the white back-porch rocker and sat in the car in good humor.

"Thanks, Jack, or should I call you Stony? It sounds like everyone else is."

"Yeah, it's pretty funny," Jackson grinned back. "Did you hear Big Red's interview?"

Sheila nodded, but frowned when Jackson mentioned the leave of absence.

"I know you don't agree with what I'm doing, but I can't stop now," he said, gripping the wheel as he focused on the road ahead and the path he chose.

"Part of me wants to say 'it's your life,' but it's our lives, too," she said, twisting in the seat to put a hand on his shoulder. "What you do affects Patrick and me and the kids. Setting up this website is admirable, but plotting revenge?" She shook her head. "I'm having a hard time with that one. You're not a killer."

"I know, and I hear you."

"Do you?"

He wanted to explain, but just sighed.

"I'm just doing what I've got to do," he said. An uncomfortable silence ensued until they at last reached the Vanderbilt campus and pulled into the parking deck, finding a spot on the third level. Jackson wanted to wait in the car, but Sheila shook her head.

"It's too hot out here. You'll be more comfortable in the doctor's waiting room. Besides, I might have to wait awhile and then go downstairs for tests and you wouldn't know where—"

"Fine. Let's go already." Getting out and looking at his watch, he wondered if he'd get away in time to meet Big Red. "What tests are you having anyway?"

Sheila didn't answer as they cut through the next row and headed to the elevator, walking past a red pickup.

In her plush office, Doctor Erica Karnoff scanned recent articles on Jackson Stone at the TenneSceneToday.com website. She looked forward to the session with him. She was re-reading the updated story on his leave of absence when a ruckus began in the reception area.

"I don't care. I'm leaving," the loud male voice boomed through the door.

"You're not going anywhere, if I have to tie you to that chair," shouted a similar, more youthful male voice that matched anger for anger.

A woman's voice shouted next. "Stop it, you—"

"Yes, stop this right now. What's going on out here?" Doctor Karnoff said firmly as she opened the door and stepped into the waiting room.

"This is all a set-up, and I'm not seeing any psychiatrist," Jackson said angrily. "Go tell your boss he's wasting his time."

"You're here to see *me*, Mister Stone. But you won't. Not today," Erica said, surprising the Stone brothers. The psychiatrist turned on the smiling sister-in-law. "Mrs. Stone, when you said you were making an appointment for your brother-in-law, I assumed he agreed to this meeting, and you were doing so with his blessing. You can't gain a patient's trust by getting him here under false pretenses. Mister Stone, I am so sorry for this misunderstanding. If somewhere down the road you would like to talk, I would be happy to arrange an appointment."

The doctor went back into her office and closed the door. Jackson appreciated her jumping on Sheila for—for what, for trying to help him? Sheila knew he would never agree to a session on his own volition. He grinned. She *could* be sneaky, a Stone after all. He looked up at Sheila, who was red-faced as others in the busy waiting room stared. Patrick put an arm around her, and pulled her toward the glass door.

Jackson watched them get on the elevator, then knocked on Dr. Karnoff's door. After a brief wait the door opened.

It surprised Doctor Karnoff to see Jackson. He was equally surprised to be standing there.

"Got a few minutes, Doc? I think I have an appointment."

6

Delmore Wolfe found Jackson once, but also found trouble when he saw him talking to that cop, which was why he fled the pub. Not to worry, he'd find him again. A long overdue "accident" awaited Stone.

Going out for lunch, maybe a late breakfast, and then to score some more weed, he turned on the crackling car radio. Gotta break down and get a newer car than this old clunker, Wolfe told himself, as he found a station with a strong enough signal for his antenna to lock on.

"And in local news," the sing-song newscaster said, "both *TenneScene Today* and Channel 11 are reporting that controversial Nashville advertising executive Jackson Stone has taken a leave of absence from the firm Martin and Robbins in order to start up the Angela's Angels website and to track down his wife's killer."

Wolfe guessed wrong that Jackson would head home after leaving work. He stepped on the gas and drove down Dickerson Pike past the football stadium and turned left on Shelby Avenue. He got to Jackson's house and kept on going without slowing down. Two groups of a half-dozen people each were walking up and down the sidewalk in front of the brick cottage. A Channel 7 newsvan was parked at the corner and the videographer set up for a live shot of the protesters. The group of sign-carrying Christian conservatives beseeched Jackson to "Turn The Other Cheek Now" and "For The LOVE OF GOD, Don't Become A Murderer." The group of atheist activists' signs of the times blared "Revenge

Is Still Murder" and "YOUR god Has Deserted You." Polar opposites in their beliefs, the two sides seemed to agree that Jackson should not kill.

Later, while sitting in line at the Burger Barn drive-thru, Wolfe remembered that Jackson had a brother—Patrick. Yeah, that's it. After paying for his burger, Wolfe whipped into the gas station and went inside. He asked the clerk for the phone book and flipped through the White Pages until he found the listings for "Stone." He ran his finger down the page.

Barry-Chad-Don-Eddie-Eric-Frank-Greg-Harold-Keith-Jackson-Lawrence-Melvin-Nicholas-Oscar-Gotcha! A finger traced right, and he memorized Patrick's address—2175 Prescott, West Meade.

Wolfe made it to West Meade in fifteen minutes. But Jackson had picked up Sheila five minutes earlier and headed to Vanderbilt. Wolfe found the Stone house, but the driveway sat empty. He planned to prowl around, but thought better of it. He didn't know which nosy neighbors might be snooping and decided to watch from a distance. A few houses down the street, he pulled over and put the hood up, then got back in his car where he could see the Stones' driveway. He didn't wait long. He had bought one of those late-night TV infomercial "Super Hearing" directional earpieces last year and used it to eavesdrop on Sheila and Patrick as they walked to the front door.

"I can't believe the way Jack acted," he heard Patrick say. "Where'd you find that psychiatrist anyway?"

"Maybe he'll make an appointment to see her."

7

Jackson cruised on autopilot as he drove to Murfreesboro. Brad Paisley's 2002 hit "I'm Gonna Miss Her" blared on Classic Country 750-AM, but Jackson's mind replayed over and over his forty-five-minute session with the psychiatrist.

"I'm so glad you decided to go through with the session, even though your sister-in-law duped you into it," Doctor Karnoff had said. "I've followed the case in the media and know how much courage it required on your part just to carry on."

Jackson told her about all the shocks of the first few hours, how he almost threw up when he saw the bloody sheets in their bedroom, all the fear, uncertainty, and confusion he experienced. Anger followed at the lack of information coming from the police, turning to rage and frustration over the discovery of Angela's body a week after she disappeared. Doctor Karnoff asked if there were times when Jackson wished that he'd died in Angela's place.

"No death wish here," Jackson replied derisively, "but I *do* wish to spend eternity with Angela at my side."

Doctor Karnoff asked Jackson how he felt about reactions from the police chief, his pastor, the media, and the public after announcing his intentions. Jackson said he anticipated strong public and police backlash from the media coverage, although it seemed more intense and divisive than he ever expected. "The biggest surprise, though, came when

212

Brother Armstrong pounded the pulpit on Sunday," Jackson said.

"You have strong religious views, don't you?" She wanted to get to the root of Jackson's attacks. "How do you reconcile desires for vengeance with your faith?"

Jackson admitted it tugged at his conscience, but remained adamant.

"I *have* to do this."

"Why, Jack?" she pressed. "*Why* are you so obsessed?"

Silence stretched into minutes as Jackson wrestled with whether or not to reveal the truth nobody else knew—not his brother or Sheila, neither the police, nor his pastor. Decision time. He'd carried this secret long enough. Client-patient rules meant it would not leave this office.

"When I arrived home that night, I couldn't find any sign of Angela and nearly flipped out on the spot. I frantically searched the house from top to bottom and what I found is why I'm determined to find the man that took the life of my wife—and the life of my unborn child. Yes, child. Angela was pregnant, according to the EPT I found. Then I found the appointment she"—he looked at his watch and shook his head—"scheduled with her OB/GYN as we speak."

Jackson shook, and tightened his lips. "She didn't tell me she was pregnant. She was going to, I think, the last night we were together for dinner out, and I invited another couple to join us. I didn't give her a chance to tell me. I had a wife and a child to protect. And I didn't. And that is why I am going to *destroy* the cursed creature that butchered my precious Angela and our little innocent baby."

In both subsequent interviews and her just-released book, the psychiatrist reflected on that turning-point moment with her new patient. Shocked, she still kept her professional composure.

"It explained everything," she said, "but I have never witnessed such an instant transformation in persona. A gentle lamb became a savage lion who hunted wolves."

HOOOOONK!

The blast from a passing truck's airhorn snapped
Jackson into the present. Memories of the conversation faded
and Jackson realized he neared Murfreesboro. He took his
foot off the gas pedal and weaved from his own right lane
into the safety lane as if slowing for an emergency, then
swerved back onto the road. Jackson wiped a tear, waving as
the truck sped by, and got his car back to speed. The
remainder of Jackson's short trip proved less eventful than
the short, painful trip down memory lane he'd just taken.
Alone with his thoughts, he assumed, but that turned out to
be not quite the case.

A couple of cars back, the red truck also slowed when
Jackson did and then resumed a safe speed that kept pace
with Jackson's car.

Jimmy Boyle sat in Murfreesboro's Roadside Cafe off
Highway 96 drinking his third cup of black coffee when
Jackson arrived. The transition from the bright sunshine to
the restaurant's dark interior caused him to blink, then two
big arms engulfed him. Jackson returned the hug.

"Man, you look great. How you been?"

Red gave that same laconic shrug that marked his
country lifestyle and attitude toward life in general. He
rarely sought the spotlight or talked much in any situation,
which made his five-minute interview with talk show host
George Dunkirk all the more extraordinary. Red would lay
down his life for his friend if it came to that, but Jackson
hoped it wouldn't.

Jackson ordered a beer and asked Boyle if he wanted
one for old time's sake.

"Naw. I quit about two years back," Red said. "It
became a problem and messed me up pretty good. I went
cold turkey; ain't touched a drop since."

Ouch, Jackson thought, as the comment hit him like a
punch to the liver. No, that's what the alcohol is doing,
pickling my liver.

"I'm thinking I should quit, too. All I need is to give the
police a reason to arrest me. I've already given them a few—
if I go through with this. That's why I wanted to talk."

Jackson asked instead for coffee—black—and they ordered dinner. They were sitting in the corner booth and Jackson noticed the furtive looks from nearby tables. Too public a setting. He glanced out the window and recognized a red pickup, realizing he'd seen it—or one just like it—several times. No idea who, or why. Hundreds of thoughts and suspicions formed. The cops, he figured, then wondered. Could be Angela's killer? Don't get paranoid, Jack. And for God's sake, don't do anything to tip him off.

Jackson couldn't make out the driver except for dark hair and sunglasses.

Paranoid about their possibly bugged conversation, Jackson ditched the original plan to pitch at Red. Instead, they talked over old times and the all-too-few times he met Angela. As they ate, they discussed Red's radio interview. When Red went to the bathroom, Jackson used the break to scribble a brief note. Among other things, it told Red how to get to his Lascassas cabin, where to find the spare key, and where to find the case Jackson needed. In the parking lot, they shook hands and Jackson whispered as he leaned in for a parting hug. As Red waved goodbye, he watched a red pickup follow Jackson out of the lot. Then Red opened his palm and read the note Jackson slipped him.

In the truck, Sergeant Mike Whitfield kept his distance as both vehicles traveled west toward Franklin—too far back, it turned out. He didn't see Jackson's car anywhere ahead now that he rounded the wide bend in the two-lane road and hit a straight stretch. Another mile and Whitfield kicked himself for losing Jackson. Hungry, he turned around at the four-way stop and headed back to Murfreesboro, where he would report in to Chief King. Then he saw it—a small wooden sign with an arrow pointing to turn right. "Birdies shot here. One mile ahead," read the amusing sign announcing the way to the Murfreesboro Gun and Golf Club. On a hunch, Whitfield checked it out. Sure enough, Jackson's car sat in the full parking lot. Whitfield called Nashville. Chief King called Murfreesboro. Officer Bobby Powell would call on Jackson.

While Jackson and his mysterious pursuer traveled west, Big Red headed east toward the Lascassas community and the cabin. After retrieving the key from the knot in the third tree on the west side of the house, Red entered and went straight to the kitchen. He gave the table a shove, kicked aside the rug and saw the loose board. One tug and it came up easily. Red squatted and wrapped his good hand around the handle. He laid the case on the table and put everything back in its original place.

Red did what he was asked without question. Jackson's brief note finished by saying to guard the case with his life and he'd be in touch. The note didn't say Red shouldn't open the case and curiosity got the best of him.

"What you got in here, Jack?"

The locks didn't budge, so Red found a wire and jiggled it in the keyhole. *Gotcha!* Red smiled, flipped the latches, and whistled. The Tokarev .30 caliber pistol. Red picked it up, twisting it in his hand, awash in a flood of memories from the incident nineteen years earlier when Jackson appropriated what the dead Red Brigade captain no longer needed. Jackson had retrieved the gun two days after he buried it, then Red never saw it again until now. And, yep, plenty of ammunition.

The Tokarev, used with great success in the Russians' defense of Stalingrad in World War II, didn't pack a lot of punch. It was crude in design, but effective for close-range killing. Red twirled the gun, examining it at close range, and then held it out in front of him.

He imagined aiming it at Angela's killer, now stalking Jack. He imagined squeezing off a couple of shots with the tip of his missing left finger.

8

Officer Bobby Powell entered the Murfreesboro Gun and Golf Club unsure of what to expect. Jackson Stone might be trying to buy a gun from someone, the call from Nashville said. Nope. Jackson just needed some practice. Once a member of both clubs and now an instant celebrity, he renewed old friendships and made a roomful of new acquaintances. Jackson borrowed a Taurus Raging Bull .44 Magnum from his old buddy Larry McDaniel, a retired Army colonel and one of the club founders, and popped off a hundred rounds on the target range. Rusty at first, he regained the form that earned him sharpshooter status in the Marines. After hitting twenty-seven bull's-eyes in a row to close out the session, he smiled as he removed his tapered hearing protectors and shooting glasses. Larry put them up.

"Nice shooting. How about signing some targets? We'll auction them at our fall fundraiser," Larry said.

Officer Powell entered the private club as Jackson signed autographs, shook hands, and told the crowd about plans for the future—if one awaited, he reminded himself.

"How's the hunt going, Stony?" A voice from the back.

"Jack, please. And I haven't gotten started yet. I'm still trying to get my website off the ground. I hope you all check it out in a couple of weeks."

"I ain't gonna do it," said farmer Ned Buchanan, another club old-timer who received a lifetime membership as part of the deal to sell the land where the clubhouse, eighteen-hole golf course, and indoor shooting range were located.

All heads swiveled from Jackson to Ned and back as if following a tennis match.

"How long we known each other?" Ned said, snapping at his suspenders.

"It's been at least ten years, Ned. You were one of the first members I met."

"And now I wonder if I ever knew you at all. What you're doin' ain't Christian, Jack."

"I appreciate your—"

"Don't pay any attention to that old fool," retired Murfreesboro judge Richard Henson snapped. "On the bench for thirty-two years, I saw plenty of scumbags that deserved the death penalty. I would've been happy to send them on their way, but it wasn't an option then. I'm glad they reinstated it."

Voices raised, then hushed, as Officer Powell grabbed their attention.

"That's enough, gentlemen. Mister Stone, I'd like a word with you outside."

The members quieted and watched Jackson follow the policeman outside. The warm air enveloped him and he broke out in a sweat, which made Officer Powell suspicious.

"Can I ask your reason for coming here, sir?"

"What's this about?" Jackson said.

"We got a report of an illegal gun purchase going down. Now I walk in and see you inciting a riot. Where's the gun?"

The suspicious officer's eyes narrowed, and Jackson found himself in another stare-down with a cop. He allowed himself to grow angrier, but maintained control.

"I no longer own a registered handgun, nor am I trying to buy one. Ask Judge Henson, he'll tell you. I thought I'd visit some friends, if it's any of your business," Jackson said, adding, "I used to be a member here."

"It *is* my business, and I don't want trouble. You better leave," Powell said, "unless maybe you'd rather go downtown and answer some questions."

Maybe he didn't. Jackson left without a fuss. He drove back to Nashville trying to figure out this puzzle. Too late to call his attorney now, so he'd call first thing in the morning.

WEDNESDAY, AUGUST 18
1

I woke up, had two cups of coffee, along with cinnamon rolls and a slice of cantaloupe, then left for the office because they wanted an in-depth look at Stone for the Sunday op-ed section. They planned a pro-con debate with the paper's religion editor, and they proposed to label the package "Stone-Cold Killer?" I thought it was a cliché, but what the editor wanted, the editor got. I faced a noon-Thursday deadline, hence the sooner-than-usual start. As it turned out, that piece never got published because of the call that came in at eight thirty on the police scanner sitting atop my cluttered desk.

"All area units please respond to a possible double-homicide in East Nashville at one-six-nine Evans Street. That's one-six-nine Evans Street," the scanner crackled.

One sixty-nine Evans. Why did that address sound familiar?

Then it hit me. I emailed city editor Carrie Sullivan and photo editor Brad Moore the address of where I was headed—the house next to Jackson Stone's.

The protesters had returned—both groups—and about twenty minutes after Jackson arose, he became aware of them. He turned on the coffee, showered and dressed. He almost put on a tie before the realization hit: No job, no more ties. He poured his first K-Cup—choosing Hazelnut over Mudslide—and went to fetch the paper.

The harried scene outside surprised him. Jackson didn't know it marked the protesters' second day on the sidewalk.

"There he is," shouted a bearded young man holding a sign which read "Put Your Faith In The Lord's Vengeance, Not Jackson Stone's."

Jackson walked between protesters and picked up the paper, shaking his head. As he neared the front walk, a tinny female voice shouted.

"Violence sucks and so do you, Stone."

"That's enough," Stone said angrily, staring down his hecklers. Each set of eyes he met dropped. Jackson cupped his hands around his mouth and shouted.

"Don't you people have anything better to do? Do you know what time it is? Get out of here before you wake my neigh—"

Jackson froze, his first hint of something very wrong. Struck by the four days' worth of newspapers on the driveway next door, he stood oblivious to the protesters' resumed shouting. He crossed the strip of grass between the two driveways and picked up the Sunday paper, looking around.

"That's odd," he mumbled to himself. Their cars were in the driveway. They weren't out of town, otherwise they'd have asked him to get their mail. He checked the mailbox. It was jammed tight with envelopes, magazines, and fliers. Jackson didn't like that and trotted to the front door, brushing by the protesters who followed him into the next yard. He tried the lock. Nothing.

He sprinted around to the back door. Also locked. A hand to his brow blocked out the sun as he pressed his nose to the bay window and peered into the open kitchen. An open mustard jar sat on the counter beside the opened loaf of bread. He saw a twist-tie on the floor, and a drawer stood open. No signs of movement or life from inside. He pounded the door, then looked inside from another angle and noticed the open door to the basement.

"Herb? Sarah? Anybody home?"

No reply. He banged the door again, smacking harder. After several seconds of silence, Jackson backed up and then crashed his shoulder to the door—once, twice. The third time the door jamb gave and Jackson burst in. The overpowering stench gagged Jackson as it brought back Gulf War memories. He stumbled outside and around the corner of the house.

"Somebody call the police," Jackson shouted at the protesters. Several did. Jackson pulled a handkerchief out of his back pocket and covered his nose and mouth. He used his forearm to push the basement door open wider and looked down the steps. *Ohmigod!* At the bottom of the stairs lay Herb, a knife protruding from his back. Jackson thought he couldn't be any more shocked. Dead-wrong. He wondered if Sarah hid down there and descended four steps to look around and saw nothing.

"Sarah?"

Jackson eased down a couple more steps, halted, and looked. Again, nothing. Stepping around Herb's body, careful not to touch anything, he turned the corner and stumbled backward.

Sarah's limp body hung from a noose.

What in the name of God happened here?

Jackson didn't touch either body or disturb the scene. Moving around Herb's body to climb the stairs, Jackson noticed the claw marks for the first time. Peering closer at the bloody scratches on the left cheek, something else caught Jackson's eye, something familiar. What's that cloth in his mouth?

2

As the first reporter to arrive at the crime scene, I spotted police and people everywhere. The protesters no longer protested. The Christian group formed a sitting circle on the thick grass, praying aloud while the atheists huddled on the other side of the driveway. Two tattooed goth girls hugged and a blond, bearded young man—who went searching for Jackson and got a whiff of the odor emanating up the steps—crawled on his hands and knees, still gagging.

I learned Jackson found two bodies inside the house. The officer wouldn't divulge any other information, so I went looking for Jackson. My cell phone buzzed, the first of many calls from city editor Carrie Sullivan. After getting her up to date, at nine oh five, I dictated what I could. Carrie filed our first online story, tagged as **BREAKING NEWS** and sent out at nine fifteen as an email alert to TenneSceneToday.com and Twitter subscribers:

2 more deaths possibly linked to Angela Stone murder case
By GERRY HILLIARD
TenneScene Today

Police this morning were investigating the deaths of two people believed to be the next-door neighbors of controversial Nashvillian Jackson Stone, who last week made headlines by proclaiming his desire for vengeance after the Aug. 3 disappearance and murder of his wife, Angela, 35.

Police won't confirm the identities of the male and female victims, whose bodies were discovered in the house at 8 a.m., by Stone. Public records identify the owners of the property at 169 Evans Street as Herbert J. and Sarah M. Fletcher.

It's the latest twist in a bizarre series of tragedies connected to Stone. It is unknown if these latest deaths are in any way connected to the murder of Angela Stone, who went missing for a week before searchers found her body in the Warner Parks area.

Stone held an extraordinary press conference last Friday to announce a vendetta which has drawn both praise and criticism. His wife's funeral was Saturday.

Return to TenneSceneToday.com for updates on this breaking story.

At the paper, Carrie took charge as reporters arrived. Shelley and Tony Smith were ordered to the scene to help me, while editors reached photographer Casey Leiber at home and told her to head to the crime scene and get something ASAP. At nine thirty, I called in.

"It's them, Carrie. It's still not official confirmation, but another cop I know said they found Sarah and Herb Fletcher dead in the basement. He didn't say how they died. The police spokesman isn't here yet, but we can run with it."

"Thanks. Help's on the way. Call back when you've got something else. Can we identify the cop?"

"We'd better not. I don't want to burn a source. Hold off if you want until I can get official confirmation. I'll try to get to the paper by noon or one, two at the latest."

Carrie hung up and filed the first of several updates throughout the day. She rewrote the second sentence, changing "police have not confirmed the identities of the male and female victims, whose bodies were discovered in the house at 8 a.m., by Stone" to "police confirmed the identities but have not released the names of the male and female victims, whose bodies were discovered in the

223

basement at 8 a.m., by Stone." Stronger, but she would not
identify them until the police did.

My story, posted for about twenty minutes, already
included five attached comments.

> At 9:18 a.m., <u>JUDY BLUE EYES</u> wrote:
> "OMG. Can't believe this. Everybody around
> Stone is dying. Are they going to question
> him?"

> At 9:22 a.m., <u>EL GORDO</u> wrote: "East
> Nashville has always been a dangerous place to
> live, but this is incredible. Lotsa unanswered
> questions, but I'd start by asking Jackson
> Stone's whereabouts."

> At 9:25 a.m., <u>CHILLPILL PHIL</u> wrote:
> "Don't overreact and jump to conclusions,
> people. We don't have all the facts yet. We
> don't even know for sure if it's the Fletchers."

The city's radio stations began reporting the Fletchers'
deaths on the nine-thirty news breaks, citing *TenneScene
Today* as their information source. George Dunkirk dropped
his planned segment on the weakening economy to discuss
the Fletchers' deaths, speculating not on *whether* they were
connected to Angela's death, but *how*. Listeners joined in,
and it made for lively—and perhaps libelous—conversation.

Other media arrived and Channel 11's Dan Clarkston
was delivering a live report on sister station All-News 111,
when police spokesman Darrin Jensen arrived. Darrin
assessed the situation and ordered the media to assemble
down the street. We all grumbled but followed him a block
away, assembling in a half-circle.

Jensen said he would release information as it became
available and that he would try to get Chief King to make a
statement at the appropriate time. Until then, he cautioned,
stay out of the way and let the officers do their jobs. Any
requests for interviews were to go through him. Jensen got
the victims' identities confirmed, and I called the paper as he
tried to keep the press in rein. It didn't work.

3

About two hours after detectives and crime scene investigators arrived, Officer Barry Mendez began searching for Jackson. Pockets of people stood behind the yellow tape barricades and confusion reigned everywhere. It took Mendez a minute to spot Stone, who walked down the street with me for an interview away from the crowd. I conversed with my head down, going over my notes and didn't realize the cop approached.

"So you sensed something was wrong when you saw the pile of papers and decided to check the house," I said. "You broke in, found the bodies downstairs in the basement. You saw Mister Fletcher lying on the floor. Now how about Mrs. Fletcher? And could you tell how either died?"

"It was just an appalling, gruesome scene," Jackson said. "I didn't see Sarah at first, then—"

"Excuse me, Mister Stone, Chief King wants to see you," Mendez said.

"Let me finish—"

"Now, sir."

Jackson left and I wondered why the cop ordered him around like that.

Chief King was studying Commander Reynolds' preliminary report when Mendez ushered Jackson to the Fletchers' backyard gazebo, which served as the temporary command post. The NCSI team continued to pore over the crime scene, accumulating evidence and taking photos. Jackson stood and waited. Mendez stood watch to ensure no interruptions. The forensics team leader came outside the house, and made eye contact with the Chief.

"Wait here, Mister Stone."

Jackson fidgeted, sat and took off his jacket. He saw the EMS crew arrive to take the bodies to the morgue. Finally, the chief returned, and sat beside him. He looked Jackson square in the eye and rubbed his chin.

"It's time for the truth to come out," King said. "Why'd you do it?"

Jackson misinterpreted King's question.

"Do what?" Jackson said, jumping to his feet. "You think I somehow figure in their deaths? You son of a—"

"No, Jack." The always-cool police chief raised an open hand as if he were a crossing guard holding up a stop sign. "I don't think you murdered your neighbor and his wife," King said in a warm, soothing tone that made Jackson sit back down. "I do think you've acted rash and foolish about all this vendetta business, but you're not a murderer—yet. No, what I wanted to know is why you broke into the house and didn't wait for our men to arrive. It's dangerous, and you might have tampered with a key piece of evidence or disturbed the crime scene. It jeopardized the entire investigation."

Jackson thought about it, agreed, and nodded. "You're right, sir. I didn't think, I just acted on instinct, and I apologize. I didn't touch anything; you've got the report."

"Apology accepted," King said, moving on. "And if you think of anything to add to that report, let Commander Reynolds know."

King lapsed into a long, silent stretch, and Jackson squirmed until the chief came to a decision.

"The most curious part of the captain's report is when you stated having noticed what appeared to be some type of cloth in Herb's mouth. Did it look like this?"

Jackson gasped, looking from the chief to his hand and back to the chief, too shocked to speak for several minutes. He recognized a pair of lacy, red Simone Perele underwear he gave Angela for her birthday last March.

After Jackson identified the underwear—saying it sure looked like Angela's—King decided to bring Jackson up to speed on the investigations. For what King planned, he desperately needed his cooperation.

"Somebody's gone to a lot of trouble to make it look like Herb Fletcher caused your wife's death. We found these in the back of a drawer upstairs, along with some other personal items from your wife. We found another pair in Sarah Fletcher's purse. The third pair—what you described to detectives as a piece of cloth—somebody crammed those in Herb's mouth. Judging from the signs of struggle, it wouldn't be too big of a leap to conclude that Sarah found out about the affair between Angela and Herb."

"No affair occurred," Jackson all but shouted.

The chief remained calm. "From the facial bruising, it wouldn't be too hard to suppose that Herb slapped Sarah when confronted with the affair. From the DNA under Sarah's fingernails and prints found on the knife in Herb's back, one would construe that Sarah fought back and stabbed Herb, who fell down the stairs. No confession or suicide note, but it seems Sarah couldn't live with the shame of what Herb did to Angela or her attack on Herb, so Sarah took her own life. The investigations are over, and the cases are closed to everybody's satisfaction. Fears in East Nashville are calmed, and people get on with their lives—including you, Mister Stone."

Jackson looked ready to explode when the chief raised a hand again to stop him.

"The problem is it's all too tidy an explanation. Nothing's ever as it seems. Somebody wants us to think we've got all the answers, so we're going to see how that plays out. Then if I've guessed right, that somebody's going to come looking for you, Stony, as they're calling you on the radio. So I'm here to ask for your help. Will Stony stick his neck out to catch a killer?"

Jackson almost laughed out loud, but just stared sullenly at the chief. A Stony silence.

What do you think I've been trying to do?

Stony had his own agenda. Stony needed to work alone. Stony needed to get there first.

4

I got back to the paper about twelve thirty after Chief King's media briefing and compared notes with young reporters Shelley Finklestein and Tony Smith. I added a few King quotes to the online story which by then already drew more than three hundred comments, many by the same posters and going off on several irrelevant tangents.

I pounded out my twenty-inch mainbar on the day's events and made a couple of minor changes my editors requested. I also looked over the copy from Shelley and Tony, offering a few suggestions which they seemed to appreciate. Her piece focused on the Fletchers, who they were, and why this tragedy occurred. His article took a look at how three brutal deaths in a three-week span rocked a close-knit community, how it might affect local businesses, and he quoted Commander Mark Reynolds on how citizens shouldn't fear for their safety.

After all that, I returned to the Sunday piece I'd begun to write hours earlier. It was less than scintillating prose, but I planned to polish it on Thursday morning. I sent Carrie a copy for her input and feedback, then reviewed my mainbar, already sent to the copydesk for the final edit. I still wanted to check Casey's photographs, but Carrie seemed pleased with the choices. I planned to look at the online slideshow before I left for the night.

For me, the most intriguing part of the morning concerned one quote from Chief King during his briefing. Asked about possible connections between Angela's murder and the deaths of the Fletchers, the chief refused to be pinned down.

"Of course, the cases are being examined for similarities . . . No, I won't elaborate or speculate," he said. "Another question?"

The chief would not go into how the Fletchers died; the press would have gone nuts if he'd told us it looked like a murder-suicide. The media would have demanded to know why. But there were ways of getting that information out. For me, the word came from Commander Reynolds. I caught him just before he headed back to the East Precinct, and we talked for fifteen enlightening minutes. As it turned out, Reynolds did not tell me everything, just what the chief wanted leaked. He refused to be quoted.

After talking it over with my editors—Publisher Andrew Polk made the final call—we decided to go with the new information linking the three deaths. My story cited "sources close to the investigation" as confirming "certain similarities in the slayings." The newspaper policy is to avoid unsourced stories but exceptions can be made for incidents like this one.

My mind kept going back to King's comments. I thought it a rather poor pun when King said, "We will look under every rock and stone during this investigation."

One of King's favorite catch-phrases, it got me to wondering about a hidden meaning. The police said they'd officially ruled out Jackson as a suspect in his wife's death, but what if? The case clearly revolved around Stone. Three slayings in two houses side by side? I don't believe in coincidences, but couldn't fathom the connection.

On a whim, I decided to call Doctor Erica Karnoff to tap her thoughts. I wanted to talk to her anyway for my Sunday piece and hoped it wasn't too late.

5

By five o'clock the East Nashville neighborhood had returned to a semblance of normalcy—if the yellow police tape marking off the Fletchers' entrances could be considered normal. Jackson sat in his den wishing for a six-pack, looked at the clock, and turned on Channel 11 to watch Clarkston's remote broadcast from next door.

"Police have yet to classify it as either a double homicide or murder/suicide or reveal whether it's connected to the recent death of next-door neighbor Angela Stone, who was murdered at her home almost three weeks ago. Angela's husband, Jackson, made the grisly discovery this morning."

Video showed two stretchers being wheeled out and loaded into ambulances, police swarming the scene, and interviews with Chief King, Jackson, and several neighbors. The chief had interrogated Jackson privately, telling him to keep all the details to himself. Jackson had tried to honor that request, evading most media questions.

"I'm surprised that I didn't notice anything wrong sooner," Jackson heard himself say on the television. "The last time I saw Herb was at Angela's funeral. Sarah stayed home, and the last thing he said was that he was going to go home and try to talk Sarah into coming by to visit the family. But they never showed."

Clarkston kept pressing Jackson's buttons to get the emotional response he wanted for the camera. That's how TV guys operate.

"Police indicated the Fletchers died several days ago," Clarkston said. "Is there reason to believe their deaths are in any way connected with your wife's?"

Of course they are, you idiot, Jackson thought, seething inside.

"Of course not," he said, keeping calm. "Other than the fact that they lived next door, I'd call it just a tragic coincidence. Sarah and Herb were having problems."

Conducting interviews is like pitching, a mix of insightful off-speeds with probing curveballs or forceful fastballs. Sometimes it's a perfect strike; other times you get shelled.

"There are unconfirmed reports of physical evidence linking the three deaths, that Sarah Fletcher took her own life after discovering an affair between Herb and Angela," Clarskton said. "Can you shed new light on this tragedy?"

Jackson had anticipated the ambush statement, just not that quickly, and he felt a need to defend Angela's honor.

"That's a lie. It makes me sick to hear stuff like that. Herb and Sarah were friends, and that's all. You need to get your facts straight before you go repeating garbage like that. You'll hear from my lawyer."

He'd stalked off and started yelling at the police spokesman, but the cameras didn't show that. They stayed on Clarkston, who to his credit aired the confrontation with Jackson. Clarkston finished his report unflustered, though he felt sick inside. Had he blown his shot at working with the *Ed and Tara* show?

Jackson looked at his watch. Time to leave for the Wednesday evening services at church. He'd missed the weekly church dinner, but he needed to be in God's house after such a horrifying day. As Jackson opened the car door, his cell phone rang. Big Red.

"I'm leaving now."

Jackson made his way across town. He didn't notice the big red pickup keeping a loose tail on him.

Delmore Wolfe all but howled as he watched the taped confrontation.

"Whooooo-haaaaaa! Way to go. Herbie, the lady-killer. And Sinister Sarah."

Wolfe knew it would be a matter of time before the press got wind of the underwear, but it happened faster than he expected. In his mind, spinning a new fantasy, it meant the cops would stop looking for Angela's killer. The cops' evidence confirmed the "affair" and that Herb in fact murdered Angela when she tried to end the tryst.

Wolfe flashed an evil grin as he watched Stone erupt at the reporter and stalk off. It was a modern American tragedy. The only thing missing? The final act—the demise of Jackson Stone.

He felt like celebrating his best day since arriving in Nashville a month before. Seeing Clarkston ask Jackson about the "love triangle" struck Wolfe as award-winning journalism. Feeling cocky and feeling the glow of freedom, he felt sure "the pigs will squeal over solving this one"—that Angela died at the hands of the next-door neighbor with whom she had a torrid fling, that Sarah Fletcher killed Herb after confronting him with what she discovered, that Sarah then committed suicide. Case closed.

A night to remember, he decided as he pulled into the Got Spirits! liquor store near the Vanderbilt campus. He stood in line with four fifths in his two hands. Behind him, a raven-haired woman holding a bottle of Chablis answered her cell phone.

"Hello, Mister Hilliard. Yes I'm headed home, but I have a few minutes. It's funny you should ask. I met with Mister Stone yesterday afternoon."

Wolfe froze as he handed the clerk the cash, and his ears perked up.

"Yes I think it helped him a great deal," she said. "It took a while, but he opened up at the end. This isn't for print, but I'd call it an excellent session. I fully comprehend why he's doing this. I'm afraid I can't discuss details, not even in general terms. You know the doctor-patient relationship is confidential. . . . Yes we're meeting again tomorrow."

Wolfe got in his car, then watched Erica fall into her Fiat and pull into traffic. Wanting to get in Stone's head and the doc's pants, he set out after her.

Some twenty minutes and eight turns later, Delmore Wolfe found himself semi-lost. He followed the speedy Fiat south/southwest out of the city to Old Hickory Boulevard and turned right on the state route which doubled as the dividing line between Davidson County and Williamson County's Brentwood. A quarter-mile more and the Fiat turned left into a gated community of large, lush stone homes and manicured, flower-filled yards.

Wolfe slowed and watched a slinky arm reach out of the car and punch a passcode into the scanner, then he stepped on the gas and sped on. As he wondered about the psychiatrist's identity, it dawned on him just *where* he was. Wolfe approached from a different direction the last time he was here, but recalled the part of the park where he buried Angela's body.

Snatching Angela had proved no problem, although she was "a gamer" and put up a fight. But he reeled her in as easy as catching Ole Mister Catfish in the Arkansas River a dozen years earlier. Her pet dog actually became the first Nashville victim. It had growled at his stealth approach. He had noticed it earlier when leaving Sarah's house and came back prepared.

"C'mon, boy," he'd said, "have a bite of this tasty burger." When it got within striking distance, he struck. The tire iron made a nice crunching sound. "Reminded me of Granddaddy's coon hound, 'cept this one didn't make a sound." Then he headed for the house. "Just warming up."

Angela had gotten Jackson's call from the Charlotte airport about five, saying he would be late, that mechanical problems had cancelled his flight, but the airline had re-routed a plane from Atlanta to fetch stranded passengers.

She had picked at dinner and watched a little TV, but remained too disturbed from seeing Sarah with that guy in her kitchen. She couldn't get the image out of her head, that lustful look of evil on the man's face.

Angela must have thought her friend insane to betray her husband in their own kitchen, Jackson would later say, knowing his wife's moral compass. How in the world could sweet Sarah, her closest friend for a decade, wind up *on the floor* with that man? Caller ID, checked later, showed Sarah calling several times that afternoon, but Angela wouldn't have accepted any calls with explanations for that behavior. Maybe Angela had perceived that man to be insane, too. He looked insane in those few seconds and what if he . . . no! The thought had horrified Angela.

She switched off the television, flipped off the lights, and went upstairs. The steaming sprays of the shower felt wonderful beating down on her back and shoulders, but couldn't wash away the day's awful events. When her fingers wrinkled and her skin turned bright pink from the pulsating shower, Angela turned off the water, dried, put on her pajamas and robe, and settled on the king-size bed. She might have tried to read to keep her mind off things. Police would later find an open paperback on the night table. The title: *The Neighbor's Dirty Little Secrets*.

Getting inside had proved no problem for Delmore Wolfe. The itinerant handyman slipped on Latex gloves and picked the back lock. Downstairs lights off, check.

The scene Angela had witnessed earlier that afternoon in Sarah's kitchen rattled her to the core. What purpose, what destiny in God's great name, could viewing that obscenity serve? If everything did indeed happen for a reason, as she believed, why did she witness that despicable act? Perhaps she was there at that moment in time to scare off that man, to keep him from harming Sarah. But Sarah's betrayal of Herb would have been an uncrossable line for Angela.

Angela would have been dead-certain that no matter how close they'd been in the past, she didn't want to talk to Sarah ever again.

She wouldn't.

6

(This is Wolfe's verbatim journal recount of his assault on Angela, with some scenes reconstructed for clarity.—GH)

I knocked all lovey-dovey on the wall as I neared the bedroom, whistling 'Hungry Like THE Wolfe' like I always do when it's time to have some fun. She sounded SO happy to see me.

"Jack! I didn't hear you pull u—"
Her smile vanished, vocal chords tightened. Stepping into the doorframe, blocking her way out, stood the strange man she'd seen with Sarah on the kitchen floor. Dressed in black, wearing rubber gloves. He set his smartphone on the dresser, pushed "record," and flashed an emotionless smile. And in the other hand, behind his back, something else.
"Hiya, Angie baby. Remember me?" Wolfe swung his tire iron as he came fast at her. But Angela reacted quicker than expected. She rolled off the far side of the bed as the tool struck the feather pillow. She shrieked.
Wolfe wrote in his journal about how he loved that moment when his startled victim cringed in absolute terror at the stark realization of impending doom.

That was so fuh-reakin' cool, glad I got it on camera. I'll savor that one a long, long time.
She kinda suprised me by moving that quick. We had a hot date ahead, a Luv Connection thing. She saw me with her hot little friend this afternoon and I knew she dug me. Chicks always have. I could see it in her eyes, how bad she wanted me. Just like Aunt Cora, she begged for it, and more! And you can't

dissaspoint them, right? Her little friend saw how much Angie baby wanted me and started hissy-fitting. Angie baby was so mad she cut out. For that, I'll cut HER heart out and then get back to my sweet-hot Sarah.

The impact of the tire iron had exploded the pillow like a downy duck hit with both barrels. Angela fled for the door and her life, but Wolfe angled and cut off her escape. He grabbed for her arm and missed, but latched onto a handful of the light blue bathrobe and jerked her back. The tire iron broke ribs, but not her spirit, as she collapsed to her knees.

She panted, playing hard to get and thought she could scare me by saying, 'You won't get away with this. My husband will be home any minute. He'll kill you. You don't know his temper.'

Wolfe laughed, back-handing her. She smacked the wall, blood flowing from her nose.

'Ooooh, I'm sooooo scared, baby,' I said, and popped her again, landing a Joe Frazier uppercut that put her on her back. 'Maybe I'll wait up for him, after I'm finished with you.'

Angela fell back on the bed, and he pounced atop of her, beating her into humiliating submission. She tried to knee him. None of that, he told her, and threw his haymaker. She didn't reply that time. The jarring blow shattered teeth and her mouth filled with blood. Angela passed out.

It was taking too long, and we had a long night ahead. I wanted to take her for a ride, and wasn't taking no for an answer. I never do. No ALWAYS means yes.

Wolfe went to the garage, found a roll of duct tape, and first bound her ankles so she couldn't kick, then pulled her arms behind her and wrapped her wrists. He then tore off pieces and double-covered her mouth. He lifted the slight, unconscious woman over his shoulder, took her downstairs, found the car keys, and dumped her in the trunk. Unhurried and unworried, he glanced over the city map he'd bought.

When someone reads this someday, they're gonna want to know why I took Angie baby way across town to that particuler park instead of one closer to her house or maybe dump her in the river. Short answer, I just got in town and wasn't ready to leave yet, so I didn't want her body found too quick. But on a hot August night, the moon shinin' bright and I was feelin' all right. Just me 'n Angie baby.

Wolfe had pulled into the most secluded part of the park that he could find and went to enjoy his remaining time with Angela. Under a full August moon, he anticipated seeing her shimmering, lithe body in the moon glow. Instead, Wolfe howled. Already dead, her lifeless eyes stared at him.

Looked like she tried to twist loose in the trunk and suffucated. No fun at all!

Showing true Texas verve to the last, Angela must have scratched the duct tape from her mouth on a piece of metal; it pulled in the wrong direction when the car hit a bump and covered her nasal passages, cutting off her air supply.

She'd been so hot and was already cold. Well, a man's gotta do what a MAN's gotta do.

The rest of Wolfe's journal entry was too sick and twisted to record. Suffice it to say he took out his sexual perversions and frustrations on the body. Finally spent, he dug the grave, covered it with bits of brush and drove back near the motel, where he left the keys in the ignition. Police would find her stolen car months later at a Tulsa flea market.

Jackson needed to picture Angela's final moments on Earth as being peaceful. He knew she would miss life, would miss him, but look forward to seeing her grandparents and her Lord and Savior, Jesus Christ. Jackson liked to think she offered one final prayer that he would someday, somehow find her killer and bring him to justice.

He wanted to believe, to hope, to pray, her final earthly thoughts focused on him.

7

Attention to detail is the key for any good reporter or columnist, and I seem to have a knack for seeing the one little item others often overlook, that would help explain the bigger picture. And I know how to read people, when I'm hearing a lie, when somebody's trying to cover up facts, and I can draw the truth out of them. That psychology class still ranks one of the best I ever took, and it also helped me learn the value of remembering birthdays, anniversaries, names, faces, places, and events.

Those memory tricks came into play when I clicked on the online slideshow attached to my story on the Fletchers' deaths. Photographs ranged from investigators looking for clues to the body bags being taken out of the house, from a worried-looking Stone talking to two detectives to the fearful looks of neighbors gathered outside the house. There were other pictures of the Fletchers as well, from past social gatherings to several taken of Herb Fletcher at the visitation for Angela.

I spent a long time studying one particular photograph. I remembered seeing it in print, but cropped into a tight mug shot of Herb. Now I stared at the same photo online, but saw the full frame, and what I saw bothered me. The picture revealed a snaking line of people, stretching from near the front door of the funeral home all the way down the driveway. Fifty or sixty people could be seen in the frame. All in various poses, caught without being aware of the shot being snapped. One fifty-ish man scratched his ear, while an older couple dressed in somber black looked ahead. A young woman straightened her daughter's skirt. The thirty-something man smiled as he chatted up a young woman, probably about Angela, but maybe about the weather. Near the front of the line, Herb mugged for the camera. All the people in line bore one thing in common—all except one. All the other figures in the photograph faced the camera. That solitary figure with his back to the lens? A young, well-dressed man with his long, dark hair pulled into a ponytail. About seven or eight feet from the camera, he headed away from the line, toward the parking lot. Something about it struck me as odd and made me think of the famous *Life* magazine photo from the 1950s of all those people sitting in the movie theatre wearing those funky 3-D glasses. If one person left off those glasses, he would stand out from all the rest. That's how this visitation photo struck me, and I couldn't help but wonder why the man with the unseen face picked that exact moment to leave the line. People leaving the visitation room were routed to the parking lot through another exit. In my recollection of the visitation, I couldn't envision this young man in line behind Herb Fletcher, because I had focused on talking with Herb at the time. I zipped through the rest of the thirty-frame slideshow and saw no other picture of the unseen young man. Or his back, I should say.

Good reporters, like good detectives, listened to that inner voice that bugged them from time to time, and played hunches. Curious to see the face of that individual, I wondered why he left in such an apparent hurry when he stood in line so long. Maybe on his lunch break and running late to get back to work. Or maybe because Casey and I showed up to talk to Herb, and he didn't want his picture taken. I called the funeral home to ask director Arthur Greaves to see security tapes, but he'd departed for the day.

When one road's blocked, there's always a detour. I picked up the telephone and dialed my good friends over at Channel 11. As a professional courtesy—Dan Clarkston later admitted he thought he might glean something about the possible connection between Angela's murder and the

Fletchers' deaths from me—Clarkston called Greg Pittard, and they met me at the front counter.

We spent twenty minutes quick-scanning footage. Near the end, I thought I saw the right segment, but I'd check closer when I got home. As a dodge, I asked to see the first five minutes at regular speed, then wanted to see it again in slo-mo. Then I requested a DVD of the entire segment. Clarkston nodded, and Pittard returned in five minutes with my copy.

"Thanks for doing this on short notice," I told Clarkston as we shook hands. "It's been a crazy day, hasn't it? Who would have thought the Fletchers would wind up dead, too? I've never covered a story quite like this."

"I know what you mean," he said. "I'll be glad when it's all over. But I don't think that's anytime soon. So what's your angle?"

We were two competitive journalists jousting, so I lobbed a softball.

"I'm researching for the Sunday piece we're doing on Stone," I lied. "I wanted to see if you captured any interaction between Stone and Fletcher at the visitation that I might have missed. We've got a mug shot of Herb but nothing else. I didn't even know him until you interviewed him that first night. Nice piece."

"Thanks. He seemed harmless." Clarkston shrugged. "You believe that about something between him and Angela and then Sarah killing him after he killed Angela?"

I expected that to come up in the conversation, but thought I'd have to work it in. I wanted to keep him off-balance, so I threw my curveball.

"I'm not so sure," I said, shrugging. "I heard some of it, but couldn't get it confirmed on the record so we didn't toss it out there. However, I did include a line that Stone denied a Channel 11 report that the three deaths were somehow connected."

"Well, just great," he said, somewhat glum. "Hope you at least spelled my name right."

One more and the inning would be over. "So how's the New York gig going?"

"We're still talking. Maybe I can get you on the show as an expert. Maybe you can help me get Stone to agree to appear."

A lot of maybes, I thought, and zipped the fastball. Strike three!

"Yeah, maybe. First, though, I've got a killer to catch."

8

Mike Whitfield wished he *was* in rehab. A lot more exciting than this, the Metro police sergeant yawned as he weaved through traffic, while keeping a reasonable distance behind Jackson's Honda.

Chief King called Whitfield after his fruitless conversation with Stone and ordered him to stick to Stone. He said Jackson refused to aid the police in the plan to lay a trap for the killer, but that didn't mean the chief planned to end surveillance. Now more than ever, King confided, he felt the murderer would come after Jack. They didn't yet know why the Fletchers died and would need to find the killer to answer those questions. They were, of course, pursuing all leads, but if the chief proved correct that the killer pursued Jack, then Whitfield would be there to prevent another tragedy. Whitfield's supposed rehab ran a week. The chief said that could be extended if necessary—but for how long?

An exhausted Whitfield had followed Jackson for two days, a move to jump a full pay grade from sergeant to lieutenant. The chief would've loved for him to be Jackson's shadow twenty-four/seven, but settled for eighteen-hour days. They just hoped for the right eighteen hours. What if an attack occurred in the middle of the night while Whitfield napped? They talked it over and the chief considered pulling a shift himself.

Whitfield watched Jackson turn into the church parking lot, then he drove around to the opposite side of the church and parked behind the bushes where he could keep an eye on

Jackson's car. Services lasted an hour? He dug out his cell phone and dialed for backup.

"Is this your one phone call? How's lockup?" officer Barry Mendez answered smartly, recognizing his partner's number.

Whitfield laughed. "I'm out on parole. You busy?"

"Never for you. What's up?"

"I'm out here in Bellevue and wondered if you could meet me in about twenty minutes at Red Caboose Park."

"I'm leaving now."

Enlisting help seemed like the right move at the time, but Whitfield's plan backfired, and three hours later, he flew into a state of half-panic, half-rage. Whitfield didn't know if he should call the chief or not. Jackson had disappeared!

About five minutes before Jackson's arrival at Belle Rive Baptist, pal Big Red pulled into the church parking lot. He went inside to use the bathroom and stayed in there as Jackson arrived. Jackson joined the service conducted by Reverend Armstrong. After Red washed his hands, he walked outside to wait for Jackson and have a smoke. Stepping around the side of the building to light up, he saw Jackson's car—and dropped the matchbook. Half-hidden by a large oak, Red realized he'd seen the red pickup before. It followed Jackson out of the parking lot at that restaurant in Murfreesboro. Red ducked behind a bush and watched another five minutes before the pickup pulled away, then he re-entered the church.

"Jack."

"Where you been buddy? I saw your truck outside," Jackson whispered back.

"Jack!" A more urgent whisper. "Remember that red pickup truck you saw in the 'Boro? It's outside."

"Outside where?"

Armstrong didn't break stride in his sermon as he saw the two men slip into the hall where he saw them talking. They clasped hands and Jackson alone returned to the sanctuary.

More than a handshake, they swapped car keys. Big Red got in Jackson's car and waited. Forty-five minutes later, the red pickup returned. Red pulled out of the lot, making sure to be seen, and headed for the interstate.

Whitfield smiled at seeing Jackson's car still in the church parking lot. His conversation with Barry Mendez had taken longer than expected as he explained the situation. Essentially, Whitfield wanted Mendez to help keep tabs on Jackson around the clock; he'd clear it with the chief in the morning. Mendez listened to Whitfield's explanation and agreed to take over surveillance for the sergeant as soon as his shift ended at ten p.m., and Whitfield would resume watching at four a.m.

Whitfield saw Jackson's car pull out of the lot and into the evening traffic. He noticed a more erratic driving style. The car weaved around vehicles without the use of turn signals, then sped up without warning. Whitfield roared through a yellow light so he wouldn't lose Jackson. The car whipped onto the Interstate 40 East ramp—again without using his turn signal—and zipped toward Nashville at eighty miles per hour. On the east side of town, Jackson's car then headed toward Murfreesboro as storm clouds darkened the horizon off to the southwest.

Heavy traffic thinned as they reached the Murfreesboro area. Whitfield wondered where Jackson was headed, but assumed he headed for the property near Murfreesboro he co-owned with his brother. But Stone's car zipped past the first Murfreesboro exit, then the second, then the third, the fourth, the fifth interchange.

"Okay, so where are you going, Jack?"

A half-hour passed, and so did a brief shower before the turn signal ahead flashed. He exited in Manchester. The car pulled into a gas station—and Jackson Stone didn't get out!

"What the . . . ?" Whitfield quickly figured out the red-headed stranger must be Stone's friend, Jimmy "Big Red" Boyle. Whitfield kicked himself at how he'd been outfoxed.

He sat there considering his next move. Should he confront Boyle or continue to follow him to see where he'd wind up? Should he call the chief and give him the bad news that he'd screwed up? Boyle finished filling the tank, paid outside with his credit card, and took off. Whitfield followed for another half-mile and Jackson's car pulled into the Golden Calf steakhouse's parking lot. Boyle went inside and took a window seat.

Red watched and waited to see what the man in the red pickup would do next. The waitress came over, and Red asked for a booth, saying he expected a friend. He ordered sweet tea for both of them as Whitfield headed into the restaurant. Red sized up the man walking across the pavement. The stocky man took off his sunglasses as he entered the building. The waitress pointed in his direction. Red smiled and held up a hand missing a finger.

"Hello, Red," Whitfield said in a serious but amiable tone. This guy wasn't the enemy, just misguided like Jack. He tried to gain Red's trust.

"Jimmy Boyle," came the not so trusting reply. "Just my friends call me Red."

"I'm Jack's friend. His guardian angel. Where is he?"

Jackson stayed at church for the rest of the evening service and a half-hour after that as Brother Armstrong cornered him and wanted to talk. They went to the church offices upstairs and faced each other.

"I wanted to see how you're doing after this morning," the pastor said. "That must have been quite a shock, finding your neighbors like that."

"Yes sir, it was."

"Is there any truth to what they reported on Channel 11, that Herb may have murdered Angela? I saw him at the visitation and find it impossible to believe."

"It's not true," Jackson assured him. "None of it is. But somebody out there has tried to build a convincing case. The chief isn't buying it and wanted me to help lay a trap for Angela's killer who in all probability also murdered the Fletchers. I declined."

"But, Jack, I thought you wanted to find the killer."

It took several minutes for Jackson to explain his refusal to go along with the chief's request. He told his minister about Angela's pregnancy, how he had to make things right for his wife and their child. How he didn't protect them when he should have, so he had to see this through. Jackson wanted his pastor to understand his motivation in case something happened to him in the next forty-eight hours.

"Only one other person knows what I've told you, Brother Bob." A smile crossed his face. "By the way, did you start doing confession on the side?"

The preacher laughed. "I'll pray for you and Angela and your unborn baby. They're in heaven and someday—not too soon, I pray—you'll all be reunited in the Lord's arms. But maybe there's another way to satisfy this yearning."

The preacher's earnest pleas brought back the old doubts that Jackson wrestled with, since it went against everything he'd ever learned in church. Never a saint—far from it during his wilder college days—meeting Angela proved the salvation he needed after all he witnessed in the Persian Gulf. Some called what happened to Angela a test of faith, and maybe it was, Jackson agreed, recalling their conversations. He said he prayed for answers and still awaited a sign.

"I don't know if you'll ever get all the answers you want, but the Lord provides. Have faith, Jack. Don't ever lose faith." Angela had always told him the same thing, Jackson recalled.

Off in the distance came the first rumblings of the late summer storm.

"I'm trying, Brother Bob. Everything I've shared with you tonight is between us, right?"

"You have to ask?"

"Yes I did, I'm sorry to say. I've got to go, but if anything happens to me, explain to Patrick and the police why I've been doing this. Let the world know."

"Let's pray together."

Reverend Armstrong and Jackson Stone clasped hands and bowed their heads as another peal of thunder clapped.

9

While I enjoyed zinging Clarkston, I decided I would have to show my gratitude someday for this gold strike. After fast-forwarding through the DVD, I found the segment I sought. The videographer filmed an eight-second pan shot of the snaking visitation line and in about the last three seconds near the end of the line, you could see Herb Fletcher. I slapped at the pause button and then zoomed in on the frame as much as the controls would allow. Fletcher appeared to be talking to the young man with dark hair tied in a ponytail behind him.

I squinted and studied the profile. Yep, absolutely, positively. One hundred percent the same man I'd seen leaving the scene in the photo now posted at TenneSceneToday.com. The same solid build, the same jacket. Trees shaded his eyes, but a shaft of sunlight broke through the leaves and highlighted a crooked smile, then panned on past and cut to another scene inside the funeral home. I shook my head, wishing for a full frontal image of the man, but at least it was something to go on.

My cell phone camera captured several pictures off the paused television screen. The grainy images on the DVD might not be admissible evidence, but if the man walked past, you'd recognize him from the digital snapshot.

"Okay, now what?" I said, thinking out loud. No clue as to the man's identity, why he attended the visitation or left so abruptly, but something about this guy failed the smell test. More than ever, I wanted to learn all about this man.

I wanted to know his background, something, anything. Maybe I could crack this thing wide-open after all.

Briefly, I let my imagination run wild. A member of Jackson's church or possibly a friend of Patrick Stone, there to pay respects. He attended because Angela used to babysit him on Friday nights as a teen-ager, when the wild-child third-grader's parents needed a date night. The man got a call from his wife about the overflowed toilet and that's why he left so suddenly. The guy remembered that he forgot to turn off the stovetop and rushed home before the house burned. The man joined the visitation line . . . to size up Herb? Or Jackson Stone?

"Okay, enough," I said, shaking my head as Jill entered the den to see if I wanted a drink. I needed one, but declined. Outside, lightning crackled, and the storm built in intensity.

Decisively, I placed my first call to Jackson Stone's cell phone number. Straight to voicemail, so I left a message and fired him the image off my cellpix.

"Jack, it's Gerry Hilliard at *TenneScene Today*. I've come across a photo of someone I'm trying to identify from Angela's visitation and thought you might help. Thanks."

I left the same message on Patrick's answering machine, and tried Reverend Armstrong, who didn't recognize the description, but said he might if he saw the photo.

"Try Jackson again in a little while. He just left here about fifteen minutes ago."

"Thanks, I will. Was Patrick with him?"

"No I didn't see either Patrick or Sheila tonight. Jackson attended with another friend who didn't stay long."

I hung up and glanced at my watch. I wasn't about to call my police contacts, spokesman Darrin Jensen (whose job description included fielding late-night media calls) or East Precinct Commander Mark Reynolds. Usually, I'd call Sergeant Mike Whitfield, but I'd been spoon-fed and swallowed the rehab story and didn't know how long he'd be there. Thinking about Whitfield led to another idea. If the front door's locked, try the back one. I dialed the precinct.

"Gerry Hilliard at *TenneScene Today*. Is Officer Mendez still on duty? . . . Yes, I'll hold."

Barry Mendez, whom I'd interviewed last Friday with Whitfield, was speaking on another line when his telephone buzzed.

"So what's this Red guy saying?" he asked Whitfield. "How did he and Stone manage the switch?"

"All I know for sure is that they traded cars at the church. I might arrest Boyle for interfering with an investigation. He'd be out in a few hours, but he might think about helping Stone the next time."

"That's if there's a next time. Did he know Stone's plans?"

"He wouldn't say, even if he did. But I doubt Stone told him."

"So whaddya want to do?" Mendez said. "Wanna put out an APB for Stone?"

"No," Whitfield said. "Put out an APB for Jimmy Boyle's truck. That's what Stone's driving now."

Finding Stone wasn't going to be easy since they were looking for the wrong vehicle. He dropped out of sight, thanks to Big Red and a crusty bartender.

After leaving Reverend Armstrong, Stone walked outside, stood under the covered walkway, and looked around the parking lot. The preacher's car sat in its designated spot, seven away from Red's truck. Perimeter's all clear. Feeling safe, he unlocked the pickup and drove across town as the rain poured.

Red had asked Jackson what his plans were, and Jackson said he'd call. Not exactly the truth, but not a lie, either. Operating on instincts, Jackson formulated a general plan that depended on how fast it came together. He'd call Red tomorrow.

The truck hit a puddle of standing water as he pulled into the near-empty parking lot at Eddie Paul's Pub. The rain had slowed to a drizzle, just like the crowd. Weeknights were slow at the East Nashville eatery after nine o'clock.

One couple sat in the corner, and four guys hovered at the far end of the bar watching the baseball game. Jackson took a stool in front of Louie, who was already cleaning up.

"Hi, Louie. How's the bursitis?"

"I sure didn't expect to see you today of all days," Louie said. "That's a heckuva thing about Herb and Sarah."

"We need to talk—alone."

"Last call," Louie announced. Ten minutes later, they were alone. Jackson turned down the beer, then the cup of coffee that Louie offered.

"I don't need anything to drink. I need your help."

There was no hesitation. Louie had waged his war in the rice paddies of Vietnam and stood ready to aid a brother in uniform.

"There are people looking for me, and I don't want to be found."

"Who's looking for you, Jack?"

Jackson always shot straight and needed the barkeep to understand the dangers involved. He wouldn't blame Louie if he changed his mind, but didn't think he would.

"I'm not sure. I'm guessing the police, but it might be whoever killed Angela—and Herb and Sarah."

"You're kiddin' me," Louie said. But he didn't rescind his offer to help.

Jackson shook his head. "The cops think he may come after me next. I hope he does. The cops wanted me to sit still and let him come, then they'd close in. I said no."

"You wanna find him first, don't you?" They both grinned, though Jackson's more resembled a grimace.

"They say the only person who knows you as well as your wife is your bartender. I guess they were right. So I need to disappear until I figure this out."

"Why don't you go to that place you got in Murfreesboro?"

"Actually, I wondered if I could sleep on that couch in the office."

"Not a problem."

Louie came around the bar and led Jackson to the office, handing off the front door key.

"Just lock up when you leave in the morning. Stick the key under the mat."

They walked outside. It stopped raining, but steam rose off the streets. Jackson appreciated that Louie didn't ask a lot of questions.

"I might stay an extra night if that's okay. I'll let you know. And one other thing, can I borrow your car?"

Before the bartender could answer, Jackson walked to the passenger side of Big Red's big truck and opened the door. He reached under the front seat and dug out a small case. He then handed the keys to Louie.

"One last request. This is another friend's truck, and the cops might be on the lookout for it now. Drive it home and park it in your garage, or behind the house, but don't get caught driving it, or you'll be answering a lot of questions."

Louie again didn't hesitate, just accepted the keys Jackson held out.

"Good luck, Jack. You brought your toothbrush and shaving kit, huh?"

With an ominous grin, Jackson unlocked the case, flipped the clasps and opened it to Louie, who whistled. Inside, the untraceable Soviet Tokarev .30 caliber pistol.

"Something like that."

Louie's turn to smirk, only not so grim. "Good hunting, Jack."

10

I gave up on anybody returning a call so late. I reached Patrick, who didn't recognize the description and didn't know his brother's whereabouts. I tried Jackson's home, his cell phone, and via text message. The cop Mendez hadn't called either; I assumed he was out on a call or forwarded the interview request to Commander Reynolds or the police spokesman. I planned to call Reynolds first thing in the morning. I stood to go to bed, yawned and my cell phone beeped.

"It's Barry Mendez, Mister Hilliard. Hope it's not too late. I just got off duty and grabbed a quick bite."

"Not at all, officer. Thanks for calling. Have you talked to Mike lately? I wondered how he's doing."

Mendez answered with caution.

"We talked tonight, as a matter of fact. Sergeant Whitfield is fine. This isn't for the paper, is it? I don't want to be quoted."

"Nah, we're just talking," I assured. "I like Mike a lot and felt concerned about him. We've talked over cases before, you know? He sometimes steers me in the right direction on a story. It keeps me from printing an error and having to write a correction. We talk on the record when it's appropriate."

I let that sink in and plunged ahead.

"Along those lines, I think we can help each other on this Angela Stone case. I'd call your partner, but since he's in rehab, I tried you. This is not an official request, by the way."

Mendez hesitated. "How long will it take you to get to Antioch? There's an IHOP right off the interstate."

"Forty to forty-five minutes," I said, looking at my watch. "I live out in Hendersonville."

"Hop on down," Mendez said, and hung up. I went to tell Jill, who was already asleep. I kissed her and turned out the light.

As it turned out, I wasn't alone in not getting to bed at a decent hour. Jackson gave up trying to get comfortable lying on the lumpy couch at Eddie Paul's Pub in East Nashville.

After scrounging around the bar for some food, digging out some nacho chips, shredded cheese, and salsa, Jackson opened a diet soda, resettled on the couch, found a newspaper, and read the small item about Whitfield's suspension. Old news, so he flipped through old golf magazines, and others on fishing and hunting.

Jackson figured he better get some rest and cut off the lights. But he couldn't shut off his mind and kept thinking about finding Sarah and Herb and his meetings with the police chief, the reverend, and Red. He wondered how that goose-chase had worked, and it pleased him to make Red's truck disappear. He hoped he would have time to get one of those disposable phones tomorrow, maybe several if he wanted to stay ahead of the cops, or whoever. He thought about Red, but figured he could take care of himself.

Tired but not, Jackson rose and turned on the television. An old movie might put him to sleep. When he lifted the newspaper on the side table, he saw the control device for the security system. Hooked into the portable TV, it allowed the bar manager to review the last two weeks' worth of video surveillance. The newspaper article he read earlier about Mike Whitfield's suspension made him think of the warm meeting with the sergeant and his wife. That led to a thought that even though the man in the red pickup wore dark hair and a mustache, he bore the same build as the blond officer.

On a hunch, Jackson decided to check the security cam. It took a minute to figure out how to rewind through the system, but soon he saw himself sitting at a table with the

Whitfields on Monday night. Jackson reflected that Angela would've liked the young couple. He saw his demeanor change over the night, going from sober to almost sloppy drunk. He rewound the tape and counted his beer intake that night—one, two, three . . . six, seven, eight!

"Man, he should have arrested me. I'm surprised he even let me get in the car."

It disgusted Jackson and made him wonder how he ever let himself go like that. And why hadn't Angela ever said anything? He shook his head. The security tape reinforced the thought that Jackson clearly must confront a drinking problem to deal with on top of everything else. Well, one thing at a time. First, try and catch a killer. He'd overlooked some clue, but couldn't figure out what. Jackson had watched long enough, it was time to sleep. About to hit the pause button, he paused himself—then scanned back and watched again.

The tape showed a lean, dark-haired, young man come into the Pub, order a drink, then stare for several minutes at Jackson and the Whitfields, who were about twelve feet away and laughing. A look of recognition came over the mysterious man's face, and he threw some money on the bar and hustled out, turning away from their table like he didn't want to be recognized.

"That's odd," Jackson said. He didn't know the face, but would never forget it. Jackson hit the print button, then turned out the lights, and soon fell asleep.

The strange young man's face haunted his dreams.

THURSDAY, AUGUST 19
1

I wheeled my car into the IHOP parking lot just off I-24 and Bell Road near old Hickory Hollow Mall and entered. Just after midnight, the start of a new day, Mendez waved me to his table. Seated with his back to me, a thick, dark-haired man I didn't know. Another cop or maybe a friend Mendez met after his shift ended.

"I hope you don't mind that I invited someone else," Mendez said, apologizing to the man across from him who looked around.

"I thought only my hairdresser knew," Sergeant Mike Whitfield said. "Have a seat."

"And I thought you were drying out," I said, glad to see him. It would make what I in mind easier to pull off. "Did you bust out? It's good to see you even if I wouldn't have recognized you."

A few more barbs were traded, then the real meeting began.

"So who gave you permission to call in a reporter?" Whitfield asked his partner.

"Nobody." Mendez shrugged. "He called, asking about you. Said he wanted to show you something."

I took my cue as Whitfield shifted attention. I opened the cell phone, and clicked open a photo taken off my television screen.

"Either of you seen this man before?"

Whitfield studied the pictures, and then handed the cell phone to Mendez. He shook his head.

"Who is he?" Whitfield asked.

"I have no idea," I said, "but I'd sure like to. At our website is a photo of this man leaving the visitation. He took off right as I showed up to talk to Herb Fletcher. I found some video from the visitation which showed them together near the end of the line chatting away like best friends. I've described him to some folks tonight and nobody recognized him. I can't say why, but I feel like he's somehow connected to this case. Something ain't right."

Whitfield studied the photo again. You couldn't see the man's dark eyes because of the shadows, just a twisted smile bathed in sunlight. Whitfield didn't say it, but he thought I might be right.

"It's kind of hard to make him out," Whitfield said. "Got any other pictures?"

"Just the video at home and it's not much better."

"I'd like to get a copy," he said, handing me back the cell phone.

"I thought you might. I'd like to help, but—"

"Your journalistic principles?"

"Something like that." I figured they'd understand. But, no.

"We can get a subpoena and charge you with interfering in an investigation," Mendez said. A look from Whitfield silenced him.

"Yeah, I suppose you could. I'm going to have to talk to my editors in the morning. On another subject, what's up with the dye job and fake story about going into rehab? I'm feeling kind of used right now, Mike. I'm going to have to tell my editors about that, too. Maybe there's another story I need to write."

"Hold on," Whitfield said. "Let's talk this out, and I'll explain what I can."

"Not unless it's on the record," I snapped.

We all sat in silence for several minutes. I thought about getting out so late and what I hoped to accomplish through Mendez. I didn't want a golden opportunity to pass, and that made up my mind, so I stood, said I'd be right back and headed for the bathroom. I caught Mike's eye and left my cell phone on the table. In no hurry to get back, I washed my hands twice and then raked my comb over my hair. Long enough.

I never asked, and Mike Whitfield never volunteered any information, but here's what I *suspect* happened while I waited in the bathroom. I *suspect* Mike's eyes followed, and when he heard the door lock, I *suspect* he picked up my cell phone and forwarded a copy of our mystery man's cell photo to his own email address. I further *suspect* that Sergeant Whitfield put the cell phone back on the table moments before I emerged from the john because it sat *precisely* in the same position as when I left for the bathroom.

As I said, these are mere suspicions. But as I came out of the bathroom, Whitfield stood.

"We talked it over," he said. "I don't think this is the right time for an on-the-record conversation. Keep your trap closed, and I'll do the same." We shook hands and walked to our cars.

"Nice not talking to you. But I want to be the first person to hear if something breaks."

"My boss will call your boss," Whitfield said and drove off.

I got home about one-thirty, bothered a little about what I *thought* occurred. I would also report the meeting to my boss.

The stage was set for quite a showdown, and I would be right in the middle of it.

2

Storms returned Thursday morning, and the Midstate buzzed over the deaths of Sarah and Herb Fletcher. Traffic at TenneSceneToday.com reached an all-time high with over eight hundred hits on my front pager, with bloggers speculating on why Herb killed Angela, how Sarah killed Herb, and what role Jackson played in their deaths. The editors kept libelous and abusive comments in check, but as soon as they deleted one, three more were posted. A sample:

At 4:10 a.m., HOOSIERDADDY wrote: "It looks like Jackson got his revenge; how hollow he must now feel. Hope your soul was worth it, murderer."

At 4:47 a.m., DETERMINATOR wrote: "In response to JONAS, my guess is the killer is still out there and Stony will catch him and feed him to the fish."

At 5:10 a.m., MITSU wrote: "The big question is why the Fletchers are dead. There MUST be a connection to all three murders. If Stone killed Herb he had reason."

At 5:59 a.m., BUZKIL wrote: "Stone Stone. I bet he killed all three."

At 7:10 a.m., PASSION FLOWER wrote: "I know the passing of the Fletchers is news, but the media coverage is sensationalized. You make money off these tragedies. Shame on you."

At 8:32 a.m., RETCHIN' GRETCHEN wrote: "All of you people act like vultures. And not just

260

the media, but those who write this jibberish.
You should be ashamed. You make me sick."

At 8:55 a.m., Chief King scanned page after page at the newspaper website, awaiting Whitfield's call. So far the routine reports addressed what Jackson did, where he ate, who he met, if he'd made any progress toward finding the killer, if anyone suspicious seemed to be following him.

At 9 a.m., King's private telephone buzzed. He answered on the second ring.

"We've lost Stone, but we have a lead on a suspect," Whitfield reported.

King's irritation at losing Jackson abruptly shifted to excitement. Finally, a break.

"I just emailed you a photo of a person of interest. It's not a great shot, but maybe the lab boys can enhance it," Whitfield added.

For the next ten minutes Whitfield filled in his boss on the past twenty-four hours, from his decision to bring in Mendez to where he lost Stone, from his fruitless interrogation of Big Red to the APB put out on Red's truck, from Mendez's late-night phone call to the meeting with me. Whitfield expected to be fired, taken off the case, or demoted. None of the above.

"You make finding Stone priority one, and I'll start trying to find this man," King said. "Get Mendez to stick with Boyle. Let's see if Stone contacts him again."

"I still have a job?" Whitfield asked, somewhat incredulous.

"You've made some mistakes, but Stone could have pulled that switch on anyone. He's pretty clever and shouldn't be underestimated," King said, controlling his anger. "You should have called before you brought in Mendez, but we might not have this photo if he hadn't known he could talk to you, so things even out. We need to get back ahead on this. Mendez is reassigned to you. I wish the newspaper wasn't involved. I'm going to call over there. Get back to me."

At 9:20 a.m., King hung up and dialed *TenneScene Today* Executive Editor Judy Flint. Her secretary said Mrs. Flint was in a meeting but would he please hold. Danise knocked on the door and entered. Besides Judy and me, the intense meeting consisted of city editor Carrie Sullivan, Managing Editor Ken McGuire, and Publisher Andrew Polk. I felt thankful for the interruption. I'd called Carrie from the house and when I got to the paper, they were waiting for me. I felt like the guest of honor at a mid-August barbecue. The main course.

"Chief King on line two," Danise announced.

"We're finishing up here," the editor said. "Tell him I'll call back in ten minutes."

Danise left, and Judy turned on me, a disgusted look on her face.

"You can leave, too, Mister Hilliard," she said. Judy and I have a very good relationship, but she's STILL the boss.

After I left, Judy went ballistic. "I want him off this story. Assign it to Tony or Shelley."

"Don't overreact, Judy. He's been so far ahead on this story it would be a real mistake to pull him now," McGuire said.

"He's compromised our ability to gather the news fairly and impartially."

"That's bull," Carrie said. "Gerry's the best reporter we've got. You know we've cooperated with the police on investigations before—last spring on the East Nashville rapist case, as a matter of fact."

"That was different," Judy fired back. "That perv mailed us a letter bragging about his crimes. It was evidence."

"And it helped catch him, did it not? And Gerry was all over that story, too."

Publisher Andrew Polk, prematurely gray for his forty-two years, again proved the voice of reason. And the boss.

"The police are going to owe us one," Polk said. "If we hand them key evidence, we'll demand an exclusive."

Judy backed off. "All right, Andrew, it's your call. Everybody back to work. And tell Hilliard no more phone calls to the cops without talking to me first. I don't care what time it is." She dialed the police chief.

At 9:30 a.m., Carrie lectured me how she once again saved my butt, when my telephone rang. Jackson Stone, the caller ID said.

"Where did you get this photo?"

3

Delmore Wolfe sat in his car around the corner from Jackson's house, waiting and trying to watch through the steady rain that streaked the windows. He couldn't see much, but his Super Hearing earpiece picked up everything. He had driven past the house twice and down the alley behind it, spotting no cars and no signs of life.

A police cruiser approached, and he ducked from view. Fortunately, the cop didn't stop to check out his parked car. Everybody parked on the street in the close-knit community, where most of the cottage houses and Victorian homes were built in the early twentieth century and attached garages were rare.

Wolfe grew angry. He counted on finding Jackson so he could follow him to that hot little psychiatrist. Jackson had scheduled a session with her, and Wolfe wanted one, too. He tried to think where Jackson might be this early. He sat outside the house for an hour or so, growing anxious and more paranoid. He lit another cigarette and washed a handful of pills down with the last sip of Jack and Coke, driven by demons that would not let him rest until he found his quarry. He picked up sounds of another car approaching. A red pickup pulled into the driveway. He couldn't make out the features of the dark-haired man who got out and banged on the front door. Wolfe turned up his amplifier.

"You in there, Jack?" No answer. The man walked around the house checking the back door and peered into windows. He left forthwith. Wolfe stayed.

Jackson yawned, rolled his neck, flexed his shoulders, and rubbed at his lower back, still getting over the lumpy couch. He made coffee and got a paper at the market across the street from Eddie Paul's Pub. He twice read my story and the sidebars. None of it went as far as television coverage in trying to connect the deaths. Our article quoted Stone as denying Channel 11 reports.

Jackson worked at his second cup of coffee trying to decide what he would do today to speed up his search when a ravenous hunger hit him. He started to go back to the market, but decided to get going. He wanted fresh clothes for his eleven a.m. appointment with Doctor Karnoff, but didn't want to swing by the house. He didn't know if the cops would be there, but didn't want to chance it. He'd disappeared and wasn't ready to resurface. He got in Louie's silver Malibu and tuned into George Dunkirk's talk show as he drove through the rain to the Greasy Spoon diner for breakfast. Five minutes of mindless radio chatter and speculation about what happened to the Fletchers wore him out.

"If they knew," Stone muttered as he slammed the car door, wishing for enlightenment himself.

After ordering, Jackson decided he wasn't going to Murfreesboro just to change clothes. An "emergency" suit hung in the spare bedroom closet at his brother's house. As he opened his cell phone to call Patrick, he noticed a photo in his inbox. The waitress brought breakfast, but Jackson never noticed. After five minutes of staring at the picture, that's when he called me.

I stayed cool in front of Carrie. She'd climbed out on that proverbial limb for me, and if she learned I was talking to Jackson about the photo I'd shown to the two officers overnight, no amount of explaining would help. But I wanted to gather more facts and fill in holes before bringing it to her attention.

"I'm sorry, Mister Jones," I said. Carrie bristled at the interruption to her stern lecture, "but I'm working exclusively on the Stone murder case. I'll pass on your number if you'd like."

Jackson immediately understood I couldn't talk.

"I've got an appointment at Vanderbilt at eleven. I can meet you by the Parthenon in about an hour," Jackson said. "At the picnic shelter."

"Sure thing. Good luck to you, too, sir."

I hung up and tried to be attentive to Carrie's sermon about a right way and a wrong way to track down a story, that I had come *this* close to getting fired or reassigned, that I'd better call Judy before I pulled another stunt like that.

"Sure thing," I said, glancing at my watch. "Listen, I've gotta go. I'll call *you* when I've got something."

Carrie tried to be mad, but couldn't. I took care of a few things at my desk, logged off my computer, grabbed my notepad, cell phone, and mini-recorder, then, like Elvis, I left the building.

As I pulled out of the newspaper parking lot and headed toward West End, Channel 11's Dan Clarkston turned the ignition in the car and pulled out of the gas station across the street.

"So where do you think he's going?" asked videographer Greg Pittard, who filmed with his small hand-held camera as they trailed me.

"I'll pull up beside him at the light and ask him," Clarkston said.

Still stinging from my verbal jabs of the previous night about closing in on the killer, Clarkston figured something on the DVD gave me the clue I sought. We enjoyed competing against each other and now more than ever, Clarkston wanted to kick my butt on this story. After I left the station last night, they went back and reviewed the first five minutes of the video five times—the only part I'd asked to see more than once. I'd done so for the purpose of throwing them off the scent. They behaved as I expected, just the way I would, had roles been reversed. It almost worked. Clarkston recognized faces in the footage and tried matching names. He wanted to look one more time, but

Pittard said his shift ended ten minutes ago and headed home. So Clarkston restarted the playback unit. He watched the first five minutes and decided to look over the whole tape. Another five minutes passed before an urgent need to go to the bathroom hit. Clarkston didn't turn off the scanner. When he got back, it neared the end of the tape. There was Herb in the line.

The mustached man behind him looked somewhat familiar, but Dan couldn't put a name with that face. Where had he seen that guy before?

Clarkston couldn't figure it out, so he decided to let me do the legwork, and he would be there to grab the spotlight.

The chase began, with Desperate Dan running second.

4

Jimmy Boyle was driving too fast on Interstate 24 West, slogging through the driving rain on his way to Nashville when his cell phone rang. He recognized Jackson's number and put the call on speaker so he could keep both hands on the wheel.

"Hello," Big Red said.

"Where are you?"

"I'm passing the Smyrna exit now. I should be there in about forty minutes. Where you calling from?"

"I'm almost at my brother's house, and then I'm going to swing by Vandy. Can you meet me at the Parthenon?"

"Why sure, Jack. I'm in my brother's car. I left yours in Lynchburg. You were right about being followed. That cop sure looked mad. But I didn't tell him nothin'."

"Did he give you his name?"

"Yep, but I don't remember. Let's see. Oh yeah, Mike something. A big, dark-haired fella, called himself a friend of yours, but I didn't trust him."

Jackson smiled. He wasn't alone in the stealth department.

"Well, well. That's interesting. Pretty stocky, with narrow eyes?"

"Yeah, you nailed him."

"All right, Red, see you in a little while. Be careful, though. They might still be watching you. Let's meet by the picnic shelter."

Red looked in the mirror and spotted a Tennessee state trooper keeping pace with him about ten car lengths behind.

"Oh man, you might be right," he told Jackson. "There's a highway patrol—wait, he's getting off the road. Looks like you got nothin' to worry about. Seeya in a few minutes."

Red hung up and watched the trooper exit as he crossed into Nashville's Davidson County. Actually, Red should have been looking ahead. He passed a black car just pulling onto the interstate. It kept pace with the oblivious Jimmy Boyle, who tuned in to the oldies channel.

"Thanks for your help, Trooper," Barry Mendez said as he took over in the unmarked police car.

"Let us know if we can be of further assistance," the state cop radioed back.

"All right, Red. Where are you taking me?" Mendez said.

Delmore Wolfe felt stoked, and not just from the drugs. His gamble paid off. Tiring of sitting outside Jackson's house, Wolfe had spent an hour prowling around East Nashville for Jackson's car.

He swung back by the Stone house and took a sharp left. Another cop car did a drive-by. Wolfe reckoned others sought Jackson and decided he better find him first. Then a cool thought crossed his mind. They're going to arrest him for Herb's murder. I bet that's why the cops are looking so hard for him. They're closing in.

Another thought wiped the grin off Wolfe's face, and his chest tightened.

He might be at the psychiatrist's office right now.

Panicking, Wolfe entertained one last possibility.

Maybe he's gone to see his brother.

Wolfe hit the gas, and it took about twenty minutes to reach Patrick Stone's home. A silver Malibu sat under the carport canopy, one he hadn't seen before. He parked down the street for about five minutes, waiting to see who came out of the house. His Super Hearing device picked up muffled sounds inside before the door opened and a man came out. Wolfe couldn't tell who because the umbrella obscured his view. He cracked a window for a better look as an umbrella lowered.

"We're late for our appointment," Wolfe said as he glimpsed Jackson Stone's profile. Jackson backed out of the driveway and took off. So did Wolfe. With all his plans falling into place, he contentedly followed Stone to his meeting.

But time was running out for Mike Whitfield, frantic to find Stone. He left messages at various phone numbers, and sent emails, then visited Stone's brother at his Brentwood office.

"My wife arranged for Jackson to talk to a psychiatrist the other day, but neglected to tell him about it until we got there. He got mad and we left and haven't talked to him since," Patrick said.

"If there's anything you can tell me to help me find Jack, or if you should talk to him, please let me know," Whitfield said.

"There is one thing. A reporter left a message last night describing a . . . I don't know, suspect? It sounded like he wanted to warn Jack about him."

"Yeah, I know. I talked to the reporter last night. We're looking for the same guy. I think he's looking for Jack."

That worried Patrick. He presumed Jackson could take care of himself, but might not be thinking straight. If the cops were worried . . . .

"What is the name of the psychiatrist Jackson saw?" Whitfield asked.

"Doctor Erica Karnoff. She's over at Vandy."

Whitfield thanked Patrick, then dialed Chief King's private number as he sped back to Nashville.

"Sir, I'm headed Vanderbilt to meet with a Doctor Erica Karnoff. I'll keep you posted."

5

The storm that hung over Nashville had approached from the southeast, welcome relief from the heat wave. Temperatures had hovered around one hundred degrees for the past two weeks. It was the middle of hurricane season in the South, and when one moved inland in such dry conditions, the ensuing downgraded storm could still come so hard that flash floods overloaded sewers and sent water backing into the streets. It was one of those days.

Cars splashed sprays five feet as they hit the standing water along West End. Thunder boomed as the storm settled in above the Vanderbilt campus. Across the street at Centennial Park, lightning lit the dark skies like spider veins.

On a typical August day, the park teemed with sunbathers, joggers, mothers pushing kids' strollers, businessmen eating lunch, grandparents and grandkids feeding the Lake Wautauga ducks, homeless men panhandling or scrounging through the garbage cans for food, and musicians playing guitars or fiddles or banjos or bongos.

But the rain kept everyone away from the sprawling park, home to the Parthenon, an exact replica of the ancient wonder in Athens, Greece, which boasted magnificent columns topped by pediments of gods, goddesses, warriors on horse-drawn chariots, centaurs, Minotaurs and gryphons. Inside the temple stood a forty-three-foot-tall, gilded statue of Athena, the Greek goddess of wisdom, with a thirty-five-foot spear and shield at her side, and in her right palm, Nike, the goddess of victory.

271

It was under renovation, almost finished with one scaffold remaining.

Jackson approached Centennial Park from the west side of Nashville, followed by Delmore Wolfe, hot on the scent. Unaware of the tail, Jackson dialed Doctor Karnoff's office.

"This is Jackson Stone," he told the receptionist. "I have an eleven o'clock appointment with Doctor Karnoff, but I might be a few minutes late."

"I'll let her know," she said. The other line buzzed, and she punched it.

"This is Sergeant Whitfield of the Metro Police Department. I'd like to speak with Doctor Karnoff."

The receptionist connected Whitfield. He explained to Doctor Karnoff the urgency for the call, that Jackson Stone's brother had mentioned the meeting that went awry the other day, that he carried important information for Jackson pertinent to the investigation into his wife's death. Mike wondered if Jackson rescheduled for another day.

"As a matter of fact, we went ahead with the meeting. He has another appointment at eleven this morning," Doctor Karnoff said. "I'll be glad to let him know you're looking for him."

"Actually, I'm on my way there now. I won't take more than five minutes of his time. I promise"

Erica hung up, and her secretary buzzed again.

"Mister Stone called and said he might be late for his appointment."

Red approached downtown from the east. Already late for his Nashville appointment with Jack, he might run even later. Was he still being followed or just being paranoid? He noticed the black car behind him about five miles ago, and it kept pace. Jackson's vanishing act wasn't going to be blown by him. Red exited and headed downtown instead of toward the park, then dialed the last number on his cell phone. The trailing car also turned right.

"I may be a few minutes late. I'll try to lose him, but if I don't make it, you know why."

I drove by the Parthenon and around algae-stained Lake Wautauga to the back side of the park before I stopped and ran over to the picnic shelter under an umbrella that didn't keep me dry.

Despite the storm's intensity, I couldn't help but notice the lone car pull past me. What I didn't notice was Clarkston driving his wife's car. He could be devious, too.

The wind picked up, and I looked up at a stripe of lightning on the other side of the park, followed by the echoes of a cracking limb.

"Mind if I join you?"

I whipped around so fast I strained my neck. Dan Clarkston, the next-to-last person I expected to see at the park, closed his umbrella. I tried to answer as nonchalant as possible.

"Why sure, Dan, have a seat," I said, patting the bench. "You doing weather stories now?"

"So who are you meeting?"

"It's lunchtime, and I wanted to get out of the office on such a beautiful day," I said in a sarcastic tone. "Why you following me?"

"I don't know what you saw last night on that video, but I want some answers, and you're going to provide them. Start talking."

"Is this on or off the record?"

Clarkston got in my face. "Cut the bull, Gerry. You owe me."

Stone arrived and headed our way. Pittard got out of Clarkston's car to join us.

"Okay, I'm meeting with Stone. I told you about the Sunday profile I'm working on. I planned to suggest that he do your show, but I don't know now. I don't like being followed."

"What show?" Jackson Stone asked as he caught the end of the confrontation.

"*Ed and Tara*," I told him, and nodded Clarkston's way. "Dan here invited me to be a guest on the show with you if you'd agree to do it. I could use an all-expenses paid trip to New York City, Jack. Start packing."

"Oh, I am," he said, a cryptic statement that we'd only later come to understand.

"How about it, Jack? I think you've met my cameraman, Greg."

They shook hands. Clarkston pressed for an answer.

"I know you're here to meet with Gerry. He thought maybe you would be willing to do an exclusive with me after you've finished your interview with him. I don't have anything scheduled the rest of the day, so I'll be glad to wait. In fact, I insist."

The look I gave Stone told him to accede, and he picked up his cue, smiling.

"I'll tell you what," Jackson said. "My time's kind of limited right now. Why don't I swing by the station this afternoon? We'll talk about New York. It's time to take the story national, I guess. Right now, I'd like to talk to Mister Hilliard. Alone."

Dan smiled and left as if he'd won this round. He'd lost again.

The cat-and-mouse contest that was being played with Clarkston wasn't the only game of hide-and-seek in Nashville that stormy morning. Sergeant Whitfield made it from Brentwood faster than expected. About to enter Doctor Karnoff's medical office, he answered his cell phone.

"I've been spotted," Officer Mendez told his superior. "I've been following Red, and it seems like he's doing everything he can to stay away from the Vanderbilt area. We've been driving around downtown for fifteen—wait, he's pulling over and getting out."

"Don't lose him," Whitfield said. "Stone's supposed to be on his way here, but he might meet Red first. Call if Stone shows."

Big Red played country music tourist on his first trip to Nashville since the last Gulf War veterans' reunion. Despite stormy conditions, tourists roamed everywhere and at ten thirty a.m., country music blared from several venues. Red entered Bert's Beer Barn and ordered a house draught and a cheeseburger. Officer Mendez found a vantage point where he could watch and wait.

Red also waited, trying to figure how he could slip out undetected by that smart fella outside. Red didn't care about his identity, just that he lost his pursuer. Red put a couple of dollars in the collection can to benefit Angela's Angels.

A few miles away, Whitfield hoped Jackson would surface soon, whether at Doctor Karnoff's office or downtown. He'd warn him to be on the lookout for the mystery man in the photo. Jackson and I waited, too, for a break in the case. We didn't wait long.

6

I stood with Jackson under the protective picnic shelter watching it rain and watching Clarkston's car pull away. Alone at last, or so I thought.

Wolfe kept his distance, whipping his car into one of the park's side entrances once he saw where Jackson was headed. He parked on the far side of the lake, grabbed his Super Hearing device and dashed across the park's open field to the Parthenon. Climbing the massive steps of the structure and using the columns as cover, Wolfe closed to within a hundred yards, but needed to cut that distance in half to listen in on our conversation. He backtracked and came up on the other side of the lake. Moving within range, he stepped from behind the tree cover to take a spot on the stone bridge. The rain didn't bother him as much as what he heard.

In fact, it almost blew his mind.

"I guess we're going to New York," I told Jackson. "I don't know if that's what you planned, but it explained our meeting without raising more suspicions."

"So let's see what you've got."

I opened my cell phone, clicked on the photo, and handed Jackson a manila envelope. He looked at the visitation picture of the man's back and compared them.

"It's not very good," I said, "but at least you can see the profile and most of his face. That other shot ran full on our website. You can see they're one and the same."

Jackson handed the cell phone back, reached in his jacket pocket, and unrolled the photo printed off the security cam at Eddie Paul's Pub.

"I was about a dozen feet away when this—"

BOOM!

A lightning bolt shattered a nearby tree limb, the thunder clap instantaneous. Exploding in Wolfe's brain, it nearly burst his eardrums. He didn't scream, but yanked the Super Hearing earpiece off his head and backpedaled, teetering on the bridge. So Wolfe didn't hear the rest of my conversation with Jack.

"Sheesh, was taken," Jackson finished, handing me the printer image.

Jackson stared at the charred tree. I looked at the photo and then toward the movement I saw from the corner of my eye. It was *the* last person I ever expected to see at Centennial Park.

"Jack, you're not going to believe this," I said, trying to remain calm and not give anything away. "The man in this photo? He's about fifty yards behind you."

Jackson froze, but his eyes flashed left and right like an abacus, calculating.

"You're kidding! Where? What's he doing?"

I squinted over Jackson's shoulder, watching a dazed Wolfe rub at his temples, trying to regain his senses and his balance. Wolfe looked up and saw me staring.

"He's on the bridge by the lake. Looks pretty disoriented, maybe from that blast. "Wait. Looks like he's leaving."

Jackson stepped into my field of vision and locked eyes with me.

"I'm going to my car. Got to find him. You follow him on foot, see where he's going, call me, and tell me what kind of car he's driving. Do you understand what I'm telling you?"

I understood the situation, all right. I understood Jackson's intentions.

"It's him, isn't it?"

"That's what I'm going to find out."

277

Jackson bolted for the parking lot as recriminations racked his brain. He should've brought the Tokarev with him. But why take it to a meeting with a reporter? Who is this guy? Did he kill Angela and the others? If so, he's dangerous. If not, why's he following me? How'd he find me? As Jackson reached the car, he dug the Russian pistol from under the seat and tucked it in his waistband. Putting the car in reverse, Jackson hit speed-dial.

"Red, I need you now," he shouted, straightening the tires and peeling out.

Realizing he'd been seen, Wolfe headed for his car. He'd stalked enough victims to know danger lurked, caught in the rain, in an open field, exposed and with no plan of action. The tire iron and a knife remained behind in the car over a quarter-mile away. His powerful hands were killing weapons. But he'd feel better if armed.

Still stuck downtown, Red needed a distraction so he could go find Jack.

"Where's the bathroom?" he asked the bartender, who produced a key.

Red left a twenty on the bar and went to the back, ducking around a corner. He unlocked the door, then went to the bar's emergency exit and pushed open the door. Officer Mendez entered when Red went to the back. When he heard the distinctive beep that meant the emergency door opened, he sprinted to the rear of the bar. The door stood wide open. He ran out to the alley and looked both ways. Empty. Mendez pulled on the locked bathroom door. He cursed and ran back into the alley, desperately needing to find Boyle.

Inside the bathroom, Red felt the tug on the door and waited two minutes before exiting. Outside, he hailed a cab. As the taxi pulled away, so did Mendez. The chase resumed.

7

Jackson Stone pulled into the main lot, tires screeching on the wet pavement as he hit the brakes and got out of his car. He headed for the temple and made a quick recon around the perimeter, then cut between several columns. No sign of the man, but Jackson worried that he might lurk behind one of the columns or on the other side. He might never find him at this rate, but the guy couldn't leave without being seen. Jackson headed for the entrance.

As Jackson launched his war, I waged one myself as I tried to think the situation out before committing to his plan. Could I be a responsible reporter and a responsible citizen at the same time? I'd pointed Jackson in the direction of the man whom we were certain murdered Angela. Did that make me an accessory? Was a crime in progress? I tried calling Sergeant Whitfield, but the line buzzed busy. I dialed the direct number for Executive Editor Judy Flint, who expressed her concern for my safety after I explained the situation.

"Forget the story and get out of there, Gerry. Let the police handle it. I'm calling Chief King."

Judy hung up without giving me a chance to argue for staying. I knew I should leave, that I could be fired for disobeying a direct order. But how many times in a career did a story like this come along? I'd often asked myself: If I'm on an airplane about to crash, with time for one final call, would it be to my newspaper or my wife? The answer came more easily than I imagined.

I would stay, even if it meant boarding a doomed flight on the last story I would ever cover. I turned back toward the Parthenon as the driving storm grew ever stronger.

On the far side of the museum, Jackson wiped rain from his face as a hysterical woman came running out.

"Call the police!"

Jackson grabbed her by the shoulders as she broke down and he nodded inside.

"Are you okay? What's going on in there?"

"I work in the gift shop," she sobbed. "A man came in and I heard Mrs. Nelson shout. I found her on the floor. I just ran."

Jackson gave the woman his cell phone, told her to call the cops, then ran inside and saw the unconscious woman in the corner, a bloody gash on her head. Feeling a pulse, he knew she was alive, then he felt the tension of knowing he didn't have long before the cops arrived. He didn't know if he pursued Angela's killer, but no longer doubted that the man posed a danger. Cautiously, he moved into the museum, fingering the trigger.

Jackson turned the corner and stepped on glass from a shattered display case. The placard identified the missing piece as a fifth century B.C. dagger belonging to the great warrior Phideas. So the man was armed. Jackson kept his back to the wall as he climbed the stairs to the museum's main level and entered the cavernous temple where Athena towered at the empty room's far end. Eerily quiet after a few wet tourists fled from the loud screams, Jackson felt certain at least one other person lurked nearby. He clicked a cartridge into the gun chamber.

Beginning a methodical search pattern, he slipped around the giant, two-tiered Greek columns supporting the Parthenon's colossal roof. Twenty-three plaster-white pillars, three right behind Athena and ten down each side, separated the main chamber. Each imposing Parthenon column stood about three feet around and spaced some six feet apart, meaning that someone who didn't want to be discovered might never be found in this deadly version of hide-and-seek. Moving into the temple to begin his search, Jackson saw nobody and the lone sound came from his shuffling footsteps. But that meant the man on the move could be as stealthy as he. Maybe waiting to strike first. Jackson went on his first hunting trip at age ten, but never for bigger game or with higher stakes—not even in the Gulf War. Jackson's objective? To flush out his quarry.

"Why'd you kill Angela?"

His shout echoed through the chamber, startling Wolfe as he circled for a killing blow. He froze.

"What did she ever do to you?" Jackson growled, desperate to know.

Wolfe couldn't tell where Jackson hid, the way his voice reverberated.

"Wrong place, wrong time, man," Wolfe answered, adding a phrase Jackson heard many times over the past three weeks. "I'm sorry for your loss."

Jackson shifted to his right, then backpedaled. But he wasn't backpedaling from his mission.

"I'm going to kill you," he said.

"I was thinking the same thing," Wolfe replied.

8

I couldn't reach Whitfield, who was on the phone with the officer trailing Red's cab.

Red figured he'd outfoxed the officer, but he couldn't get through to Jack, who sounded frantic a few minutes earlier. He wasn't going to let Jackson down or let him die if he could help it. He'd find Jackson fast.

"Step on it, mister. I'll double the meter," Red said and tried Jackson's cell phone again. This time, a hysterical woman answered and asked if the police were on the way yet. Red cussed a blue streak, but the cabbie couldn't understand his Lynchburg accent.

Less than two miles away, Sergeant Whitfield hung up with Mendez, apologized for the interruption, and returned to his conversation with Doctor Karnoff as they waited for Jackson, already two minutes late for his scheduled appointment.

"Explain again why it's so imperative to find Mister Stone," Erica said. There were strict codes of ethics, and she followed protocol. Prior knowledge of a crime about to be committed required her to tell authorities or face possible charges. But what did she know? Nothing more than what the media reported, except, she reminded herself, the true motivation behind Jackson's desire for revenge. Should she tell this police sergeant and betray a confidence? Technically, Jackson had withheld information pertinent to an investigation.

"I have a picture of a man we think may be involved," Whitfield said, reaching into his hip pocket for his cell phone. "I want to see if Jackson can identify him."

"May I see it?"

Whitfield punched up the image, then handed it to Doctor Karnoff, who prided herself for her cool demeanor in dealing with emotional patients. She gasped.

"I saw this man yesterday."

Before Whitfield could react, the phone rang. Mendez.

"I thought we were headed your way, but it looks like Boyle might be going over to Centennial Park instead. His cab's in the far right lane. There's still no sign of Stone."

"Jackson called here, said he might be late. Maybe that's why. Call if you spot him."

Whitfield wanted to know where the psychiatrist saw this man and if she knew his identity, but the cell phone rang again before he could inquire. This time it was Chief King, scrambling out the door himself and strapping on his gun.

"Get over to Centennial Park now!"

As he bounded down four flights of stairs, Whitfield called Mendez.

"What's your ten-twenty?"

"Boyle just pulled into the park. I'm about to."

"Don't lose him. Stone's there, and so is our mystery man. I'm on the way."

9

Jackson narrowly avoided the dagger thrust, thanks to his war-honed instincts for survival. The stakes raised, just one would walk away.

Jackson had moved around the columns, pressing his back against the slabs to steady his aim. In a dual role as both hunter and hunted, his foe found him first. He admitted killing Angela, which told Jackson he conceded responsibility for the Fletchers' deaths and who knew how many more.

Jackson worked his way down the right side row of columns when the silence shattered, making him jump as it echoed throughout the chamber.

"Jack! I didn't hear you pull u—."

Angela? What the—

A shiver ran up his spine at once again hearing a golden voice, now silenced, but he understood the recording was supposed to distract him.

"Hiya, Angie baby. Remember me?"

What did he mean, they'd met before, Jackson wondered as his heart thumped in his chest. Barely conscious of his breathing, he calmed himself and tried to focus on the very real danger somewhere in front of him.

"You won't get away with this," his wife's struggling voice echoed. "My husband will be home any minute. He'll kill you. You don't know his temper."

The shock of hearing his wife's voice again produced the opposite psychological effect on Jackson.

It was meant as a diversion to lure the hunter into a death trap, but the recording sent an icy coldness through Jackson as he moved from post to post. His nerves tingled, all senses heightened. Not there. Not around that one. That one? No. All clear. On to the next one.

The tape kept playing. Her killer's bullying voice echoed. "Ooooh, I'm sooooo scared, baby. Maybe I'll wait up for him, after I'm finished with you."

Shutting down the recording became Jackson's priority in order to corner his quarry. The sounds of the scuffle and his wife's panicked screams seemed to come from the far side of the room. Holding the gun with both arms extended, he sprinted over there. His heavy footsteps were covered by the voices, and he ducked behind a column.

While continuing his methodical search of the temple, Jackson remembered saying that he'd wanted vengeance, not justice. But what he felt coursing through his veins was a cry for justice from souls whose lives were stolen by this hellish beast, including Angela, his unborn child, the Fletchers, and how many others? For days, Jackson had put himself in the crosshairs to flush out this animal. But he also endangered other lives and that weighed on him. Now at the crux of a life or death decision, the question was, did he keep the killer pinned and wait for the police to arrive, trying to make a citizen's arrest, or end it here and now? Jackson's paradigm shift in thinking began, but any decision would soon be taken out of his hands.

"God, protect me," he prayed. He found the smartphone behind a column, freezing as he glimpsed video of his wife's final struggle. He squatted and tapped the off button. Danger lurked, but the gun made him feel safe.

Wolfe's survival instincts kicked in as well. Silence and surprise were the keys as his prey neared. Once on the move, Wolfe sought the perfect moment and place to strike. Time to finish off Stone fast and get gone before the cops arrived.

Dropping to one knee behind a large cast sculpture of a Greek wrestler's torso, Wolfe savored the moment when Stone moved within range, the way he waited for all his victims. That's it . . . closer . . . closer . . . the ancient weapon felt so good in his hands. As Jackson knelt and turned off the recorder, one death scene ended, and the time for another arrived. Wolfe came up swift, expecting to rip through flesh and organs until he connected with bone.

Jackson would never quite know for sure what made him turn at the last second. Maybe a flicker of light caused by Wolfe's sudden movement, perhaps sheer intuition, possibly God's divine intercession on his behalf, a prayer being answered.

But it sure sounded like Angela.

Unlike the tinny smartphone recording he'd heard, this voice of his guardian angel hadn't been that tiny whisper one often hears described or reads about in those books on being touched by an angel in an afterlife encounter. It came as a full-throated shout in his left ear.

JACK!

He whipped his head around just in time to see Wolfe rising for the kill. The Russian pistol saved Jackson's life as ancient metal met modern, but the parry caused him to lose his grip and sent the gun skittering across the floor.

That vile grin angered Jackson, who didn't need a weapon to put down a rabid animal. A spinning kick blocked the next thrust toward his midsection and sent the blade flying. Now with both unarmed, the odds were even again. Just the two circling, looking for an opening in the ultimate winner-take-all.

Jack's powerful right would have done tremendous damage if it had connected solidly, but it grazed a whiskered chin as his foe danced in and out. Wolfe's bull-rush pinned him against a headless statue, and the force of the attack sent Jackson reeling, but he threw an uppercut that jarred Wolfe and gave room to maneuver. He whipped two jabs in Wolfe's face and followed with an overhand right that would have dropped many men. Wolfe roared at the stream of blood from his nose that splashed both and again dove. Jackson went down hard. Wolfe's steel-toed boots broke ribs, and Jackson just avoided a crushing head-stomp. He grabbed the leg and twisted hard. Knee ligaments popped, and Wolfe screamed, but didn't go down.

Instead, the pain focused Wolfe not on his desire to kill, but to flee. Survival instincts kicked in, and he needed time to recover. His good leg flashed out and clipped Jackson's head, breaking his grip, and nearly his neck. Wolfe limped for the emergency exit and scrambled out the door. The steps were slippery and he almost fell, then hit the open field.

I entered the Parthenon and assessed the situation. Shocked to see the woman on the floor, I pressed forward when I saw her breathing. I heard police sirens in the distance and moved faster. As Wolfe scrambled out the far exit, I saw Jackson lying on the floor and rushed to his aid.

"Where'd he go?" Jackson rubbed his tender ribs. It was difficult to draw a breath, but he fought through it.

"I came in that way. Nobody passed me. He must've gone through there."

Outside, Big Red arrived and sought out his old buddy. He missed Jackson at the picnic shelter, couldn't find his own truck. He didn't know of the vehicle switch with the bartender. The cab drove by the bandshell, then around the lake, back to the picnic shelter. Following the cab and watching for signs of Stone, Officer Mendez saw me entering the Parthenon. Mendez stood watch on the wrong side of the museum, or he would have run smack into Wolfe. Red took up a position on the right side, having left the cab to search for Jackson on foot. Red and Wolfe saw each other about the same time. The latter spun and headed back to the Parthenon.

Red wondered why that guy running in the rain by himself suddenly turned around. The emergency exit opened again, and there stood Jack, his shirt torn and holding his arm to his ribs.

"Which way did he go?"

Jackson used the same hand signals that had saved their hides more than once during the Gulf War. Red went left and Jackson right. Inside the museum, Mendez called an ambulance for the unconscious woman, searched the upstairs chamber and found the gun Jackson had lost, then retreated the way he'd come. Whitfield, still a minute away, hoped he wasn't too late because of traffic.

I emerged after Jackson, and watched the west side of the rectangular museum. Red studied the north side, looking for possible hiding places in the grove of trees near the lake. Mendez left from the south exit and looked for the ambulance, as well as the man they were chasing. Jackson scanned the south side and open field as far as the tree line.

Wolfe had vanished into thin air, like Jackson did at his very first press conference when he announced his quest for vengeance.

We were all looking in the wrong direction.

Jackson wasn't alone when he exited the Parthenon, or Wolfe might have attacked. But because of my presence, Wolfe figured the only way out was up. Rain made the renovation scaffold slippery and his leg hurt, but whether from the drugs in his system or acting on pure adrenaline, Wolfe scrambled up the ninety-foot framework. He'd hide on top of the museum, let the cops think he got away, then descend at sundown and get out of Nashville. Another thunderclap drew Stone's attention. When he looked at the dark sky, he saw Wolfe scrambling over the slanted rooftop. Jackson missed his gun. He began climbing.

Ninety feet above the ground, Wolfe wished for more pills. He wished for an end to the rain. He wished he'd never come to Nashville. He wished himself anywhere else. None of his wishes were granted.

Whitfield arrived and found Mendez, the injured woman—and me. He cursed and made me promise to leave or at least pull back as the ambulance arrived. The cops looked for Stone and their mysterious stranger. Both were gone.

Jackson almost gave in to the rib pain, but prayed for strength to bring this killer to justice. He vowed to make the world understand his motives. If he survived the day, he promised God.

"I need you, Lord," Jackson said, gasping. "Don't desert me now, don't desert me now."

The tropical-force wind and rain picked up again, as did the life-or-death risks. Not ready to die, Jackson would make that sacrifice if necessary to bring down this killer.

He reached the top of the scaffold and peered over the bars, which shook something fierce in the wind. Wolfe lay on his stomach, his arms wrapped around the base of the gryphon statue that sat at the roof's apex, and not looking Stone's way.

The smart thing, Jackson knew, was to descend and let the professionals take it from here. It wasn't like his quarry had anywhere else to run or hide.

But Jackson couldn't do that. The only thing left to him in this world, the only thing that mattered now, the only thought coursing through his mind, driving his body forward—bring down the killer. For Angela.

He inched onto the roof and dropped low, trying to keep from being blown off by a gust. He struggled for footing but gripped the dimensional tiling that made up most of the Parthenon's roof. The latest restoration project included the addition of a state-of-the-art sunroof above Athena to add natural lighting to the museum. Sun filters allowed more light or darkened the room below depending on outside conditions. Sketch artists loved the way it changed lighting on Athena; administrators loved how it saved on enormous light and heating bills.

The wind slowed somewhat and Jackson rose to his knees to scoot further up the roof. He hoped to reach Wolfe, still clutching the statue, before being spotted. He knew how it would go down, how *they* could go down if seen. Jackson wrestled loose a piece of the tile roof to use as a weapon. His grip slipped, and he almost went tumbling. A jagged lightning streak flashed across the sky, drawing Wolfe's attention.

289

Lit up in the darkened sky the way stage spotlights focus on Toby Keith or Taylor Swift in a live performance, the way the neon on lower Broadway made nightlife come alive, this light show almost caused the death of Jackson Stone.

Wolfe's screaming curses matched the peal of rolling thunder as he saw Jackson. The lightning crackled again, and Jackson could see madness in Wolfe's eyes so it shouldn't have been a total surprise that Wolfe sprang directly at him. Only one way down, only one final descent remained for Wolfe.

"Damn you to hell." A guttural snarl as he leapt at Stone.

Jackson saw the final assault in slow-motion and rolled with it. The movement kept them from pitching off the roof onto the concrete below. Instead, their momentum carried them backward toward the new section of roofing. They rolled, punched, kicked, scratched, and bit each other as they fought for any edge. More blood flowed. Wolfe got to his feet first and lashed out with steel-toed boots, breaking more ribs. Wolfe tried to stomp the life out of Jack, who somehow managed to roll out of the way of that size thirteen, triple-E deathblow aimed between his eyes. Jackson could count the crossing patterns on the sole of the heavy black boot about to crush his head. He would later recall the one overriding thought from that harrowing life-or-death instant: To let go and let God take control of his fate. And though perhaps it was the fierce winds, Jackson would swear to closest family and friends that it felt like he'd been pushed.

Either way, Jackson Stone's head no longer lay where Wolfe's powerful stomp connected with the sunroof. Tiny cracks in the glass rippled like a rock tossed in a still pond, spreading in all directions. Within seconds, the sunroof's integrity gave way. So did the glass.

Jackson understood the fall and the feeling. On a 2009 weekend excursion to Six Flags Over Georgia in Atlanta, Angela had dared him to go with her and Patrick on that 200-foot, dead-drop thrill ride. Jackson said no way, that he'd watch the kids with Sheila while they threw up their lunch. Angela laughed and called him "a wuss," and Patrick joined in, "Scared, big brother?"

His manhood challenged, Jackson reluctlantly took his place in line with Angela and Patrick. They were strapped in standing up and lifted sixteen stories. Then they fell, plunging toward the ground in a heartbeat. The braking system kicked in at the last second before they splattered on the concrete. After being unstrapped, Angela turned pale and looked ready to puke.

Jackson swore he'd never do anything like that ever again, yet it happened again, except this time with no braking system. The jarring sensation of the cracked sunroof giving way awakened every nerve. His eyes opened wide to see a shocked Wolfe either plunging or lunging toward him.

Jackson twisted in mid-air just enough to spare his life. A golden rod flew past his head and Jackson reached out; it seemed like someone extended a pole for him to grab and be pulled out of this nightmare. He clutched at a yellowed barber pole, and his downward descent slowed. He still landed hard, dislocating his left hip and breaking his right leg in three places. But he lived. Jackson said a Hallelujah and opened his eyes, collapsing on his back on the shards of glass.

Wolfe's fall had been broken, too. Suspended some thirty-five feet above Jackson was the impaled body of Delmore Remus Wolfe. The spear of Athena, the goddess of wisdom and prudent warfare, struck him square in the chest. Shocked eyes registered his final surprise, and lifeless orbs stared as his mouth hung open.

Red reached Jackson first, with me a close second. Bringing up the rear, the two policemen arrived in time to witness his near-fatal plummet.

"Man, I'm sure glad to see you alive," Red said.

"Me too," Jackson said and passed out. Another ambulance arrived and took him away.

As Chief King and more police cars arrived, I stepped back unnoticed and then moved to a quiet corner of the downstairs art gallery. I first called my wife to assure her and say I'd be home late, then phoned my city editor, Carrie Sullivan, with the breaking news. She first fired off emails to the publisher and executive editor, telling them of my safety, then ordered every available reporter and photographer to Centennial Park. But editors and reporters read over Carrie's shoulder while she pounded out my dictation about the final Parley at the Parthenon, as the next morning's headline trumpeted it.

I composed my thoughts and began.

"Open paragraph. A miracle occurred at the Parthenon on Thursday morning. Period. New paragraph. Less than a week after swearing vengeance against the man who brutally murdered his wife Angela comma Nashville's Jackson Stone survived a final showdown with an as yet unidentified man who tracked Stone to Centennial Park and tried to add another victim to his bizarre Nashville killing spree. Period. New paragraph. The confrontation in a driving rain ended with Stone surviving a seventy-foot fall through the Parthenon's new sunroof and his assailant's death by impalement as he landed on the spear of Athena. Period. New paragraph. Stone comma injured in the fall comma was rushed to a nearby hospital. Period. The extent of his injuries is not yet known. Period. New paragraph. Check back at TenneScene Today Dot Com for updates. Period. Close."

"Incredible! Great job, Gerry," said Carrie, breathless and giddy at the same time. "Help's on the way. Call back when you've got an update."

Jackson Stone's ordeal was almost over, but mine had just begun. That's how newspapers work. I had interviews to conduct, facts to gather, deadlines to meet. It would be a long year.

EPILOGUE

It's Monday, February 13, 2012, and Jackson Stone's trial ended last Friday at ten fifteen a.m., following four days of testimony and one overnight of deliberations. Yes, there was a trial following the Showdown at the Parthenon, as it came to be called. Some people didn't think there should have been a prosecution. They thought Jackson was a hero. But law enforcement couldn't—or wouldn't—let a man go around making threats about getting vengeance.

I spent the rest of Friday talking to witnesses, lawyers, policemen, and jurors, then headed to the office. Our comprehensive coverage for the Saturday paper included a mainbar from me, sidebars from Shelley Finklestein and Tony Smith, columnist Cheryl Hanson's perspective, a breaking news editorial, six color photos, three informational breakouts, and a timeline chart.

After covering the trial for the paper, I began organizing all the pieces of the puzzle—all the information, evidence, journal entries of the killer, and charges against Jackson Stone. Like I said earlier, I was just a reporter who got a little too close and became part of the story. Now that story was mine to tell.

Below is a recap of the aftermath.

Delmore Wolfe

Wolfe's identity remained a mystery at first. His fingerprints were not on file anywhere, and no photographs existed besides the newspaper and the coroner's.

The old blue Firebird with Arkansas plates was not registered in Wolfe's real name. Wolfe's identity was finally revealed following the discovery of his journals, when the Dickerson Pike motel day clerk called police a week after the showdown, after he saw a picture of the man in room thirty six on *Ed and Tara*.

Jackson Stone's Recovery

An ambulance crew stabilized Jackson's ribs, hip, and leg immediately after the fall and transported him to the emergency room at Centennial Hospital, just across the street from the park. Surgeons inserted a steel rod into his right leg, broken in three places. The hip easily popped back into place, with no nerve damage. Doctors taped ribs, cleaned up facial cuts, and diagnosed a concussion. Jackson spent a month convalescing at his brother's house before the hard cast came off, and he wore a walking cast for another month. Then he went to rehab every other day for another three months.

Today, he still walks with a slight limp.

Charges against Jackson Stone

The investigation continued well into 2011 as the district attorney's office filled an entire storage room with evidence of atrocities committed by Delmore Wolfe, as well as mounting evidence against Jackson. The DA listened to Jackson's explanations, along with Allenby's pleas, and weighed evidence against Jackson. On October 14, 2011, the district attorney called a press conference to announce formal charges against Jackson Stone. He asked that bail be set at two hundred thousand dollars since Jackson had no prior convictions and did not seem a flight risk. Jackson's brother posted his bail, set at fifty thousand.

The Judgment of Jackson Stone

The court convened at 9 a.m., on Monday, February 6, 2012, with Judge Morris Wright presiding. District Attorney Logan Trulowicz studied the eight-man, four-woman jury.

He would have preferred an all-male jury for this trial, concerned that women would be more sympathetic to Jackson's cause of trying to avenge his wife. Three of the men were black, as were two women. A third female juror was Hispanic, and the fourth white.

"Justice is why we're here," Trulowicz said. "*Justice* is what Jackson Stone, in his own words, said he did *not* want when he held his press conference on August thirteen of two thousand and ten. He wanted revenge, ladies and gentlemen. *Not* justice.

"That, in itself, is a premeditated action, and Mister Stone is fortunate to not have been charged with first degree murder. But he is here on a lesser charge of voluntary manslaughter. Why? The law is not without compassion, and Mister Stone already paid a great price with the loss of his wife, Angela. But that does not . . . that cannot . . . excuse his actions and wanton disregard for the law. You men, you women, today you are the dispensers of justice. Today, you are the defenders of justice."

The prosecutor explained why they were there, and the stakes.

"The state intends to show that the charge of voluntary manslaughter is the justice that Mister Stone deserves for his actions that morning at Centennial Park. He *must* be held accountable for the death of another individual, no matter how despicable a monster that other person was. Jackson Stone is on trial here today, *not* Delmore Remus Wolfe. You must keep that in your thoughts at all times.

"We will prove that Mister Stone knew his actions would be dangerous, and that he acted with reckless disregard, and that his actions resulted in the death of another human being. He plainly stated that desire when he said he wanted revenge for the death of his wife, not justice. He was unwilling to let the police act, to let the court system act, to mete out justice. You must not allow that attitude to prevail. You must cast aside your feelings and your sympathies for the loss of his wife, and act as the impartial arbiters of the law."

One of four panelists who spoke with the media after
the trial ended, Juror number five said he felt troubled by
what he perceived as Jackson's blatant disregard for the law,
that he had always instructed his two children daily to abide
in the law and practice good citizenship. Now the defense
asked the self-employed insurance agent to free a man who
stepped outside the law to pursue an admitted course of
vengeance. He tried to reconcile those feelings, he said.

Juror number nine, a large black man with an
intellectual air, who wore glasses, was a tenured aerospace
professor at Tennessee State University. He wanted to hear
all the evidence before making up his mind, doing his best to
remain impartial.

Junior number twelve, the Hispanic woman, stood tall
in the closed deliberations despite her diminutive stature. A
forty-year-old, fifth grade schoolteacher in Antioch, she said
the turning point came at eleven-thirty last Thursday night,
when they broke for the night and returned to their hotel
rooms to sleep on it. The next morning, after breakfast
together, they returned to deliberations and returned a
unanimous verdict within an hour.

"Basically, I just reminded (juror number five) of the
defense attorney's opening remarks," she said. "He laid his
cards on the table and didn't try to Bee-Ess us none."

Stan Allenby rose to address the jury, knowing the DA
scored some points, but he remained confident that he could
sway the panel back toward Jackson. Allenby's strategy
proved effective. The jury seemed impressed with the no-
nonsense attorney's passionate defense of Jackson. Allenby
flailed his arms like swatting at flies.

"First, forget any temporary insanity plea. We reject
that defense and demand nothing less than twelve verdicts of
not guilty."

He squinted and began his own slow, methodical walk
before the jury, looking each member in the eye, sizing them
up as he paused in front of each of the twelve.

"Not guilty," Allenby said righteously to the first one.

"Not guilty," he indignantly proclaimed to the second and followed with ten more paces and ten more stares.

"Not guilty. Not guilty. Not guilty. Not guilty. Not guilty. Not guilty. Not guilty. Not guilty. Not guilty. Not guilty."

When he reached the end of the jury box, he shook a finger at his client, and all eyes followed him.

"We will show why you should set Jackson free, declaring him not guilty to all the world. We are asking a great deal, I understand, and it is not something we ask of you lightly.

"The alternative to finding Jackson Stone not guilty is to do as the district attorney asks and find Jackson Stone guilty of voluntary manslaughter. The alternative is to send Jackson off to jail, to punish him and put him in shackles for the next several years of his life. Jackson does not deserve that fate, but it is all up to you twelve men and women.

"If after weighing all the facts, you can find Jackson guilty of the crimes for which he has been charged, then Jackson is ready to accept his punishment."

The attorney straightened his backbone and continued. "But Jackson is a strong man, and while he does not wish to lose his freedom, he will not lose his convictions. His faith sustained him throughout this ordeal, and he convinced me that what he did was with the noblest of intentions. It's my job to convince you, to *explain* to you, why Jackson does not deserve prison."

Allenby smiled and patted his chest.

"Me? I think Jackson deserves a medal and a ticker-tape parade down Broadway. If you want to see insane, let's focus on the killer this trial is really about. Delmore Remus Wolfe. District Attorney Trulowicz wants you to see this case in black and white, following the letter of the law. He doesn't want you to think about the devil, Wolfe, no longer on this earth. He doesn't want you to see the faces of Wolfe's fifty-plus victims, including Angela Stone, Sarah Fletcher, and Herb Fletcher here in Nashville.

"But I say to you, remember each and every victim. Don't you dare forget them, and don't let Jackson Stone become the final victim of Delmore Remus Wolfe. Here's why Jackson Stone should be allowed to go free."

For effect, Allenby counted off the reasons for "not guilty" votes on each finger.

"One, Jackson Stone did not stalk Delmore Wolfe. Jackson didn't even know the killer's identity when Delmore Wolfe tracked him to the Parthenon that morning.

"Two, Jackson Stone acted in a responsible manner, invoking his right to make a citizen's arrest when no police were around. Delmore Wolfe had attacked another innocent woman inside the Parthenon, and only Jackson Stone could prevent his escape.

"Three, the gun with Jackson's fingerprints on it was a war relic he brought along for protection. His wife and neighbors had been murdered, so it seemed reasonable to think his life might be in danger. And that gun, in fact, saved Jackson's life when used to block the killing knife blow that Wolfe aimed for Jackson's midsection.

"Four, Jackson Stone did *not* kill Delmore Wolfe. Wolfe did that to himself atop the Parthenon while trying to crush Jackson's head with his steel-toed boot. He missed and broke the sunroof, causing Jackson to plunge seventy feet, dislocate his hip, and break his leg in three places. The exhibit, Athena's spear, broke Delmore Wolfe's fall, and he died—a shame for those of us seeking justice, because *he's* the one who should be on trial here, not Jackson Stone."

The emotional lawyer wound it down, bringing his knees together and putting his hands together as if praying, speaking quietly.

"I humbly ask you for an acquittal of Jackson Stone. Let him try to rebuild his life the way doctors rebuilt his shattered leg. Send him home with his family and friends. Stand up, and strike a blow for justice. Thank you."

District Attorney Trulowicz called Chief King, Sergeant Whitfield, and several other material witnesses to the stand. On cross-examination, Allenby would hammer at his own strategy, suggesting self-defense without calling it such. The last exchange with Chief King proved another turning point.

"Chief King, would you call Jackson Stone's behavior criminal?" Allenby asked.

"Yes sir . . . and no sir," the large policeman said, squirming in the tight witness box. The answer made the DA squirm, too. He had counted on Chief King to help nail down a conviction.

"I find that a bit confusing, sir. Can you clarify your answer for us?"

"Jackson Stone's words were inflammatory, divisive, and threatening on several levels," King said. "I warned him personally, and at my own press conference that the law is the law, and that he must obey it like anyone else. I warned that any actions on his part could result in charges like the ones he is facing. It concerned me that his actions would impel others to follow his lead, and the streets of Nashville would become a bigger shooting gallery than they already are."

In this shrewd game of high-stakes poker with Jackson's life on the line, Allenby played his ace in the hole. "Chief King, would you call Jackson Stone a criminal?"

"No sir," the police chief answered, refusing to look at the glaring district attorney.

Allenby did not visibly smile, but his eyes sparkled as he faced the jury.

"What, Chief King, would you call Jack?"

This time the police chief spoke to the glaring prosecutor, matching him stare for stare.

"I would call him a hero."

If Trulowicz felt concerned, he didn't show it as the prosecution rested its case.

The defense attorney took over, and called a number of character witnesses, including Doctor Erica Karnoff, Reverend Armstrong, Jimmy (Big Red) Boyle, Patrick and Sheila Stone, and Louie the bartender.

They all testified to the mental state of Jackson Stone during that period, that nothing they did or said could sway Jackson from pursuing the course of action that he did, and how much they loved, admired, and respected him for what he'd done.

Then, to the surprise of many, Allenby called Jackson Stone to the stand.

Allenby breezed through his portion, asking Jackson to clarify several points about how he wrestled with his faith when he decided to go down that road, and whether he ever intended to carry out his stated goal of vengeance.

"That's a tough one to answer, but I'll try to explain. It wasn't that I thought the police couldn't find Angela's killer, or that I could do their job better. I just wanted to make something happen. She deserved that much, if I wanted to live with myself."

"How did you try to lure Angela's murderer out into the open, Jack?"

Jackson fidgeted like Chief King in the witness box, knowing he must make the DA, the judge, the jury, and fellow Nashvillians understand his going public with a professed vendetta.

"Simply, I made myself a target," Jackson said. "The murderer had killed and gone into hiding, and I just tried to flush him out."

He went on to explain hunting trips with his father and the lessons his father taught him.

"My dad and I were out one fall Saturday hunting in northwest Davidson County when I was ten or eleven," Jackson recounted. "We heard a couple of shots, and a few minutes later we came across two hunters standing over a big buck that one bagged with his rifle. My dad saw the salt block used to lure the deer into the open."

Jackson shifted slightly, talking to the jurors. "Deer love salt and real hunters hate it," he said. "My dad cussed the two hunters and told them to get outta there before he called the game warden. They left without the deer. I'd never seen my dad that mad. Walking to the truck, he explained his actions toward the hunters."

Jackson's voice dropped an octave, mimicking his late father's inflections.

" 'That ain't sport, son; that's killin.' That's what he said and I never forgot it or how easy it was to lure an animal out of hiding with a baited field. I just made myself the murderer's next target. I believed if I did or said something outrageous to infuriate him, he would come after me. Then either I or the police would stop him."

The attorney started to ask another question, but Jackson interrupted.

"A minute ago, you asked whether I intended to carry out my vengeance. I'd like to answer that. Talking about my dad reminded me of something," he said, folding his hands. "Those two guys I mentioned? There's a difference between hunting and killing. I'm a hunter."

Jackson paused, waiting for the final question. "And do you feel any remorse how it all played out?"

A deep, whooshing sigh and the curled shoulders told the true weight he bore. "Every day. For Angela, for Sarah, for Herb. Not for their murderer."

"Thank you. That's all, your honor."

District attorney Trulowicz fired off plenty of questions, but just one mattered. It was the question so many of us asked since the first day, one that until then went unanswered. Why?

"Angela was pregnant when she died." Jack's voice cracked as he tried to stare down the unflinching district attorney. "I think she wanted to tell me the night before she died, but I asked if she could wait until I got back home from a business trip."

His whole body slumped as he spoke.

"She never got the chance to tell me, and I'll always be haunted by the fact that I denied her the opportunity to share her joyous news with me. I'll always feel guilt that I should have protected my wife and my child."

The courtroom made a collective gasping noise at the revelation, and the muted lawyers summed up their cases.

Every heart in the courtroom ached for Jackson, and the case went to the jury at six p.m.

After a working dinner, the jurors discussed the finer points of the laws, reviewed evidence, and called it a night. At nine the next morning, they met, took a poll, and returned to the courtroom at ten a.m.

At ten fifteen, Jackson walked out of the courtroom a free man.

The hunt was over. Justice had been served.

And I'm getting back to work. I've got a book to write.

AFTERWORD
A PERSONAL NOTE FROM JACKSON STONE

I wasn't sure I wanted to participate in this project when Gerry Hilliard approached me after the trial, feeling it was a chapter of my life that I was ready to . . . never truly close, but at least put some distance behind me. I wanted to focus on the future, and not dwell on Angela's senseless murder.

But I put off a decision for a week, and prayed on the right thing to do. Ultimately, it became clear that I should give Gerry my input and support. He seemed determined to write this book, so this way you will get the unvarnished truth, at least from my perspective. Gerry did not surrender editorial control, and we agreed to disagree over some of his conclusions and observations.

I wish this book didn't need to be written, that Angela and I could have grown old together, but it wasn't meant to be. Even as I move forward, not a day goes by that I don't think of her. That will never change, but I have much to accomplish in this world before I am with Angela again. Gerry agreed to contribute a portion from the sale of each book to the foundation I started in Angela's memory. There are many worthwhile victim's rights organizations out there; please consider supporting one.

May God bless Angela's spirit . . . and you.

—**Jackson Stone**, *August 3, 2012*

ACKNOWLEDGMENTS

This book would not have been possible without Jesus Christ, my Lord and Savior, in my life. He has opened so many doors to me and led me down a path that resulted in this book. Many thanks to my wife Bennie Wood, my late father Tom Sr., and family including Brian Chumney, Tracey Carroll, Jennifer and Michael Darling, Ray Hylton, Stephanie Lowe, Kristy Oldham, Larry Riley and Cheri Sanders. I appreciate editor Kathy Rhodes, cover designer Katherine Campbell and photographer Nora Canfield. Several former colleagues at *The Tennessean* offered critical feedback, including John Seigenthaler, the former editor and publisher and now chairman emeritus, as well as Sandy Campbell, Nick Sullivan and Larry Woody. Information, inspiration or support came from former Middle Tennessee State mass communications professor Jerry Hilliard; authors Jaden Terrell and Clay Stafford; the Killer Nashville and Sisters In Crime organizations; my Franklin critique group (Sandy Ward Bell, Suzanne Brunson, John Davis, Micki Fuhrman, Ruth Lebovitz and Michael J. Tucker); Nashville Writers Meetup members, including Kathleen Cosgrove, Lily Wilson and Robert Mangeot; Steve Brodsky, Michelle Honick, Rachel Joiner, Woody Murray, Carolyn Sullivan; East Nashville police officer Chris Jones; Dr. Mike Shelton, my pastor at Bellevue Baptist Church; psychologist Dr. Charles Ihrig; the late Stan Allen, an attorney, boxer, manager and friend; and late *Tennessean* columnists John Bibb and Jerry Thompson. I hope I've made you all proud.
—**Tom Wood**, *August 2013*

Made in the USA
Charleston, SC
20 September 2014